A CASE OF
CONSPIRACY IN
CLERKENWELL

A Freddy Pilkington-Soames Adventure Book 3

CLARA BENSON

MOUNT
STREET
PRESS

MOUNT STREET PRESS

Copyright

ISBN: 978-1-913355-12-8

ClaraBenson.com

Cover design by Shayne Rutherford at
wickedgoodbookcovers.com

Interior Design & Typesetting by Ampersand Book Interiors
ampersandbookinteriors.com

CHAPTER ONE

DESPITE THE THIN covering of frost on the ground outside, the meeting-chamber inside the Tradesmen's Hall was hot and stuffy, warmed by the presence of three hundred men (and a sprinkling of women) packed together like so many hundredweight of cabbages into a space that was too small for them. Outside could be heard the clatter of hooves and the rumble of motor-cars and omnibuses on the busy London thoroughfare which led in various directions towards Threadneedle Street or Poultry or Lombard Street, and thence to a thousand other places in the city. The sun, in cheerful mood, sent a dazzling ray of light through the tall window, which had evidently not been cleaned in some time. The errant sunbeam passed unheeding over the dust particles that danced in the air, and directed itself determinedly onto the shining bald head of a man in the third row, who seemed to be uncomfortable at the attention, for every so often he twitched irritably and put his hand up to shield his eyes—although he could not do much more than that, for fear of causing a disturbance. At the front of the room, on a dais, the Minister for Labour had already been speaking for thirty-five minutes, and looked set to continue for quite as many more, for he had much to say and a willing audience of uneasy business-men who were seeking reassurance.

'It is not a question of denying the working man his rights,' he was saying, 'but of ensuring that the country retains the stability which has served it well for so long. We have all heard of the terrible events which have occurred in Russia. Are the workers any happier for it? I say they are not! No, it is not through Communism that a better society is created—rather, it falls to the leaders, the business-men, to set the example to the people of this great nation of ours. I come here to assure you that this Government has no such radical intent—'

His voice droned on. At the back of the room, a small gaggle of press-men sat, listening attentively and bending dutifully over their notebooks—all except one, a young man who appeared to have drifted off to sleep, for he was leaning to one side, his head resting against a pillar, his eyes closed, a gentle smile playing across his face. Occasionally he shifted and his eyes opened a little, then he would murmur something and settle back down. The seasoned old reporter next to him cast him an amused glance and gave him a nudge, but the young man slept on, the very picture of peaceful contentment. The reporter shook his head and went back to what he was doing.

At last the Minister's speech came to an end and the audience applauded politely. A few questions were taken, which the Minister somehow contrived to answer without actually communicating any information, then he gave a dry little smile, excused himself, and left. There was a great shuffling and scraping of chairs as everybody rose to do likewise.

At the sound of the applause, Freddy Pilkington-Soames had woken with a start and was now frantically scribbling down what little he could, seemingly unaware that his hair was sticking up all on one side.

'Late night?' inquired the old journalist.

'I don't know how it is,' said Freddy with a faint air of puzzlement, 'but I certainly *meant* to be in bed by midnight. What did the old boy say? Anything interesting?'

'They're going to sell Buckingham Palace and use the money to send all the miners to the seaside this summer,' said the other.

'*What?*' said Freddy, looking up.

The man snickered.

'Just my little joke. You didn't miss much. He made no promises but said what he thought they wanted to hear. What do you expect? These business-owners are all looking for an excuse to cut wages, but the Government isn't keen on that, as they know they'll be out on their collective ear sooner than you can say knife if they allow it, since it was the workers who voted them in. At the very least, there'll be another general strike. So he took the safest course and said a lot of pretty words that all add up to nothing. It seems to have kept them happy enough—for now, at any rate. We'll see whether they're so polite when their own employees start making threats against them. Hallo, what's going on here?'

They both looked round. Most people were still in the meeting-chamber, collecting their things and preparing to leave, but through the open door could be heard sounds of a disturbance.

'Trouble?' said the seasoned old reporter, and left the room hurriedly. Freddy followed. In the entrance-hall, a few people were hovering hesitantly, as though wondering what to do. The Minister for Labour was standing by the large double doors with his secretary, looking annoyed, as an official of the Tradesmen's Hall bobbed about them in agitation and two men in ceremonial uniform barred the way out as politely as possible.

'This is most inconvenient,' said the Minister. 'I had no idea such a thing was planned. Why was I not informed of it?'

'We had no idea of it ourselves, sir,' said the anxious official. 'It seems to be quite a spur of the moment protest. There are at least a hundred people outside, however, if not more, and they appear a little heated, if you'll pardon my saying so. Might I suggest leaving quietly through another door? We have a small side entrance that would perhaps be more suitable for the occasion, although there is not enough room to allow everybody out that way.'

'But how are they all to leave, then?' said the Minister's secretary, a young man with an air of great efficiency. 'Surely you don't intend to send three hundred people out through the front door of the building to face an angry rabble?'

'Certainly not,' replied the official. 'After you have left, we shall wait a few minutes then announce to the people outside that there is no use in their staying any longer, since you have already gone. Once they have dispersed, we shall allow everybody else to go.'

'Hmm, hmm, perhaps you are right,' said the Minister, with a glance at his secretary. 'Very well. If you would be so good as to show us the way. Come, Chivers.'

The official, looking slightly relieved, led the two men off. The crowd of business-men were now spilling out into the entrance-hall, and another official immediately stepped forward to request that they wait a few minutes, since there were pro-testers outside. There was some huffing and muttering, but most appeared inclined to wait as instructed. Not all, however; one tall man in particular seemed reluctant to have his progress impeded by such a minor obstacle. He strode up to the men in ceremonial uniform.

'Never mind that,' he said. 'Open this door at once. I don't have time for this sort of thing.'

The ceremonial uniforms politely suggested that he wait, but the tall man would brook no opposition; and since they were not, after all, police, the ceremonial uniforms had no choice but to unbar the door. Immediately a shout went up outside. Then there came the sound of chanting voices, although it was difficult to distinguish what was being said, since they were not calling in time. Freddy craned his neck to look through the door, and saw a throng of determined-looking men and women, many holding placards, standing in the square in front of the Tradesmen's Hall, held back by a number of policemen. The tall man curled his lip disdainfully and descended the steps, pointedly ignoring the crowd of protesters. Others followed suit, emboldened by the presence of the police. Alas for their confidence! For as they emerged from the building, the crowd became excited and surged forward, pushing the policemen aside. The chanting became louder and more urgent as the protesters formed themselves quickly into a line, giving those leaving the building no choice but to pass closely by them in order to escape. The tall man ignored the jeers directed at him and hurried off, followed by a few other brave souls.

'Get back, now!' bellowed a police sergeant. He waved his truncheon in a manner which left no doubt that he was perfectly prepared to use it, and with a few barked instructions soon saw the protesters pushed back away from the building. More people now began to come out of the Tradesmen's Hall. One by one at first, then in larger groups, they emerged and hurried off as fast as they could, the shouts of the hecklers ringing in their ears. Freddy, meanwhile, was standing just outside the entrance, watching the scene with interest and reading the placards, most of which ran along a familiar theme. At length he descended the steps and approached a middle-aged woman wearing several rosettes and carrying a sign which said, 'WHY NOT WOMEN?' He was just about to ask her a question when another shout went up, and he turned to see that reinforcements had arrived in the form of another ten or twenty policemen. Unfortunately, the new arrivals seemed to be under the impression that they had been called in to prevent a revolution, rather than keep a small group of political protesters in order. They began barking orders and shoving the little crowd back even further with their truncheons, to keep them away from the people emerging from the Tradesmen's Hall. The woman with the rosettes was knocked almost off her feet, and gave a yell of indignation. She was saved just in time by Freddy, who caught her by the arm, but her placard fell to the ground and was immediately trampled underfoot.

'Here!' she cried indignantly. 'Isn't that just like the police?'

Within a very few minutes the crowd seemed to swell, the shouting grew louder and angrier, and it became difficult to distinguish between protesters, police and escaping business-men. An egg was thrown and hit a policeman. Other comestible missiles followed. Freddy ducked just in time to avoid a half-eaten apple. He was being jostled about most uncomfortably, and was starting to become alarmed. This would undoubtedly make a much more interesting story for his newspaper, the *Clarion*, than the Minister's speech, but only if he could survive long enough to write it. Abandoning the woman with the rosettes—since she appeared perfectly capable of looking after herself, and was in fact at present attempting to knock off a constable's helmet with a rolled-up umbrella—he pushed his way out of the crowd with some difficulty, and emerged, clothes pulled about and notebook crumpled, by the railings outside the Tradesmen's Hall. There he found a stocky young man who was watching the proceedings with detachment and conversing with an earnest-faced girl in a shapeless hat. The young man started when he saw Freddy, then grabbed his hand and pumped it up and down.

'Hallo, old chap!' he said enthusiastically. 'Haven't seen you for ages. Have you come to support the cause, or is it still the old business?'

'Hallo, St. John,' said Freddy, somewhat less enthusiastically. 'I thought you'd given all this stuff up.'

'Well, I have, strictly speaking,' said St. John Bagshawe. 'I decided I was getting too old for all the explosions so I retired from active campaigning. I'm press these days, just like you.'

'Not really?' said Freddy in surprise.

'Yes. Oh, on a much smaller scale than you, of course.' He rummaged in an inside pocket and brought out a rolled-up pamphlet printed on cheap paper. Freddy took it.

'"*The Radical*," he read. '"The Weekly Newspaper of Revolutionary Socialism."'

'Rather good, isn't it?' said St. John. 'When the pater died he left me a little money so I decided to put it to good use.'

'You mean you started this paper?'

'Yes. Father was always very fond of penning worthy articles for the *Church Times*, you know, and I think he would have been proud to know his youngest son had followed in his footsteps. It has rather a good circulation, as a matter of fact. Two thousand copies a week, all around the country.'

'"We must not baulk at the prospect of violence," read Freddy, "for it is a necessary evil if we are to create a society in which aggression and fear are truly things of the past. When our brothers and sisters have been educated to understand the beauties and the virtues of a truly Communist society, only then can we truly claim—" I say, did you write this? You've used "truly" three times in two sentences.'

'Have I?' said St. John, disconcerted. 'Bother, so I have. We can't afford a copy-editor yet.'

'I didn't know your father was a Communist, by the way,' said Freddy.

'He wasn't. He hated all that stuff.'

'But you said he'd approve of what you were doing.'

'Well, he would certainly have approved of the fact that I write for a newspaper. But no,' conceded St. John, 'I dare say he'd have been pretty apoplectic at the content. I say, do let me introduce you to Ruth.' He gestured to the earnest-faced young woman, who had been writing busily in a notebook. 'Ruth, this is Freddy Pilkington-Soames, my old pal from school. Freddy, Ruth Chudderley. Ruth is my assistant at the paper. She's awfully clever—knows more than anyone about Socialism and that sort of thing, I should say. She writes the women's page of the *Radical*.'

The young woman nodded briskly.

'How do you do?' she said. 'And are you allied to the cause?'

'Not as such,' said Freddy. 'I find causes exhausting. Much better to leave them to people who have the time to dedicate to them.'

She looked him up and down.

'Yes,' she said thoughtfully, as though she had reached some conclusion from her examination. Freddy glanced down, half-expecting to see that he had buttoned his coat up the wrong way.

Scuffles had broken out between the police and the protesters. St. John and Ruth Chudderley watched with mild interest.

'Perhaps we ought to get out of the way,' suggested Freddy, as a shoe went flying overhead.

'Good idea. Rather a decent show today, don't you think?' said St. John, as the three of them removed themselves further away from the mêlée. 'Quite a successful little do.'

'If you say so,' said Freddy. 'Do you count the success of an outing according to the number of arrests?'

'Not at all,' St. John assured him. 'But you can see we've got them rattled. Look how many police they've sent.'

A small crowd of people had now broken away from the main group, and had gathered around a bronze statue of some long-dead worthy in breeches and a periwig.

'Hallo, what's happening now?' said Freddy.

'It's Trevett,' said St. John. 'He's never happy unless he's making a speech on a public monument. Oh, bravo!'

A man of gallant and striking appearance had shinned up the plinth, and was now standing next to the frozen worthy, one arm about its neck and the other gesturing towards the Tradesmen's Hall. A loud cheer could be heard from onlookers.

'Who's Trevett?' said Freddy.

'Ivor Trevett,' replied St. John. 'He's the President and Chairman of the East London Communist Alliance. He's going to shake things up a bit, you'll see.'

The man had begun proclaiming eloquently, to the great appreciation of his audience. Ruth Chudderley was watching him, her eyes gleaming.

'Now *there* is the man who ought to be running our nation, Mr. Pilkington-Soames,' she said. 'I suggest you write his name down now, as you will be hearing it a lot more in future.'

Even from where they stood, across the crowd they could hear the booming sound of Trevett's voice as he made an impassioned speech. Several times he clenched his fist and raised it into the air, to the sound of cheers. His mannerisms reminded Freddy of something.

'I should have thought he'd be better off on the stage,' he said.

'Why, yes, Ivor was an actor for some years,' said Ruth. 'But he found that the public were not appreciative of his talents and abilities, and in the end we were fortunate that he decided to employ them to better purpose.'

'Lost one too many parts,' Freddy said to himself.

Several policemen were trying to push through the crowd towards Trevett, in order to bring him down from the statue, and were meeting resistance at every turn. Trevett laughed and wagged a finger at them, and continued his speech, quite unconcerned.

'They're going to arrest him,' observed Freddy.

'Oh, they always arrest him,' said St. John. 'He'll be disappointed if they don't.'

And indeed, within a very few minutes two police constables had pushed their way to the front of the group and dragged Ivor Trevett down from the statue. He was conducted away, struggling and shouting, but with every appearance of enjoying himself immensely. The police were now getting the upper hand of the more unruly of the protesters, while those who had come to stand peacefully with a placard began to disperse, since everybody had now left the Tradesmen's Hall and the doors had been shut.

'Well, I suppose we'd better be off,' said St. John. 'A splendid little outing, what? That ought to give us plenty to talk about at the meeting next Tuesday.'

'Where is Sidney?' said Ruth, looking around. 'Are there funds to get Ivor out? I seem to remember we were running low.'

'He was somewhere about with Peacock and Dyer,' said St. John. 'Ah, there he is—look.'

Ruth was already making her way towards a round little man who was standing on the edge of the crowd. St. John turned to Freddy.

'Well, cheerio,' he said. 'I look forward to seeing what you make of all this in your piece. Mind you put in all the details.'

'I'll do my best. I'm only surprised you weren't the one being arrested,' said Freddy.

St. John gave a guffaw.

'I told you, I don't do that sort of thing any more,' he said. 'I've found a much more effective way of getting things done.' He held up his dog-eared copy of the *Radical*. 'The pen is mightier than the sword, as they say.'

'But what about all that stuff you said about violence?' said Freddy.

'Mere metaphor,' said St. John airily. 'You don't really think I approve of killing people, do you?'

'I should hope not,' said Freddy.

CHAPTER TWO

TWO DAYS LATER, Freddy was surprised to receive a letter that he did not understand at all. It came from an address near Whitehall, bore an unfamiliar letterhead and an official stamp of some kind, and was signed by someone he had never heard of. The letter itself politely requested his presence at the address indicated at eleven o'clock that same day.

Freddy was naturally very curious, and arrived punctually at the place in question, which turned out to be an unassuming building in a discreet side-street. He announced himself, and after a short wait was conducted up to the third floor, where he was ushered into the presence of a man wearing a pair of round spectacles that gave him an owlish look.

'Hallo, Freddy,' said Henry Jameson.

'Hallo, sir,' said Freddy. 'I didn't realize the letter was from Intelligence.'

'I was out yesterday and someone else signed it for me,' said Henry. 'But even so, I thought it wisest not to be too obvious to start with. One never knows. Take a seat.'

Freddy did so, wondering what exactly Henry Jameson meant by his somewhat cryptic remark, but before he could pursue the question, there was a soft knock at the door and someone poked his head round apologetically, waving a piece of paper. Mr. Jameson excused himself and went out, which gave Freddy the opportunity to look around him and take in his surroundings. For a man in such a position of power, Henry Jameson seemed to require little ostentation or show, for the room was furnished economically—sparsely, even—and contained the bare minimum number of chairs and tables required to avoid causing an echo. Yet despite the plainness of it all, Freddy could not help noticing that the apparently modest chair in which he had been directed to sit was perhaps the most comfortable chair he had ever sat in. And now he came to look more closely, he could see that everything appeared to have been designed with an admirable attention to function and a disdain for waste. The desk in front of him was bare apart from a blotter and a square inkstand. A bookshelf to one side of the room held a selection of books which, to look at their arrangement, seemed to have been chosen for their ability to fill the shelves perfectly without a gap. Even the solitary plant in a pot standing on a table had been placed so as to create the maximum aesthetic effect with the minimum of effort. Ten plants in any other room might have looked far less decorative. Freddy already knew better than to underestimate Henry Jameson, but here was further evidence that anything he wanted done would be carried out with the greatest efficiency and the least fuss.

At last Henry returned and sat down at his desk.

'I see you've been doing well at the *Clarion*,' he said. 'I read your recent piece on the problems in Ireland with interest. You seem to have quite a firm grasp on the question.'

'Thank you, sir. I did a little reading on the subject before I began,' lied Freddy. As a matter of fact he had been late with the article, and in a panic had gleaned most of its content from a half-remembered conversation with an elderly Irishman with whom he had spent an uproariously drunken afternoon at the race-track a few weeks earlier.

'I see,' said Mr. Jameson. He regarded Freddy over his spectacles while Freddy tried not to shuffle in his seat. 'I expect you're wondering why I've invited you here,' he went on.

'I am, rather,' said Freddy. 'I say, I haven't done anything wrong, have I?'

'I don't know. Have you?' said Henry with polite interest. 'If you have, I suggest you keep it to yourself. You don't want to get into trouble. No, it's nothing like that.'

He paused, as though wondering how to begin.

'I dare say you remember certain events which occurred two years ago, the last time we met,' he said at last.

'At Fives Castle? I should say I do,' said Freddy. 'Difficult to forget, that sort of thing. Spies and dead bodies all over the place. Not the usual sort of Hogmanay party at all.'

'No,' agreed Henry Jameson. 'Luckily we managed to keep it quiet and the story never got out, thanks partly to you. It's not every press-man who knows how to hold his tongue, but I was pleased to find you did. And now you must show me you can do it again, because I am about to tell you some things which must remain entirely confidential—even if you don't like them. Is that understood? Do I have your word?'

'Certainly,' said Freddy, sitting up straighter.

'Very well. Then I don't suppose it will come as any great surprise to you to hear that what I have to say pertains to your friend Bagshawe.'

'St. John?' said Freddy. 'What's he been getting up to this time?'

'That is the question,' said Henry. 'Yes, that is very much the question.'

'I mean to say, I know he went through a hot-headed phase a year or two ago, but I saw him the other day, and—oh!' said Freddy, in sudden realization. 'You know that already, don't you? That's why I'm here now.'

Henry merely smiled approvingly, and Freddy went on:

'At any rate, he told me he was done with all that sort of thing. He's started a newspaper, and has gone all respectable.'

'The *Radical*,' said Henry. 'Yes, I have seen the publication in question.'

'Full of the usual rot, of course. I don't think he'll ever give up the Communism, but he did say he'd stopped setting fire to things. Seemed very pleased with himself, as a matter of fact.'

'Was he telling the truth, do you think?'

Freddy thought.

'As far as I could tell,' he said after a minute. 'He's not exactly an intellectual prodigy—you saw that yourself at Fives—and he was so fearfully keen to tell me how he'd settled down that it never occurred to me that he might be lying. Besides, I rather think there's a woman in the picture.'

'Ruth Chudderley,' said Henry.

'Oh, you know her, do you? Anything on her?'

'No,' admitted Henry. 'As far as we can gather, she is what she appears to be: a young lady of good breeding and a contrary enough disposition to offend her family by taking up with the Communist cause. I don't suppose you've ever considered taking it up yourself, have you?' he added casually.

'Good heavens, no!' said Freddy, surprised. 'I shouldn't dare. Half my family have titles, including my own grandfather, and my mother would flay me alive if she thought I was conspiring against them. Besides, they throw jolly good parties, and that takes money,' he added as an afterthought.

'Quite,' said Mr. Jameson dryly.

'What makes you think St. John has been doing something he oughtn't?' said Freddy.

'Well, I can't say for certain he has been. In fact, he may have nothing to do with it at all. But after what happened at Fives, he is naturally the first person to come under suspicion.'

'Suspicion of what?'

A look of vexation passed briefly across Henry Jameson's face.

'That's just it,' he said. 'I don't know. And I don't like it.'

He sighed and gazed down at his desk. The position of the blotter seemed to displease him. He shifted it one inch to the right, looked up and began:

'You know, of course, about the unrest we've been seeing in recent years, with the miners, the dock-workers and other trades—the papers have written enough about it, so I shan't bore you by giving you a summary of what's been going on. Suffice it to say that things were rather unpleasant for a while.

However, they seemed to have calmed down a little lately with the election of the new Government.'

'*Seemed* to have calmed down?' said Freddy. 'You mean there's something afoot?'

'Oh, there's always something afoot,' said Henry with a wave of the hand. 'But most of it can be safely disregarded, or at least cleared up with a minimum of effort. The miners aren't happy, and the mine-owners aren't happy, and I dare say lots of other people aren't happy either, but generally speaking they're content to shout at one another and threaten all sorts of dire things, and march about a bit, then the whole thing blows over and we all go on as before. But this is something quite different.'

'In what way?'

'We've started to receive reports from a number of sources,' said Henry. 'They began a few months ago, and at first we disregarded them as more of the usual stuff, but they've become so frequent and insistent recently that we've had to start paying attention. You know that there's plenty of serious unrest happening in other countries at the moment. Normally that doesn't concern us unduly, but lately I've begun to wonder whether there mightn't be a danger of it spreading to Britain. We've been keeping an eye on things in the North—Manchester, and Newcastle, and Sheffield, and all those sorts of places—and there have been loud mutterings about calling another general strike, which I should have dismissed as exaggeration had it not been for the fact that we've also noticed a lot of unusual toing and froing between the unions and the Communists in the past few months.'

'But aren't the unions and the Communists hand in glove anyway?' said Freddy.

'Yes,' said Henry. 'But this is something else entirely. I can't disclose anything more at this stage, I'm afraid, but you can take my word for it that our intelligence is sound. What I can tell you is that the activity seems to centre around the Labourers' Union.'

'Oh? I thought that was one of the more sensible unions.'

'It is, as a rule,' said Henry. 'It's headed by Rowbotham, whom I should call solid—not to say dull.'

'Yes, I've heard him speak,' said Freddy feelingly.

'He's fairly moderate as these men go, and has many loyal followers, and we regard him as a stabilizing influence on the other, more excitable unions. So long as he's in charge the workers ought to be kept in check one way or another. Unfortunately for him, a substantial minority of his members would like to see him replaced by his deputy, John Pettit, who's a firebrand and an avowed revolutionary. Pettit has many supporters who would be only too glad to stir things up if he came to power. I don't mind telling you I'd be very concerned if they decided to try and oust Rowbotham—or perhaps even just ignore him altogether and act off their own bat.'

'Is there such a plan, sir?'

'I have no proof of it, but my instinct tells me that *something* is going on, and I've learned never to ignore my instinct.'

'What do you think is going to happen?'

'The most obvious possibility is that they're organizing some sort of violent protest, or a riot of some kind, but it had occurred to me that they might even be planning another general strike, but in secret this time.'

'Could that be done without your finding out?'

'If they could recruit enough small groups of men in each of the unions, it might be possible,' said Henry. 'Personally, if I wanted to instigate such a thing, I should start by engineering simultaneous lock-outs at several mines or factories, and putting the blame on the employers. Then I should have agitators in place to rail against the rich men and inflame the mood of the workers until they downed tools and walked out. Yes, planned carefully enough it might be feasible. That would be the worst possible eventuality, of course, although I'm not especially keen on the thought of a riot either.'

'And do you think St. John has something to do with all this?'

'It's possible. His past history counts against him, but even if he's not directly concerned in the thing, we suspect that his newspaper is being used as a means of communication between the conspirators—if conspirators there be. We've been keeping an eye on the personal advertisements, and have seen a number of messages that were evidently in code. They might be quite innocent, but taken together with what we already know, they're suggestive. Yes, very suggestive indeed.'

'I see,' said Freddy, wondering where all this was leading.

'By the way, have you heard of a man called Anton Schuster?' said Henry.

Freddy frowned.

'Schuster? Not the philosopher chappie?'

'The very same,' said Henry. 'He and his wife left Vienna and moved to London a few months ago. Schuster had published a number of articles that were slightly too radical for Austrian tastes, and he was finding things a little hot at home, so he settled here and immediately threw himself into the Communist cause. He is a member of the East London Communist Alliance, so your friend knows him.'

'And what has he to do with all this?'

'I should like very much to know that myself,' said Henry. 'You see, the intelligence reports I've been telling you about only began to reach us after his arrival here.'

'Coincidence?' suggested Freddy.

'Perhaps,' conceded Henry. 'But I'm not a great believer in coincidence as a rule. I find it easier to believe in design than in accident where this sort of thing is concerned.'

'I see,' said Freddy again. 'Very well, if I understand correctly, you suspect a conspiracy of some sort, but you don't know what it is. What am I to do about it, though? Always supposing you didn't invite me here just for the pleasure of giving me a lesson in current political developments.'

'I didn't,' said Henry. 'No, I want your help in finding out what's going on.'

'My help? Why me? Surely you have men in place who can do a better job than I can?'

'We have agents and informants,' said Henry, 'but they can't do everything. None of them went to school with St. John Bagshawe, for example. As an old friend of his you are in a position to get information out of him that he would never confide to someone of another class, or even someone from another school.'

'The old school tie, eh?' said Freddy. 'I'm not certain I like the idea of spying on a friend, even if he is an ass.'

'Remember, you mustn't repeat what's been said here, even if you don't like it,' warned Henry.

'Of course not—I gave my word. I say, do you really think he knows something? I know one could comfortably scoop the entirety of his grey matter up into a teaspoon, but I should have said he was harmless enough.'

'Even after the disaster he nearly caused at Fives Castle?'

'Well, yes,' said Freddy. 'There is that, I suppose. It was idiotic of him, but it was unwitting rather than malicious.'

'He was taken for a fool,' said Henry. 'Are you sure it couldn't happen again?'

'No,' admitted Freddy.

'And even if he knows nothing of what's going on this time, it's still possible he's being used through his newspaper, through which it would be easy enough to pass on information without his knowledge.'

'What exactly is it that you want me to find out?'

'We're missing a clear link between the Communist Alliance in London and the union men in the North,' said Henry. 'Oh, I know the Reds pledge general support and contribute to funds for those suffering hardship, but I'm almost certain there's another, more direct connection between Anton Schuster and what's going on at present, and I want to know what it is. We've been keeping an eye on Schuster's post, but he's far too careful to give himself away that easily. If he is communicating with his radical allies, then he's not doing it through the mails.' He gave a sigh that might have denoted frustration.

'My job is to keep the country safe, Freddy, but I can't do that if I don't know what I'm supposed to be keeping it safe *from*. Now, are you willing to help me?'

Freddy considered a moment.

'Very well,' he said at last. 'One ought to do one's duty, I suppose. You can rely on me to do everything I can to find out this threat, whatever it is, and report back.'

'Splendid,' said Henry with a smile. 'I hoped you'd say yes. Now, the East London Communist Alliance meets on Tuesday evenings at Clerkenwell Central Hall. I suggest you trot along there quite openly as a reporter from the *Clarion*, and tell them you're writing a story. If I know anything of these small, radical groups, they'll be only too happy to be given the chance to pontificate for the benefit of the public, and will welcome you with open arms. Schuster in particular is rather fond of himself, and tends to gather acolytes around him wherever he goes. I should like you to talk to him and his wife. Pretend to be a little awe-struck, if you must. They won't tell the press anything important, naturally, but it can't do any harm to get yourself admitted to his inner circle of admirers.'

'What about Ivor Trevett?' said Freddy. 'He looked like something of a trouble-maker when I saw him the other day.'

'Yes, we have our eye on him too,' said Henry. 'He's their leader, so one would suppose that he knows well enough what's afoot, but we haven't been able to pin anything on him yet— or on anyone, in fact.' He looked at his watch and rose to his feet. 'I have a meeting with the Prime Minister shortly, and I see we've already been talking longer than I expected. Now, don't forget: keep your eyes and ears peeled for anything that might suggest there's something nasty in the offing, and report it to me if you do.'

'I will, sir,' promised Freddy, standing up likewise.

'You mustn't come here—at least, not without an invitation—but you may telephone or send a telegram if needs be.'

'Wouldn't it be simpler to speak to your man on the spot?' said Freddy. 'Who is he, by the way?'

'I'd rather not tell you just yet,' said Henry. 'We find it's safer that way. You might be seen together, and we don't want them to suspect they have moles in their midst. But if our agent does need to communicate with you, then listen for the phrase "purple mittens."'

'Purple mittens?' said Freddy staring.

'And you must reply with the phrase "green mittens,"' went on Henry. He saw Freddy's expression and looked slightly embarrassed. 'It wasn't my idea. I don't think these things up,' he said.

'I should hope not,' said Freddy.

They walked along to the lift. It arrived and Freddy stepped in, then as it began to descend, had a sudden thought.

'I say,' he said. 'Is this likely to be dangerous?'

'Oh, no more than you'd expect,' said Henry vaguely, as the lift compartment sank out of sight.

CHAPTER THREE

D O WE HAVE enough tea, Miss Hodges?' came the strident tones of Miss Stapleton, Vice-President of the Young Women's Abstinence Association, through the door of the small kitchen of Clerkenwell Central Hall.

Miss Phyllis Hodges, wispy-haired, agitated and breathless as she attempted for the fourth time to match the items on her list with the items required for the meeting, whirled around in a moment of panic, dropping her pencil as she did so. Where was the tea? Had she forgotten it?

'Mrs. Starkweather is meant to be bringing it,' she said in relief, after a moment's thought. 'I expect she'll be here soon.'

Miss Olive Stapleton entered the room, a formidable presence in dark brown tweed, and regarded Miss Hodges with impatience.

'What on earth are you doing down there?' she said. 'This is hardly the moment to be grubbing about on the floor.'

'I'm sorry, Miss Stapleton, I dropped my pencil,' said Miss Hodges.

'Well, get up, then! The meeting will be starting in less than an hour and there's no time to waste. Now, sugar. We were running low last time, I seem to remember.'

'Yes, I've brought that,' said Miss Hodges, on firmer ground now. 'Two pounds ought to be enough, don't you think?'

'Three might have been better. We had rather a large turnout last time, and we don't want to run out. And only the white? There are a number of ladies who prefer Demerara.'

'Oh, but I thought—'

'Never mind,' said Miss Stapleton impatiently. 'Perhaps I had better see to the provisions myself next time. A pity, as I'm rather busy and I'd hoped that you might be able to take some of the burden off my shoulders. But there's no use in asking people to do things for one if they can't or won't do them properly.'

'I'm sorry, Miss Stapleton,' said Miss Hodges meekly.

'Such a pity the Communist Alliance got the main hall before us,' went on Miss Stapleton. 'Our membership has swelled considerably in the past few months, and we're becoming very cramped now in the smaller room. I dread to think what would happen if a fire broke out. And as for serving the tea—why, it's becoming almost impossible. I think we shall have to begin stacking a few of the chairs away at the back of the room near the table at refreshments time. You can see to that, can't you?'

Since Miss Hodges had timidly put forward this idea herself only a few weeks earlier, and had been roundly pooh-poohed by Miss Stapleton for her pains, she made no objection.

'And on the subject of the chairs, do try and make sure they are put away properly this week. The caretaker is complaining that somebody has not been stacking them in the correct manner.'

'Really? But I thought—'

'Back to back, not front to back, or they take up too much space. Remember that. Oh, I forgot to mention that I received a telephone-call from Mrs. Belcher earlier. She sends her excuses, but she is quite prostrate with a terrible migraine, and will not be able to come this evening. However, she sent her girl with a list of things that ought to be attended to, since she is unable to do them. There are all this month's subscriptions to be counted and recorded, for example. They really need to be done by Thursday so we can deposit the money at the bank by the end of the month, but Mr. Bottle is still unwell, and I can't possibly do it, since I am busy all day tomorrow and have a most pressing evening engagement that simply cannot be deferred. You won't mind doing it, will you?'

Miss Hodges was also busy all the next day, and had planned to spend the evening with a friend whom she had not seen for some time. She began to make her excuses, but Miss Stapleton interrupted her with an impatient click of the tongue.

'Really, Miss Hodges,' she said. 'I don't think it's too much to ask that you do something for the cause once in a while. Why, I work my fingers to the bone for this association, but sometimes it seems to me that I am the only one, and that others are not taking their due share of the responsibility.'

Miss Hodges flushed but said nothing. It was clear that her Wednesday evening engagement would have to be postponed, for she knew not how to resist Miss Stapleton's force of personality.

'Those Communists next door are so rowdy,' said Miss Stapleton, whose mind had now wandered on to another of her many sources of vexation. 'I think I shall have to have another word with them. Why, they quite drowned out *Rise O Rise This Glorious Morning* last week with their cheering and whistling—and just at the most rousing part about rallying around the Temperance banner. And that song of theirs they sing sounds most angry and war-like. Not at all suitable for a public meeting, in my opinion—oh, who is that coming in? Is it Mr. Hussey? He is not usually this early.'

She went out, and Miss Hodges heard her calling in a loud, cheerful voice:

'Good evening, Mr. Peacock, Mr. Dyer! Never miss a meeting, I see. And how is your aunt, Mr. Dyer? Has she quite recovered from her cough? So troublesome, especially at this time of year. Oh, I am glad to hear it. What? Oh, yes, do go on, I shan't keep you.'

There came the sound of young male voices, then the slam of a door, and Miss Stapleton returned to the kitchen.

'Such well brought-up young men,' she said. 'Oxford, I believe. I can't think what they're doing mixing with those horrid radicals. Perhaps it's the fashion nowadays.'

'I spoke to Mr. Peacock just before Christmas, when he was good enough to help me carry a tray of cups,' said Miss Hodges. 'He confided to me that he did it mainly for the fun of it, although he did say he believed it was a jolly good cause.'

'Well, they ought to give it up,' said Miss Stapleton. 'I'm dreadfully afraid that they'll get into trouble when it all blows up.'

'When it all blows up?' said Miss Hodges in alarm. 'Goodness! What is going to blow up?'

'I don't know, but they're plotting something, I'm certain of it,' said Miss Stapleton.

'Oh dear! But they are always so polite and well-spoken. Mr. Dyer said they read a lot of poetry at their meetings.'

'Poetry, indeed,' said Miss Stapleton with a snort. 'They might call it poetry, but I shouldn't be at all surprised to find out that they're really communicating revolutionary messages in code. No, Miss Hodges,' she went on, 'I am firm in my belief that there is something afoot. I see them talking in corners together, and passing notes to one another when they think nobody is watching. A few weeks ago I caught Mr. Trevett and Mr. Schuster coming out of the committee-room, looking very shifty indeed. They jumped when they saw me and gave me a most unfriendly glare. Naturally I went in and examined the room when they'd gone, but they hadn't left any evidence, unfortunately.'

'Perhaps they wanted to speak about something in private.'

'Of course they wanted to speak about something in private. One doesn't plot armed insurrection against the Government in front of everybody. No, they're far too clever for that.'

'Good gracious! Do you think that's what they were doing?' said Miss Hodges.

'That, or worse,' said Miss Stapleton darkly. 'One day I shall catch them at it, you see if I don't.'

'Are we late?' said a voice, which turned out to belong to a comfortable woman of middle age, who looked as though she had dressed as an afterthought. 'Mildred, did I forget to wind my watch up again?'

'I don't think so,' said the pink-faced and hearty young lady who accompanied her. 'Hallo, Miss Stapleton, hallo, Miss Hodges. We've brought sugar. That's right, isn't it?'

'Oh, goodness,' said Miss Hodges in dismay. 'But I thought we'd agreed you would bring the tea.'

'What? No, I don't think so,' said Mrs. Starkweather. 'We didn't agree to bring tea, did we, Mildred?'

'Do you know, I'm not sure,' said Mildred. 'Perhaps we did. Although I *thought* it was sugar. Have we got it wrong again?'

'Oh dear,' said Miss Hodges, for she was certain that no matter whose fault it was, she would get the blame for it. 'Shall I run out for some tea? I think there's still time.'

'Only if you can be quite sure that you'll come back with tea and not butter,' said Miss Stapleton sharply. 'Perhaps you ought to write it down, in case you forget.'

'I say, it was most probably our mistake,' said Mildred Starkweather, seeing Miss Hodges' face fall. 'Should you like me to do it, Miss Hodges?'

'No, no thank you,' said that unfortunate person, who was only too glad of an opportunity to escape from Miss Stapleton's oppressive presence. 'I shall be back in five minutes.'

She hurried out of the kitchen, and Miss Stapleton sighed and shook her head.

'It is impossible to rely on Phyllis Hodges to do anything quickly and efficiently,' she said. 'Sometimes I think she is more trouble than she is worth, although it's hardly charitable to say so, of course.'

'She's a dear,' said Mildred Starkweather. 'Isn't she, Mummy?'

'What? Oh, yes, I suppose she is,' said Mrs. Starkweather vaguely. 'And who do we have speaking this evening, Miss Stapleton?'

'I'm afraid Mrs. Belcher has a headache and has sent her excuses,' said Miss Stapleton. 'It is a great pity, because she was going to recount one of her inspirational histories about an American gentleman of her acquaintance, who was formerly very much addicted to the bottle, so much so that all his friends deserted him and his wife left him out of fear for herself and her children. Then he was introduced to the Temperance movement, became a champion of the cause himself, and was elected to the Senate. However, I believe that story will have to wait until next week now. Fortunately, Mr. Hussey has kindly volunteered to stand in. He is so personable and charming, and the ladies like him so much—especially the poor, saved girls. They sit quite silent and spell-bound during his little homilies. Oh, who is this?'

'Hallo, hallo,' said Freddy from the doorway, as Mrs. Starkweather and her daughter turned to see whom Miss Stapleton was addressing. 'Is it the Temperance ladies' night? I didn't realize. Good evening, Mrs. S. You're looking splendid as usual. Hallo, Mildred. How long has it been?'

'Last August, I think,' said Mildred. 'There was a picnic and you fell in the river and frightened the ducks.'

'Hallo, Freddy, what are you doing here?' said Mrs. Starkweather. 'Have you come with Cynthia?'

'No, my mother's off gallivanting in the South of France at the moment,' he replied. 'Never could stand the English weather in January. Good evening—Miss Stapleton, isn't it? Freddy Pilkington-Soames at your service. I hope I'm not in the way.'

'Ah, yes, Mr. Pilkington-Soames, I remember you,' said Miss Stapleton, looking him up and down. 'I'm sorry your mother couldn't come this evening. She was quite a regular at one time, thanks to the efforts of Mrs. Belcher, who was most assiduous in persuading the ladies of her acquaintance to take up the cause. It is a pity she was not so successful in inducing them to persevere with it, but I suppose some people are not cut out for the rigours of a devotedly moral life. Now, I must go and see to the chairs. Mrs. Starkweather, would you be good enough to give me a hand?'

The two ladies went out. Freddy gave a whistle.

'I say, she's a tartar, isn't she?' he said.

'Oh, don't mind her,' said Mildred. 'Now, why are you here? Don't tell me you've decided to embrace sobriety, because I shan't believe you.'

'Naturally I shouldn't dream of showing disrespect by turning up to a Temperance meeting in anything worse than my usual state of incapacity, but as it happens I haven't touched a drop since Sunday,' said Freddy.

'That's only two days ago,' Mildred pointed out.

'Really? It seems longer. No, much as I'd like to join you this evening, I'm afraid I'm here for the other lot. I've a fancy to raise the red flag and stand shoulder to shoulder with the masses, as we join together in song and bellow lusty verses that tell how effete horrors such as myself will one day be put against a wall and summarily dispatched. Jolly good fun, what?'

'You, a Communist?' said Mildred. 'I shall as soon believe that as I shall your giving up drinking.'

'Well, no, as a matter of fact I'm here for the paper.'

'Oh, a story, is it?'

'Yes, the *Clarion* sent me along. It's not all society weddings and Lord Mayor's parades, you know. As a matter of fact, it was St. John's idea originally. He's always trying to get me to write flattering pieces about his unsightly herd, so I thought I'd take pity on him for once. But now I hear he's started his own newspaper, so I don't know why he needs me.'

'Oh, St. John,' said Mildred. 'Yes, I've read that rag of his. Miss Stapleton had a copy of it. Someone really ought to donate a dictionary to them, as the spelling's atrocious.'

'Why did Miss Stapleton have a copy of the newspaper? I can't imagine it being her sort of thing.'

'Because she thinks they're up to something,' said Mildred. 'She has a bee in her bonnet about it. Rather cracked, in fact. She's convinced they're plotting a revolution, or something of that sort.'

'Is she, now?' said Freddy. 'And are they?'

Mildred snorted.

'Go and look at them yourself and tell me,' she said. 'I've never seen a more ineffectual lot. Standing and ranting poetry for hours at a time, to no good purpose. Then half of them go home to a nice, warm, cosy house, and have their servants bring them whisky or cocoa, and the other half go home and beat their wives because as working men they're the head of the house and must needs prove it at all costs, then they all go to bed and congratulate themselves on the prospect of changing society for the better, and ignore the real poverty that's everywhere around them. As for a revolution, our ladies here would do a better job of it if they had a mind to.'

'A trenchant analysis,' said Freddy. 'Perhaps I shall quote you. They love that sort of thing at the *Clarion*. "Views of a Young Lady on the Communist Movement." How does that sound?'

'Will they pay me?'

'Unlikely.'

'Perhaps not, then. I don't think Mummy would be especially pleased,' said Mildred.

Just then two more people entered the kitchen: a young clergyman who was exceedingly fair of face, and an elderly woman who resembled nothing more than a curious and friendly goat. The reverend gentleman was introduced as Mr. Theodore Hussey, and it appeared that he was there to conduct the Temperance meeting.

'I am sorry to hear Mrs. Belcher is indisposed,' he said. 'However, I must confess I was very happy to be asked to fill her place this evening, as I have a little sermon I have been working on. "The lust of the flesh, and the lust of the eyes, and the pride of life—" you know the verse, of course. I believe it to be most applicable to some of our young women, without being too difficult for them to understand, since the parallels are quite clear—yes, quite clear.'

He then disappeared. The elderly lady watched him go with interest.

'I expect you'll get a good turnout tonight,' she observed. 'All the girls like a pretty young man.'

'You're a wicked one, Miss Flowers,' said Mildred with good humour.

'Not at all,' said Miss Flowers. 'Just an observer of human nature.'

'Anyway, they don't know he's on tonight,' said Mildred. 'They think it's Mrs. Belcher. And to be perfectly frank, I think it's the tea and shortbread that brings them—that and the free trips to the cinema—rather than Mr. Hussey.'

'Well, we'll see,' said Miss Flowers. She fished in her bag and brought out a tangled bundle of wool and a crochet hook. 'Now, I had better go and take my seat.'

'Are you here for Mr. Hussey or the shortbread?' inquired Freddy, and she gave a delighted chuckle.

'Neither,' she replied. 'I'm with the other lot. Much more fun.'

And with that she departed.

'Well, now,' said Freddy in surprise.

'Yes,' said Mildred. 'She used to come to us, but she's a little vague, poor dear, and one day she wandered into the wrong hall by mistake and decided she liked the Communists better. She's one of those women who likes to have a cause, but it doesn't seem to matter which one. Miss Stapleton has never forgiven her for deserting us. Well, you'd better get off if you want a good seat—they're starting to arrive.'

Miss Hodges had now returned breathlessly with the tea, and nobody had any more attention to spare for Freddy, so he took his leave. He passed an open door to a small office, in which Mr. Hussey and Mrs. Starkweather were standing in conversation. Further on, to the left, was the entrance to the main hall, in which the East London Communist Alliance held their weekly meetings. He glanced in, and saw a few people gathered together in groups, laughing and talking. Down a short corridor to the left just after the main hall was the minor hall, in which the Young Women's Abstinence Association met, while straight ahead of him was a door marked 'Committee,' which was standing slightly ajar. He moved towards it curiously, but before he could do anything the door opened and out came a tall, bearded man with a commanding presence whom he recognized as Ivor Trevett, in company with another man, who was elderly and of foreign appearance. They did not even glance at him as they passed. Freddy waited until they had gone then went inside, but saw nothing of interest, for the room held very little apart from a table and chairs, and was evidently used for smaller meetings.

People were now beginning to arrive for their respective gatherings. For the most part, it was easy to tell which was which, since the members of the Abstinence Association were mostly women and the Communists were mostly men; however, once in a while a man in working clothes would enter the minor hall, or a young woman of respectable appearance would hurry into the larger hall breathlessly, clutching a copy of the *Radical*. Further, it appeared that some members of the opposite houses were on very friendly terms: Freddy saw a young man and his girl arrive arm in arm, and separate with a kiss and a wave in the lobby.

'Hallo, old chap!' came a voice just then. 'You're here, then. Come to see the fun?'

It was St. John, in company with Ruth Chudderley, who wore the same aloof expression as she had during their previous encounter. She nodded at Freddy and went into the meeting.

'Is it going to be fun?' said Freddy.

'Oh, tremendously so,' said St. John. 'We've a chap this week who's written a novel about a working man who suffers a lifetime of bad luck and dies the most horribly tragic death. He's hoping to have it published, and he's going to read one or two excerpts from it. Then Trevett will be speaking, of course.'

'Ah, yes, I saw they'd let him out of gaol.'

'Just a fine as usual,' said St. John, with a wave of the hand. 'The subs generally cover it, although I think we'll have to put them up soon if he goes on the way he has been lately. And we have our Austrian philosopher, Schuster. Rather a *coup* of ours, that one. He's terribly well thought-of in Austria—well, he was until he started writing articles about blowing up the Schönbrunn Palace and had to leave in a hurry. Look here, it's about to start. You'd better go and sit down. I'll be speaking, so watch out for me!'

He hurried off. Freddy entered the large hall and looked around. The room was now almost full, but he saw Miss Flowers gesturing to him from the back row with her crochet. There was a seat next to her, so he took it, then the meeting began.

CHAPTER FOUR

IF FREDDY HAD expected to discover evidence of a grand conspiracy at Clerkenwell Central Hall that evening, he was sadly disappointed, for the meeting turned out to be almost exactly the same as any other meeting of any other organization. First of all a man stood up on the stage at the front and gave apologies for absences, and announced how much had been taken in subscriptions the previous week, and how the Committee proposed to spend it. Then the minutes of the previous meeting were read out, and one or two motions of procedure put forward, which were debated briefly and voted on. It was all singularly dull—although Miss Flowers informed Freddy in a whisper that it was a pity he had missed last week's meeting, which had mostly been spent in debating how the King was to be introduced, were he ever to come and address one of their gatherings, and, furthermore, whether one ought to bow to him. Things had become quite heated, she said—remarkably so, in fact, considering that the chances of the King ever attending an Alliance meeting were so remote as to be non-existent. However, since the Alliance had no objection to entertaining questions of a rhetorical nature, the motion had been allowed onto the agenda, and anyone who wished to speak had been given the floor. The meeting had ended at midnight, but only because the caretaker had come and threatened to call the police if they did not leave, and Miss Flowers believed—although she had not witnessed it herself—that some of the more impassioned speakers had continued their debate afterwards with their coats off in the public gardens behind the hall.

Freddy expressed his sincere regret at having missed all the fun, but had no time to pursue the subject further for just then an interval was announced, and everyone rose at once. At one side of the room a table had been set up, behind which two women stood, serving tea at threepence a time. Freddy had already paid a shilling in subscriptions to attend the meeting.

'For a political movement that doesn't hold with money, they certainly know how to accumulate the stuff,' he said to Miss Flowers. She chuckled.

'Yes, they do, don't they? Much more efficient than the Y. W. A. A. next door. *They* give their tea away for nothing, but perhaps they ought to take a leaf out of our book and start charging, because I've no idea how they keep the thing afloat. Eighteenpence a week I paid them—although the working-class women pay reduced subs of a shilling, and the poorest ones get in free if they plead hardship—and they still never seemed to have any money. I expect that's because they spend it all on sending their saved women to the cinema and Southend. Either that, or somebody's had his hand in the till. They're not all as virtuous as they like to pretend in that association.'

She nodded significantly and tapped her nose. They were now joined by St. John. He greeted Miss Flowers as an old friend, then turned to Freddy.

'I say, come and meet the chaps,' he said. 'Trevett in particular is very keen to meet you. See that round little fellow standing next to him? The one who looks like a dog waiting for Trevett to throw him a bone? That's Sidney Bishop, our treasurer. He's common enough, but he has a tremendous head for money.'

Ivor Trevett had a hearty handshake, a loud, resonant voice, and a tendency to oratory. He affected to be uninterested in the prospect of appearing in the paper, but Freddy noticed that his replies all seemed particularly polished—rehearsed, even—while his gestures and mannerisms were expansive and graceful. He wondered whether Trevett practised in front of the mirror every evening.

'That was an impressive speech you made outside the Tradesmen's Hall the other day,' he said politely. 'It seemed to be received very well.'

Trevett gave a booming laugh.

'Yes, yes, my boy,' he said. 'One always likes to take the opportunity to speak to the man in the street. These meetings in private are all very well, but here one is already preaching to the converted, in a manner of speaking. If we truly mean to overturn the established order of things, then we must get out and mingle with the common people—out into the streets, among the working men and the middle classes—yes, even among those in high society who at present look upon us askance. One day they will come to accept that they, too, will benefit from a fairer, juster distribution of wealth, even if they do not like it at first.'

'And how do you propose to achieve this fairer distribution?' said Freddy with interest. 'Do you think you can talk them into it?'

'I very much hope so,' said Trevett. 'If it can be done through the power of speech alone, then I shall not be found wanting in my duty. Better to avoid violence if at all possible.'

'Oh, yes,' said Freddy. 'Speaking is better than fighting, as a rule. It's just a pity the police at the Tradesmen's Hall didn't agree.'

'I fear that arrest is a hazard of the job,' agreed Trevett. He ran a hand through his thick, wavy mane of hair. 'However, it shall not deter me, for I am but one man, and am of little importance when set against the prospect of the greater good. It is hardly a sacrifice.'

'Ivor is such an inspiring leader,' said Ruth Chudderley, who had come to join them. 'So many men are not prepared to turn their thoughts into deeds. They are all talk and no substance, but Ivor is not a hypocrite. He has demonstrated time and time again his devotion to the cause.'

'Very true,' said Sidney Bishop, who appeared just as starstruck by Trevett as Ruth was, and in fact seemed to have no other object in life but to agree with Trevett's every slightest pronouncement, and laugh uproariously at anything he said that might possibly be construed as a joke. 'I have no doubt that one day we will see Mr. Trevett appointed to one of the highest positions in the land—perhaps even Prime Minister.'

'Enough of that now,' said Trevett to Bishop, as one commanding a dog, and Bishop subsided immediately, the picture of dejection.

Two young men now detached themselves from another group and made their way towards Freddy and St. John.

'Bother, it's Peacock and Dyer,' muttered St. John. 'I suppose you ought to meet them.'

Leonard Peacock and Ronald Dyer turned out to be two waggish types with a tendency to rag St. John. Since St. John was commonly known to lack a sense of humour, this only made them rag him all the more.

'He's a Cambridge man,' explained Peacock, the taller and more talkative of the two. 'I mean to say, was there ever an easier target?'

'A sitting bird, in fact,' added Dyer. 'Why, he practically begs us to do it.'

'Indeed. I ask you,' said Peacock to Freddy, 'is there anyone left in the world, from the smallest child to the most doting of elderly ladies, who would be such a chump as to fall for the old glue-on-a-chair trick? And yet you see before you a man who has fallen for it not only once, but three times at last count. Why, even Bishop here isn't dim enough to be fooled by it.'

'I'm glad you think it's funny,' said St. John crossly.

'Oh, it is, it is,' said Peacock, and the two young men burst out laughing.

'Are you Oxford or Cambridge?' inquired Dyer of Freddy.

'Cambridge,' replied Freddy. 'But only briefly, I'm afraid. They developed an objection to me—on purely spurious grounds, I might add—and after some negotiation it was agreed that no prosecution would occur, but that I had no need of further education and might return to London as soon as I liked.'

'Bad luck,' said Dyer with sympathy.

'But tell me, what are you doing here?' went on Freddy. 'I mean to say, St. John's had the sickness for years and is quite incurable, but you chaps seem reasonably sane.'

'Oh, come now,' said Peacock. 'There's nothing wrong with wanting to see a more equitable society, is there?'

'Besides, one meets all sorts of clever people,' added Dyer. 'Schuster, for example. A fascinating fellow, to hear him speak.'

'Ah, yes, I've heard of Schuster. I'd like to meet him,' said Freddy.

'And you shall,' said St. John. 'There he is.'

An impeccably turned-out man of about sixty with wiry grey hair was now introduced. Freddy recognized him immediately as the man he had seen emerging from the committee-room with Ivor Trevett, and regarded him with some interest. This was the man he had been sent to see. He put on his most respectful manner.

'How do you do, sir,' he said. 'I know all about you, of course. I've read several of your works, in fact. Very intriguing, the way you look at things. I've never seen ideas presented in quite such an original way before.'

Schuster accepted the tribute as his due.

'Yes,' he said, with only the slightest trace of a foreign accent. 'It is true that my mind runs in a different way from that of most people, but I fear my ideas were a little *too* original for the Government of my country. They threatened arrest, and since I had no wish to spend my declining years in prison, I and my wife decided to come to London.'

'Won't they come and find you here?'

Schuster gave a shrug.

'It seems they have no further interest in me now that I have left,' he said. 'I was a—how do you say it?—a nuisance, under their feet, but now that I am the guest of another country they do not care. British Intelligence follow me around, naturally, but they are very polite. I know the English—it is not for them, the method of hitting a man over the head and making him disappear forever. If they want to put me in gaol, they will arrest me for leaving my car in the wrong place and then somehow forget to let me out.'

There was something inscrutable about him. His manner was light-hearted, but Freddy could not tell whether he were serious or not. A woman now came to stand silently by Schuster.

'Ah, but I beg your pardon, this is my wife,' said Schuster. 'Theresa, this is a man from the press, who has sympathy with my ideas.'

Theresa Schuster regarded Freddy from under her lashes, and her mouth curved up a little at one corner. She was a dark, striking woman of thirty-five or so, much younger than her husband, and much more foreign-looking—Freddy might even have called her exotic. She held out her hand in the manner of a queen bestowing grace upon a favoured vassal.

'Yes, I see he is a sympathetic one,' she said in a voice that was as smooth as silk. 'You shall come to our house one time. We have a gathering once a month—a kind of *salon*, yes? We exchange ideas and talk, and there is much music, and drinking, and laughter, and all good things.'

'Oh, yes,' said Peacock, who was still standing close by. 'They're jolly good fun. If Theresa has invited you then you'd better accept. It's quite a privilege, you know.'

Schuster began to recount an anecdote about his days back in Vienna, and for a few minutes the attention of the little group was necessarily directed towards him. Freddy was listening too, but happened to look up just in time to see a glance pass between Theresa Schuster and Leonard Peacock when they evidently thought no-one was watching. The meaning was plain to see, and Freddy raised his eyebrows. Peacock turned his attention back to Anton Schuster, looking very pleased with himself, leaving Freddy to draw his own conclusions as to the real reason for Peacock's devotion to the Communist cause.

'Listen, I want to talk to you,' came St. John's voice in his ear, as Schuster finished his anecdote. He took Freddy to one side and glanced about furtively.

'Fire away,' said Freddy obligingly.

'It's about Ruth,' said St. John, after a moment.

'Oh?'

'I mean to say, you've seen what a wonderful girl she is, so you can see the problem.'

He looked at Freddy expectantly.

'I think you've missed out the story, old chap,' said Freddy. 'What *is* the problem?'

'Why, I want to marry her, of course!'

'Yes, I thought as much. Congratulations and all that, what?'

'But I need your help.'

'My help? What for?'

'Because she won't have me.'

'Won't she? What is it? Is there something about your face that puts her off? I shouldn't have thought there was anything particularly offensive about it myself, but one never knows with women.'

'It's not that. As a matter of fact, she says she *will* have me, but she won't marry me.'

'What?'

'She doesn't believe in marriage, you see,' explained St. John. 'She believes in free love and all that nonsense. Well, I can't have that. I'm an honourable man. She shall marry me or nothing.'

'But I thought you Communists were all in favour of the dismantling of the old systems.'

'Well, but I mean to say, there are limits,' said St. John indignantly. 'I won't let a woman ruin her reputation on my account. I mean to marry her and marry her I shall.'

'I should like to see you persuade a woman to do anything she's set herself against,' said Freddy. 'But why Ruth? She seems a nice enough girl, but I should hardly have thought she was your type. Isn't she a little too intellectual?'

'Oh, she's terribly brainy, but I don't mind that. I want a woman I can talk to.'

'But won't your mother disapprove of her?'

'Yes, I dare say she will. But Iris is marrying well, so I'm pretty certain I can talk her into the idea. One good marriage in the family ought to be enough, surely?'

'Iris? Is that still on? When is it to be?'

'This spring. I expect you'll get an invitation. Oh—I forgot, you and she had a thing for a while last year, didn't you?'

'It wasn't at all serious,' said Freddy carelessly.

'I don't know what she sees in that chap of hers. He's the most awful stiff. I'd much rather have you for a brother-in-law, although I dare say you're not interested in marriage either. But I don't see what's so terrible about it. I mean to say, that's how things have been done for centuries, and if it's good enough for everyone else it ought to be good enough for her.'

He was evidently talking about Ruth again. Freddy shrugged.

'I don't know what to suggest,' he said. 'If she doesn't want you then there's not much you can do about it except keep pegging away at her until she either says yes or takes a fives bat to you out of sheer exasperation.'

'Will you talk to her for me?' said St. John suddenly.

'Talk to her about what? Propose on your behalf, do you mean?'

'No, of course not. I meant try and convince her that I'm a good prospect.'

'My dear old ass, if she doesn't believe in marriage then what makes you think I can convince her to betray her principles and stray from the path of righteousness? Or do I mean *to* the path of righteousness? I expect I do.'

'But you're good at that sort of thing. Talking drivel until people do what you want, I mean.'

'Is that meant to be a compliment?'

'I suppose it is. You *will* have a word with her, won't you?'

'Er—' said Freddy, but had no time to finish before there was a bustle and it was announced that the meeting was about to recommence. St. John threw him a meaningful look and returned to his seat by Ruth. Freddy glanced around, and decided not to return to his own seat. Instead he stood at the side of the room, in order to get a better view of the proceedings. The first person to stand up on the stage was the man who had written the tragic novel. He was evidently unused to public speaking, and read out the first chapter of his book very fast in a monotone, without once looking at his audience, then stopped abruptly and walked off before anyone had the chance to gather their thoughts and clap. Fortunately, Ivor Trevett rose to the occasion and called for an enthusiastic round of applause. The author, who had just arrived back at his seat, went crimson in the face and sat down hurriedly. Then one or two women stood up and read poems and extracts. After that it was Trevett's turn. He took to the stage and spoke with great eloquence about last week's demonstration outside the Tradesmen's Hall. Those who had not been able to attend had missed a shining example of what effective protest could achieve, he said. Why, the number of police alone demonstrated clearly that those in power were unnerved by the determination of their opponents. Now, more than ever, said Trevett, was the time to press their advantage. The sound of the working man's voice should not be drowned out. He continued in this vein for some little time, his audience rapt and silent. Even Freddy had to admit he spoke very well, and felt an unexpected twinge of disappointment when the speech ended—surprise, too, for he had judged Trevett to be a man who was very fond of the sound of his own voice, and had assumed he would continue for longer. But he soon understood why the speech had been cut short when Anton Schuster was announced. Schuster was obviously considered an important person, and the star turn of the evening, but his speech was something of a let-down, for he was dry and quiet, and his humour went above the heads of many of those present. Moreover, his ideas were abstract and difficult to grasp, unlike those of Trevett, who constantly advocated practical action. The audience sat politely, but the applause at the end was much more muted than it had been for Trevett. Schuster seemed by no means disconcerted at this, and merely left the stage with a little bow.

The meeting was now drawing to a close, and everybody rose for the Red Flag. Freddy did not sing, for he was too busy watching Trevett, who had taken Anton Schuster to one side and was talking to him in a low voice. Schuster gave a little smile of satisfaction and nodded. Someone else was watching them too, Freddy noticed: Sidney Bishop, the little treasurer and hanger-on, was standing on the other side of the room, watching Schuster and Trevett with wrinkled brows. Freddy looked around ruminatively. He had met all the most important members of the East London Communist Alliance, he believed. It was curious to see that, apart from Bishop—and possibly Trevett, who as a former actor might easily be dissembling—they were all from the upper reaches of society. Why were the real working men not represented on the Committee? Was there really a conspiracy? And did it originate with Anton Schuster, as Henry Jameson believed? Schuster and Trevett certainly seemed to have private concerns to talk about, but they might be quite innocent matters. The only other suspicious thing Freddy had seen that evening was the look which had passed between Mrs. Schuster and Leonard Peacock—but that was easily explained away and most likely had nothing at all to do with any sort of political plot. Altogether it had been an unsatisfactory sort of evening with regard to his investigation, and he would have very little to report to Henry Jameson. Freddy set himself to pondering idly the best way in which to ensure that Mrs. Schuster did not forget to invite him to her next evening party, for it seemed to him that if there *were* anything to find out, then the Schusters' house would be the best place to start.

Just then he noticed Miss Flowers giving him a stern look, of the sort one receives from an elder on being discovered fidgeting in church. He recalled his thoughts to the here and now, and was just in time to join in with the last two lines of the Red Flag, which he sang without having any particular idea of the words.

CHAPTER FIVE

BOTH MEETINGS ENDED at about nine o'clock, and all was confusion as two hundred people tried to leave the building at once. Freddy hung back under the pretence of wanting to speak to St. John, but really in the hope of finding out something useful. As he waited in the lobby, he saw the young couple who had gone into the two separate meetings standing by the cloak-room. The girl seemed to be complaining about something. Freddy drifted across and listened shamelessly.

'They lump us all together,' she was saying. 'And some of those girls aren't any better than they ought to be. I'm not one of that sort—never touched a drop or done anything I oughtn't to have—and yet they seem to think we're all the same. They think we all need saving. Well, I don't! I'm sick of being talked down to, and I've a good mind to tell them so.'

She looked quite fierce. Her companion clicked his tongue and frowned in annoyance.

'I've told you before about those la-di-da types,' he said. 'I said they didn't understand, and I was right, wasn't I? They're nothing but bourgeois tyrants.'

'Well, I shouldn't go that far,' said the girl reluctantly. 'Some of them are all right, I suppose.'

'They're all as bad as each other,' said the man. 'But it's all going to end soon. You mark my words, my girl—soon you won't have to sit through all this nonsense, or mix with those who are beneath you. They'll stop looking down on you soon enough when they see what we've got planned. Watch out for something in the next few weeks. I've told you before, Trevett and Schuster know what they're doing. I'll be out on the streets protesting, and if you know what's good for you you'll come too.'

'Get away with you,' said the girl good-humouredly. 'You and your revolution. I'll believe it when I see it. Come on, are you going to treat me to this fish and chips supper or not? I'm hungry.'

They went out and Freddy was left to wonder whether there was anything in what the man had said. Most people had now left, but he had not seen any of the Committee leave the hall, and he was about to go and scout around a little when to his dismay he was accosted by Miss Stapleton, who just then came out of the minor hall and swooped on him with an exclamation of triumph.

'Ah, Mr. Pilkington-Soames!' she said. 'You won't mind helping us clear up, will you? I'm afraid we are one short, since our treasurer, Mr. Bottle, who usually helps us, has most unfortunately been struck down with pneumonia and is not here this evening.'

Since Miss Stapleton was accustomed to carrying all before her, Freddy could do nothing but allow himself to be swept up, much to his vexation. Fortune was with him, however: Miss Stapleton wanted him to stack chairs in the minor hall, and when he entered Freddy found that the big folding doors between the two halls had been thrown open, allowing him to see into the main hall. Nothing much was happening, as far as he could see. St. John and Ruth were just on the point of leaving, and very soon did so, but not before St. John had stared very hard at Freddy and then directed a meaningful glance at Ruth. Freddy indicated the chairs and gave an apologetic smile, and St. John grimaced, and then they went out. The Schusters seemed to have disappeared, while Peacock and Dyer were indulging in noisy horseplay as they stacked chairs in the main hall. Just then, Ivor Trevett appeared from somewhere and strode towards the lobby. In the doorway he bumped into Mr. Hussey. The two men stiffened and glared at one another haughtily, then passed on. Freddy heard a giggle by his side. It was Mildred Starkweather, who had come to help.

'Marvellous, isn't it?' she said. 'They can't bear one another.'

'Whyever not?'

'Well, it's obvious, isn't it? They're far too alike—fascinating to look at and full of S. A, although I suppose it doesn't do to talk that way about a Wesleyan minister. At any rate, you can see they each want to be top dog. Whenever Mr. Hussey comes they compete to see who can get the loudest applause and drown out next door's meeting.'

'But Mr. Hussey is a man of the cloth,' said Freddy. 'I should have thought that sort of thing was un-Christian.'

'Pfft,' said Mildred. 'Try telling that to Mr. Hussey. He thinks it's his duty to assert the superiority of the Church over the heathen Communists.'

'And I suppose Trevett wants to do the opposite?'

'I don't think he cares much, as long as people are clapping loudly enough,' said Mildred.

'I'm sorry I missed Mr. Hussey's speech,' said Freddy. 'Was it good?'

'Oh, very good. How's St. John, by the way?'

'Asinine, as usual.'

'I gather he's fallen for the Chudderley female,' said Mildred. 'I know it doesn't do to say so, but she's insufferable.'

'I—er—did get something of that impression,' said Freddy cautiously.

'I'm being a spiteful cat, of course. I only say it because she looks down her nose at me.'

'How could anyone look down their nose at you? You're a splendid girl,' said Freddy.

'She thinks I'm naïve—or at least, that's what she said. Oh, she dressed it up in a compliment, but it was pretty obvious what she meant. She thinks I'm too green for words.'

'Well, there's nothing wrong with that, is there? You're jolly nice.'

'No, she's right,' said Mildred, stacking chairs with great ferocity. 'I'm dull. Prim and dull. I come to Temperance meetings with my mother, and smile at people and make tea and never have any fun.'

Freddy was spared having to reply by the arrival of Miss Hodges, flustered as usual, who had been sent in to help by Miss Stapleton.

'Mrs. and Miss Starkweather have to leave very shortly,' said Miss Stapleton from the doorway, 'and Mabel and Jessie are quite capable of clearing up the kitchen by themselves, so you may as well help Mr. Pilkington-Soames. Do remember to stack the chairs properly this time.'

Miss Hodges gave an apologetic smile and began flapping ineffectually, since Freddy and Mildred had already made short work of the chairs. Miss Stapleton disappeared, to be replaced by Mrs. Starkweather, who put her head into the hall.

'Come, Mildred,' she said. 'It won't do to keep Burton waiting.'

Mildred said her goodbyes and hurried off, and Freddy shoved the last stack of chairs against the wall.

'I think that's everything,' he said. 'Is there anything else?'

'No, I don't believe so,' said Miss Hodges doubtfully. 'That is, unless Jessie and Mabel need us to do anything.'

Jessie and Mabel, who worked in a nearby factory and were recent converts to the Temperance cause, had no need of help, it turned out, and were already putting their coats and hats on.

'It's very dark outside,' said Freddy, glancing out through the front door. 'How do you get home?'

'By 'bus,' said Miss Hodges. 'Islington is not very far, but it's just a little too far to walk at this time of night.'

'I'll see you onto the 'bus,' said Freddy. 'What about you two girls? Where do you live?'

There was much giggling at the question, but it was eventually ascertained that the two young women shared a room less than half a mile away, and after some little discussion it was agreed that Freddy would see them safely to their door. Miss Stapleton was nowhere to be found, so they set out without bidding her goodnight. It was a clear evening, with half a moon. The streets were damp, and gleamed under the light from the street-lamps. The two girls chattered together, discussing some mysterious business of their own, and Freddy made polite conversation with Miss Hodges, who seemed fearful of putting him out—indeed, had it not been for the presence of Jessie and Mabel, it is very likely that she would have refused his assistance altogether. In less than five minutes they arrived at the 'bus stop. Freddy and the others were preparing to wait with Miss Hodges for her 'bus to arrive, but there were already two respectable-looking women standing there, who, to judge from their conversation, worked at a well-known draper's shop near Oxford Street. Miss Hodges was evidently so agitated and pained at the thought of keeping anyone waiting on her account that Freddy and the girls bade her goodnight and walked on. Once Jessie and Mabel had been safely delivered to their dingy lodgings Freddy turned back. He was not so very far from his own rooms on Fleet Street—not more than ten or fifteen minutes' walk—but it was cold and he decided to take a taxi if he could find one. An omnibus passed, and Freddy saw that the 'bus stop was now deserted and felt a brief sense of relief that he should not have to stop and make conversation with the permanently apologetic Miss Hodges. As the sound of the 'bus receded into the distance, silence fell. It was all unusually quiet for that time of night—perhaps because of the cold, and Freddy strolled along, thinking of nothing in particular. A hundred yards ahead of him he could see that some of the lights were still on at Clerkenwell Central Hall, and he decided to go in and snoop around a little if the caretaker had not yet locked up. Just as he reached this decision, he saw a dark figure detach itself from the shadows of the main entrance to the hall, descend the steps and hurry off down the street. The figure had a furtive appearance, and seemed fearful of being seen, for it glanced to right and left as it went. Freddy could not see who it was, although it was certainly a man. Whoever he was, he looked so anxious to avoid detection that for a moment Freddy considered following him to see what he was up to, but then decided against it, for the man was now some distance down the street, and even as Freddy watched, he turned a corner and disappeared.

Freddy stood looking at the building for a minute, then went in quietly. Some of the lights had been switched off, and the lobby and corridors were dim. Nobody was about, but he could hear voices coming from somewhere—perhaps the main hall. He stole up to the door and peered in. At the far end of the hall was the stage, hung with a heavy curtain that was pulled a little way across. The voices were coming from behind it. He listened carefully but could distinguish nothing that was being said. He wanted to get closer, but it was impossible to do that without walking openly through the hall. Perhaps he could approach through the minor hall instead. Yes; he could sneak in there and through the folding doors between the two halls, which were located near the stage of the main hall. There were some chairs stacked against the wall there, and it would be easy enough to crouch down behind them and avoid being seen. He turned and went into the minor hall, walking slowly and quietly so as not to be heard, and put his head carefully around the folding doors. He could see nobody, but the sound of voices was a little louder from here. He was just about to creep forward to the nearest stack of chairs when a hand came down on his shoulder and he nearly jumped out of his skin. He whirled round to see Leonard Peacock and Ronald Dyer standing before him. Dyer was just putting on his scarf.

'Hallo, hallo!' said Leonard Peacock jovially. 'Still here, are you? I thought you'd gone home ages ago.'

'I'm looking for my umbrella,' said Freddy easily. 'I thought I'd left it here. You haven't seen it, have you?'

'Don't think so,' said Peacock. 'Come back tomorrow and ask old Davis. Dyer and I are just off home now. You'd better come with us; they don't like people staying here too late.'

'All right,' said Freddy. It seemed he had no other choice, for Peacock and Dyer were now leading him out of the hall and evidently had no intention of allowing him to stay. 'Are you the last?' he said.

'Yes, I think so. The others left a while ago,' said Dyer. 'I expect Davis will come and lock up soon.'

Freddy could not say for certain that Dyer was lying, for it was always possible that he believed what he said and had not heard what Freddy had heard: the voices of Ivor Trevett and Anton Schuster coming from behind the curtain. There was nothing to be done, however; Freddy had no wish to be found out, and could only hope that his snooping would be ascribed to the natural curiosity of a press-man out for a story. Moreover, since he wanted to be admitted to the Schusters' inner circle, he felt it expedient to ingratiate himself with Peacock and Dyer—Peacock in particular—and so he walked with them as far as Chancery Lane, even though it was a little out of his way, and bade a cheery goodnight to them there, then went home and was most uncharacteristically in bed by eleven o'clock.

CHAPTER SIX

FREDDY WAS AT his desk on time for once the next day, and was immediately handed a particularly dull story about road-works. He was thinking about it and grumbling to himself when Jolliffe at the next desk put down the telephone and stood up.

'Off somewhere?' said Freddy absently.

'Yes. This murder in Clerkenwell.'

'Which murder?' said Freddy, raising his head at the familiar name.

'You know—the woman who was found dead at Clerkenwell Central Hall.'

'*What*?' said Freddy, astounded. He stared at Jolliffe, all thoughts of road-works forgotten.

'Oh, didn't you hear Bickerstaffe? Yes, the call came in not half an hour ago. A Miss Olive Stapleton. They found her this morning. A friend of Marjorie Belcher's, apparently, from that Temperance organization of hers. They're all up in arms about it.'

'But murder? But what—I mean to say, when—look here, are they sure? How did she die?'

'A dagger to the heart, apparently. There's some suspicion of robbery, I think.'

'Good God!' exclaimed Freddy. He could hardly believe his ears.

'Quite,' said Jolliffe. 'Mrs. Belcher is devastated, I understand. Miss Stapleton was her second-in-command, you see. It seems there was a meeting last night at the hall in question, and nobody saw Miss Stapleton leave, and then this morning she was discovered in a side room by someone from a club that meets in the hall on Wednesday mornings. Now, what did they say the club was? I ought to have written it down but I couldn't find my pencil.' He scratched his head and stared into space, trying to remember. 'Oh, yes. Raffia, I think it was.'

'Raffia be damned,' said Freddy. 'Why, man, do you realize I was there last night and saw Miss Stapleton herself?'

'Were you?' said Jolliffe in mild surprise. 'Has Mrs. Belcher got to you at last? I didn't know you'd gone all in for abstinence.'

'I haven't, and as a matter of fact it wasn't that meeting I was at—it was the Communists I was there for.'

'Communists?' said Jolliffe. 'Are you sure you're feeling all right, old chap? You haven't gone off your head or something, have you?'

'Don't be an ass. I was there for a—' Here he stopped, for he could not very well say to one of his fellow-reporters that he had been sent there on a story, since Jolliffe would know perfectly well that it was not true. 'I went out of curiosity, that's all,' he finished lamely.

'I see,' said Jolliffe, regarding him askance.

'Listen,' said Freddy. 'You'd better let me take this one, since I'm in on it already, in a manner of speaking.'

'Oh, but—'

'Never mind that. Here, you can have this one. Road-works.'

'What?' said Jolliffe in dismay, but Freddy had already pushed the details across to him and was putting on his coat. He then left the office in a hurry, leaving Jolliffe regarding the road-works story with disfavour.

He took a taxi and arrived at Clerkenwell Central Hall to find that a group of reporters from other newspapers had already arrived and were standing in a huddle outside the front door, for it was bitterly cold.

'Any news?' he said to the nearest one.

'Nothing we can get out of them,' said the man in disgust. 'They're a close-lipped lot. Can't even get them to admit there's been a murder.'

Freddy went up the steps to speak to the constable on the door.

'No press,' said the constable. 'You'd better go and wait with the rest of them.'

'Look here,' said Freddy. 'I was here last night and might have some useful information for you.'

'Might you, indeed?' said the policeman disbelievingly. 'You're a member of the Young Women's Abstinence Association, are you?'

'Well, I mean to say, I wasn't at the Temperance meeting. I came for the other one—the Communist Alliance, you know. But some of the Temperance ladies are friends of mine, and I helped them tidy up at the end of the meeting. I tell you, I was here last night and spoke to Miss Stapleton.'

The constable regarded him for a moment, then said, 'All right, then,' and admitted him to the lobby.

'What's all this?' said a man in plain clothes, who had about him the look of a detective-inspector. 'I told you not to let anyone in.'

'This gentleman says he was here last night and has something to tell us, sir,' said the constable.

'He looks like press to me.'

'I am press,' said Freddy, then went on hurriedly, 'but it's true that I was here last night, and spoke to Miss Stapleton.'

'I see,' said the inspector non-committally, but with a slight gleam of interest in his eye. 'And what did you speak to her about?'

'Oh, just the best way to stack chairs. I was helping them clear up, you see.'

'Indeed, sir? And are you—er—a champion of the Temperance movement?' said the inspector.

'I don't know why everybody always looks so disbelieving when they ask me that,' said Freddy. 'If I were the sensitive sort, I might take it personally. However, you're right—I'm not a member of that worthy group. I was here on behalf of the *Clarion*, watching the Communists disport themselves in the next room. After the meeting Miss Stapleton asked me to help put the chairs away, so I did that and then left.'

'I see,' said the inspector. His face was impassive, but Freddy could sense the suspicion welling up inside him. 'Do you happen to remember at what time you last saw Miss Stapleton?'

Freddy thought.

'It must have been about half past nine, I think. At what time did she die?'

'We don't yet know for certain, but most likely not long after she was last seen.'

'And at what time was that?'

'About half past nine,' said the inspector significantly.

'Don't look at me,' said Freddy. 'I had nothing to do with it.'

'Can you prove it?'

'I think so, yes. I was in company with several people while we cleared up, and we all left the hall together shortly afterwards.' He explained further what everybody had been doing the night before, and the inspector listened attentively.

'And I dare say the others will testify to that?' he said.

'I should hope so. It would be particularly uncivil of them not to,' said Freddy.

'Did you speak to Miss Stapleton when you left?'

'No, she'd disappeared somewhere, so we went without saying goodbye. I saw Miss Hodges onto her 'bus and the two girls to their door, and then went home.'

'You didn't return to the hall afterwards, by any chance?'

'No,' said Freddy. Of course this was not true, but ought he to mention it? He was not sure, for it would require awkward explanations he was not permitted to give at present, and so he said nothing.

'Did you see anything suspicious at all?'

Freddy hesitated.

'There was something—' he began.

'Yes?'

'When I passed the hall again on my way home, I saw someone slip out of the building and hurry off down the street. It might easily have been somebody who was at the meeting, although I didn't recognize him.'

'Are you sure of this?' said the inspector.

'I'm sure I saw somebody, yes,' said Freddy. 'But as I said, it might not have been anything important. I only mentioned it because of the man's manner, which I should describe as distinctly furtive.'

'Certainly a man, you say?'

'Oh, yes.'

'And you're sure you didn't recognize him?'

Freddy shook his head.

'There were a lot of people there that evening,' he said.

'Hmm,' said the inspector, and made a note. Freddy looked at him as he wrote. He had never seen the man before, but he had a quiet authority about him which spoke volumes. This was not the usual sort of policeman, and there was obviously more to this than met the eye.

'This isn't an ordinary murder, is it?' he said.

'What makes you think that?' said the inspector suddenly, and Freddy was sure his guess was correct.

'You chaps,' he said.

The inspector regarded him searchingly for a moment.

'We have no reason to believe it was anything other than what it appears to be,' he said.

'I heard something was stolen,' said Freddy. 'What was it?'

'A takings box belonging to the Young Women's Abstinence Association. It was kept in a locked drawer in the office that's used by some of the organizations which meet here, but according to Mr. Bottle, the Association's treasurer, it is now missing.'

'Was it stolen from the drawer?'

'It doesn't appear so. We assume Miss Stapleton had removed the box from the drawer prior to taking it home herself, since the lock of the drawer had not been forced. It looks as though the murderer came upon her, killed her and took the takings.'

Freddy paused, thinking.

'Look here, is that really what happened?' he said at last. 'Or is this all something to do with what was going on in the next hall?'

Again there was that searching look.

'We are examining all the circumstances of the killing,' said the inspector. 'However, at present we've no reason to believe the crime is anything other than that which it appears to be. Miss Stapleton seems to have encountered a particularly violent thief, and there was a struggle and she was killed.'

'How did she die?'

'She was stabbed with a sharp object,' replied the inspector. His manner was bland and calculated to discourage inquiry. He stood up. 'And now, if you'll excuse me, I must get back to my duties. You'd better give me your name in case I have any further questions.'

'Oh, I'm sure you will, inspector,' said Freddy cheerfully, and handed him a card. 'You'll always find me at the *Clarion*'s offices. Although it's probably safest to call after ten,' he added, as he went out.

CHAPTER SEVEN

THE GROUP OF reporters had grown, and as Freddy went to join them they crowded around him, demanding to know what he had found out—which, he was forced to confess, was very little. There were one or two grumbles of disbelief, but since it was obvious that Freddy either could not or would not say anything, they soon left him alone and returned to their vigil, stamping their feet and blowing on their hands, and leaving Freddy to reflect on his conversation with the police. He had judged it best to maintain the fiction that he had been sent by his paper to attend the East London Communist Alliance meeting, and so had necessarily kept quiet about having returned to the central hall later. But that meant he had not given the police all the information he had. He had mentioned the man he had seen leaving the hall, but had said nothing about the fact that Peacock and Dyer had remained behind after the meeting—as had Ivor Trevett and Anton Schuster. Was one of them to blame for Miss Stapleton's death? Freddy knew the police were likely to take it amiss once they found out he had lied to them, and so went to find a telephone box in order to call Henry Jameson and give him the full story. He hoped Henry would not deny all knowledge of him to the police. Mr. Jameson was not in his office, he was informed, but was expected within an hour or so. Freddy clicked his tongue in impatience at the delay and went back to join the others, for he still had a story to write. After they had all stood an hour or so in the freezing cold, the detective inspector came out and told them what Freddy knew already. The victim was a Miss Olive Stapleton, aged fifty-five. She had been found dead in the committee-room of Clerkenwell Central Hall at a quarter to nine that morning, having died in unexplained and suspicious circumstances. More information would be given as soon as they had it, but in the meantime the gentlemen of the press were advised to leave, for more details were not expected that day. The reporters wanted to know whether it were true that Miss Stapleton had been stabbed in the heart with an ornamental dagger, as had been rumoured, but the inspector would state only that she had died by means of a blow from a sharp implement. Yes, Miss Stapleton's body had already been removed, and the press would be informed of any further developments in the case as soon as the police were permitted to disclose them. The inspector then went inside, and the reporters were left to cool their heels on the steps.

Freddy waited a few more minutes then gave it up and returned to the telephone box. Henry Jameson had just arrived, he was informed.

'Hallo,' came Henry's voice at the other end of the line. 'I can guess why you're calling. Have you had lunch?'

'No,' said Freddy.

'Then come and eat, and we can talk in comfort.'

Freddy liked this way of conducting business, and approved greatly of a man who knew how to do things properly. They met in a discreet restaurant near Whitehall, but to Freddy's surprise Henry talked only of general subjects throughout lunch.

'One gets tired of talking shop all the time,' he said vaguely, and asked another question about a big story to which Freddy's newspaper had given much attention over the past few weeks, wherein it had 'scooped' its rivals most resoundingly. Freddy answered obligingly, but gradually began to notice that the questions Henry Jameson was asking were not general at all. Taken one at a time they might have seemed quite innocent, but the overall direction of the conversation was unmistakable. He was being sounded out, he realized. It appeared Henry wanted to make certain that he had taken on the right man for the job, and had not yet lowered his guard. It was a sensible attitude to take on the part of the Head of Intelligence, Freddy supposed.

'Well, do I pass muster?' he could not help asking at the end of lunch.

Henry gave a small smile of acknowledgment.

'You'll do for the present,' he said. 'Now, let's go to the park and talk.'

St. James's park was only five minutes away, and they strolled around the lake as though they had come purely to take the air. Henry—not the sort of man to volunteer information himself unless forced to do so—seemed to be waiting for Freddy to begin. Freddy took the hint.

'You know about this murder in Clerkenwell, of course,' he said. 'A Miss Stapleton.'

'I had heard something of it,' said Henry cautiously.

'She was stabbed with something, although the police won't say what.'

'It was a paper-knife,' said Henry.

'Oh?' said Freddy.

'Taken from a drawer in the office.'

'I see,' said Freddy, thinking. 'At any rate, I hear the motive was simple robbery—in which case, why Special Branch?'

'I beg your pardon?' said Henry.

'Oh, come now. It was perfectly obvious. I could hardly get a word out of them. They weren't ordinary C. I. D, were they?'

'No,' admitted Henry.

'But why?'

'Miss Stapleton was known to the police. She had three or four times reported that she believed the East London Communist Alliance were up to something, although she could provide no evidence of it—only a suspicion born of the fact that they tend to whisper conspiratorially in corners, and that once or twice she had overheard snatches of their conversation which seemed to indicate they were up to no good. The police considered her to be more of a nuisance than anything, and so did little more than record her complaints and send her on her way politely.'

'But you think there was enough in her suspicions to make it worth sending in Special Branch when she got herself murdered?'

Henry bowed his head in acquiescence.

'If there's nothing in it, then we'll hand it back to the usual chaps,' he said. 'But in view of my current suspicions as to what's been going on lately, I thought I'd better have this lot take a look at it first. And now you must tell me what you have found out—about the murder or anything else. I gather you attended last night?'

'I did,' said Freddy. 'And if you're looking for proof of what you told me the other day, I'm afraid I didn't find it—although I don't suppose you expected me to on the strength of one public meeting.'

'No,' said Henry.

'I did, however, observe events rather closely, and saw one or two suggestive things that may or may not interest you. I saw—as did Miss Stapleton, it seems—that Ivor Trevett, who is the President of the Alliance, and Anton Schuster, are prone to gathering in corners to whisper together. I also met two chaps of my sort, who claim to come to the meetings for fun. Friendly enough, top-drawer and all that, but if you were to ask me I should say they reminded me of nothing more or less than hired toughs. They found me snooping around the hall after the meeting ended, and escorted me from the premises pretty sharpish. One of them may or may not be misbehaving with Schuster's wife.'

'Indeed?' said Henry with interest. 'What makes you think that?'

'Just a look between them, but there's no mistaking that sort of thing as a rule. Whether it's got any further than a look I couldn't tell you.'

'What did you think of Schuster?'

'He does his best to avoid looking suspicious,' said Freddy. 'He knows that you chaps have your eye on him, by the way.'

'I should think the less of him if he didn't,' said Henry.

'Still, he seems harmless enough. From my first meeting with him I should have said that he is what he appears to be: an elderly philosopher and academic who's far too pleased with himself and his own ideas to bother with any sort of violent action. I should have thought he was far more likely to stand back and let someone else do the dirty work.'

'Ivor Trevett, for example?'

'Well, Trevett certainly glories in making a public exhibition of himself. I can see him taking great pleasure in standing at the vanguard, brandishing a red flag and orating furiously, although he'd make jolly sure he had a crowd of people to watch him as he did it. He craves the adulation of the public, I'd say.'

'Yes, that is a weakness,' said Henry, musing.

'A weakness? Is that what you're looking for?'

'Oh, one's always searching for a chink in the armour,' said Henry. 'The threat of police and courts and gaol is all very well, but most of these people revel in the idea of attracting that sort of attention, and it only makes them stand their ground more firmly, if you see what I mean. As a general rule, it's a much better idea to try and undermine them from within. For example, if Trevett's main fault is vanity, then we can look for ways to force him to show his hand by appealing to that part of him.'

'I see,' said Freddy. 'And what about Schuster? I suppose you would get at him through his wife?'

'Exactly,' said Henry. 'If she is prone to—er—flightiness with young men, then perhaps we can induce her to reveal information about what is happening using that method.'

He looked sideways at Freddy.

'You have a calculating expression on your face,' said Freddy. 'Schuster's an old man, but I shouldn't like to have to go three rounds with Peacock if he took offence. He's twice my size and looks pretty handy with his fists.'

'But surely there's no harm in speaking to the lady? I seem to recall from the last time we met that you had—er—something of a talent in that way. Would there be any opportunity for you to exercise it?'

'Well, there was talk of some sort of intellectual shindy. Apparently Mrs. Schuster likes to gather London's best and brightest around her to sing songs and raise glasses to the future, and that kind of thing. She mentioned inviting me to the next one.'

'That's excellent news,' said Henry. 'Do your best to go. Don't wait for a formal invitation.'

'Oh, no fear of that. My gate-crashing abilities are legendary,' said Freddy. 'And perhaps a gathering of that sort would provide a better opportunity to find out what we want to know.'

'I think you're probably right,' said Henry.

'There was another thing,' went on Freddy. 'I did hear mention of something having been planned for the next few weeks. I don't know what it is, but a young man was telling his girl that there was something afoot, and that he'd be out demonstrating on the streets when it happened. Of course, it might mean anything or nothing, since these people do like to talk.'

'There's a big march taking place on the fifteenth of February,' said Henry. 'It's to be followed by a rally in Hyde Park.'

'Is that so? He might have been talking about that, then,' said Freddy. 'Yes, that makes more sense. I suppose the ringleaders are hardly likely to pass on the details of whatever they're plotting to the rank and file, are they?'

'Not very likely,' agreed Henry. 'At some point they will have to mobilize the troops, but at what stage do they do that? If they do it too early then there's the risk of the news getting out, but if they leave it too late, then the thing might fall flat, since nobody will have time to prepare themselves.'

'But what *are* they plotting, exactly?' said Freddy. '*Is* it a general strike?'

'I'm not sure. The last one didn't work too well in the end, did it? I mean to say, the miners in particular didn't achieve their aims. I wonder whether they mightn't be taking a different approach this time. If they organize things efficiently enough then they might cause just as much disruption and draw just as much attention to their cause without everybody's needing to down tools.'

'But I thought you said Rowbotham didn't approve of such things, and was all for getting his way by negotiating with the Government?'

'Yes, I did. But while Rowbotham is certainly influential, and well thought-of among the powers that be, he's only one man, and there's no saying that some of the more excitable elements might not decide to break away and take matters into their own hands.'

'You mean supporters of this Pettit fellow?'

'Yes. The problem from their point of view is that they are relatively small in number, and without the machinery of a large union to back them up they will have difficulty in achieving anything of note. I should like to find out how they propose to do it.'

'And how do you intend to do that?'

'With your help, I hope,' said Henry. He looked about and spied an empty bench. 'Let us sit down.'

They did so, and Henry reached into his inside pocket and brought out a neatly folded copy of the *Radical*.

'You may remember I mentioned that we suspect the plotters—whoever they are—of communicating with their counterparts in the North by means of a code,' he said.

'Yes,' said Freddy, and looked on with interest as Henry opened the paper at a page that was dedicated to personal announcements.

'The usual stuff,' said Henry. 'The readers seem fond of corresponding through the newspaper, and most of it is of no interest to us at all. But look at this.'

Freddy took the paper and looked down the column. There were the usual advertisements for lodgings, second-hand books and old furniture for sale, but at the bottom of the page was a discreet announcement of the cheapest sort.

'"Daddie Dearest, close to my heart,"' he read. 'What are all these numbers? It makes no sense.'

'Not to us,' said Henry. 'I expect it's perfectly clear to those who are meant to read it, however.'

'Haven't you been able to crack it?'

Henry grimaced.

'No,' he said. 'We've had the chaps on to it, but they tell me it's most likely a cipher based on a particular book. You've probably read about the kind of thing I mean—you know, everybody in on the secret has a copy of *Alice in Wonderland*, or *Great Expectations*, or some other well-known book that anyone might own, and the code is drawn from that by giving clues to particular words. You see the first three numbers here: twenty-seven, eighteen and six. They most probably refer to the page number, the line number and the word number.'

'Oh, I see,' said Freddy. 'So the sixth word on the eighteenth line of page twenty-seven, is that it?'

'Yes,' said Henry. 'Rather a laborious way of writing a code, but it's very effective, provided everybody is using the same edition of the same book. The problem is that we don't know which book it is.'

'Do all the messages begin with "Daddie Dearest?" How revolting,' said Freddy.

'Quite,' said Henry. 'That, and other similar endearments. They vary them a little so as not to look too obvious, but they're easy enough to recognize.'

'I suppose you'd like me to snoop around and find out the name of this book? What about your man on the spot? Hasn't he found it out yet?'

'Not so far,' said Henry shortly.

'Very well, I shall do my best,' said Freddy. 'If it's humanly possible to talk the information out of someone, then I shall do it.'

'Splendid,' said Henry. 'By the way, you haven't told me anything about your friend St. John. Should you say he knows anything?'

'I didn't see him doing anything suspicious,' said Freddy, considering. 'As a matter of fact, he seems more interested in trying to persuade his girl-friend to marry him, but that's not to say he's not being used, of course. Miss Chudderley is a great admirer of Ivor Trevett. If he's up to something, she might be in on it too. I shall keep an eye on her.'

'And keep an eye on Bagshawe too. Perhaps he's not as stupid as he looks.'

'Then he must be a positive genius to have kept up the act all these years,' said Freddy. 'Now, you'd better tell me more about this murder, just in case it *was* one of our chaps. Do you think it was?'

'I think it is highly possible, yes,' replied Henry. He fixed Freddy with a piercing look. 'This is to go no further, you understand. I don't want it appearing in your paper, as we don't want them to get the idea that we know there's anything out of the ordinary in this case.'

'Certainly,' said Freddy.

'Very well. Then I shall tell you that Miss Stapleton's body was moved after she died. From the evidence we found, we believe she was killed just outside the committee-room, and her body dragged inside the room afterwards.'

'Oh? Why was that, do you think?'

'I don't know. Perhaps there were other people still present in the building, and the killer did not wish to be disturbed. But then that makes the whole thing look less like an opportunistic theft than a deliberate act of violence against Miss Stapleton.'

'I see what you mean,' said Freddy thoughtfully. 'Yes, I suppose if Miss Stapleton just happened to catch a thief in the act, and was murdered because she stood in his way, then presumably his first thought would be to escape as quickly as possible. He wouldn't want to waste time in dragging her body out of sight.'

'Exactly,' said Henry.

'By the way, I think I ought to confess to you that I lied to the police earlier,' said Freddy. 'I told them I didn't return to the central hall after I left it, but that wasn't true. I went back in to scout around.'

He explained what he had done and whom he had seen, and Henry listened attentively.

'Are you certain it was Schuster and Trevett talking behind the curtain?' he said.

'As certain as I can be,' said Freddy. 'Of course, it might have been perfectly innocent—after all, there's no law against private conversations as far as I know, but Peacock and Dyer were so fearfully keen to hustle me out of the place toot sweet that it made me more suspicious than I might otherwise have been.'

'That is very interesting,' said Henry. 'At what time was this? Do you remember?'

'It must have been tenish, once I'd walked the half-mile with Jessie and Mabel and then back again.'

'And you didn't see Miss Stapleton when you returned?'

'No. I only saw Peacock and Dyer. Was she dead by then, do you think?'

'It's impossible to say,' said Henry. 'Davis the caretaker says he locked up the building at eleven, but he did only the most cursory of inspections and didn't look into the committee-room. Presumably she must have been dead by then—unless the caretaker himself did it, but since he's about eighty-seven, half-deaf and arthritic, it seems unlikely. The doctor can only say she probably died before midnight.'

'Well, if she was already dead when I turned up again, then any one of Trevett, Schuster, Peacock or Dyer might have done it,' said Freddy. 'Or there's the man I saw leaving just as I arrived, but I told the police about him.' He repeated the story to Henry. 'Anyhow, if she died after that, then it couldn't have been Peacock or Dyer, because they left with me.'

'Might they have doubled back afterwards?'

'It's possible,' conceded Freddy. 'I left them at Chancery Lane and it's only a fifteen-minute walk.'

'And I suppose you don't know whether anyone else was still at the hall when you left? Mrs. Schuster, for example? If her husband was still there then it seems likely that she would have been too.'

'I didn't see anyone else,' said Freddy. 'But any of them might have stayed behind, I imagine.'

'They might indeed,' said Henry. 'So you see, while it *might* have been a chance thief, it might also have been one of the people who were there that evening.'

'What about this paper-knife? How did the murderer come to have it? I mean to say, if he came upon Miss Stapleton with the takings box in her hand outside the committee-room, and wanted to get it off her, he'd hardly run along to the office first and rummage around in a drawer on the off-chance that he might find a handy weapon, would he? I take it Miss Stapleton was carrying it herself and the murderer snatched it from her?'

'That seems a reasonable assumption,' said Henry. He hesitated. 'There is one other thing. When Miss Stapleton's body was discovered, it was found that she was clutching a tiny scrap of torn-off paper in her hand.'

Freddy stared, then laughed.

'Good Lord! You don't mean to say she'd found some incriminating document belonging to the Communists, and was murdered for it? This is all too Black Hand for words. What next? Was there also a message scrawled in Russian on the wall with the victim's blood?'

'If there was we didn't find it,' said Henry. 'At any rate, if it was a letter she'd found it would explain why she was holding the paper-knife.'

'She must have been wandering about with an armful of stuff,' said Freddy. 'Little wonder she didn't have a chance to defend herself.'

'Yes,' said Henry. He stood up. 'Well, that is all I can tell you at present. If I were you I'd leave the murder investigation to the police, since they seem to know what they're doing. Personally, I am more interested in finding out what the chaps of the Communist Alliance get up to in their spare time.'

'Then I'll do my best to find out,' said Freddy.

'Good,' said Henry. He turned to leave, then turned back again. 'I suggest you be careful,' he said. 'If they're the sort of people who will murder a harmless elderly lady, then they won't think twice about putting you out of the way if they happen to find you out.'

'They won't find me out,' said Freddy. 'I'm far too careful for that.'

CHAPTER EIGHT

MRS. STARKWEATHER'S SITTING-ROOM was a large one, but it was so stuffed full of divans, chairs, tables, cupboards, cabinets, indoor plants, grandfather clocks, lamps and ornaments that there was barely room for anybody to stand up in it. Mrs. Starkweather and her daughter had removed themselves and all their belongings to the flat on Upper Montagu Street from their house in Hertfordshire upon the death of Mr. Starkweather, and Mrs. Starkweather had been reluctant to get rid of anything, despite her daughter's exhortations, so whenever the two of them were at home they did nothing but bump into things and knock over vases.

Today the sitting-room was fuller than ever, since it was currently host to several of the senior members of the Young Women's Abstinence Association, who had come to talk over the dreadful happenings of two days ago. Sitting in the best armchair was a generously-proportioned woman, who was dabbing a handkerchief to her eyes. This was Mrs. Belcher, the founder and President of the Y. W. A. A. She had been quite prostrated at the news that one of her most valuable helpers had been murdered, and had just declared that she would never again set foot in Clerkenwell Central Hall.

'Now, Marjorie,' said Mrs. Starkweather in her most sensible voice. 'This is not like you at all. Do try and pull yourself together, if only for the sake of the girls.'

'I suppose you are right, but I cannot help thinking of poor Miss Stapleton and how she must have suffered,' said Mrs. Belcher, with an enormous sniff.

'But she didn't suffer, did she?' said Mildred. 'At least, not according to the police. They said it was all very quick and she wouldn't have felt a thing.'

'Do you think that is true?' said Mrs. Belcher, raising her head. 'You don't think perhaps they said it just to be kind?'

'Not at all,' said Mildred stoutly. 'I'm sure they wouldn't lie to us.'

'But how shall I manage without her?' said Mrs. Belcher. 'She was quite my right-hand woman. I am so terribly busy attending receptions, and raising funds, and speaking at events, that I can't possibly do everything, and it was such a comfort to have a capable person upon whom I could rely to take care of all the other things, such as running the meetings. She was so terribly efficient that I am afraid the Association will be lost without her.'

'I fear this is true,' said the handsome Mr. Hussey, whose particular arrangement of features was very well suited to the solemnity which such an awful occasion demanded. 'But we must not allow ourselves to be daunted by this set-back. The Lord sends us these trials for very good reason, and He shall not find us wanting. We shall pray for Miss Stapleton, and as we do, we shall ask that He send us the strength to continue her work in the same way she did—with modesty, unassuming dedication, and above all without complaint.'

There was a brief silence as those present tried to reconcile this description with their memories of Miss Stapleton, then Mildred Starkweather said fairly:

'At any rate, she was a tremendously hard worker. No-one could possibly say she wasn't devoted to the cause.'

There were fervent nods at this.

'Are you sure you ought to be out, Mr. Bottle?' said Mrs. Starkweather, looking in some concern at a man who was sitting hunched up at one end of a large sofa. 'Pneumonia is not an illness to be trifled with. You really ought to have stayed in bed.'

With an effort Mr. Bottle drew himself up to his full height, which was inconsiderable.

'I could not possibly have remained in bed in the face of such a dreadful tragedy,' he said. 'Yesterday, I confess, I should have found it a struggle to get up, but today I am really much better. Yes, truly, I should say I am on the mend now.'

Here he was assailed by a coughing fit which lasted several minutes. After it was over, he brought out a handkerchief and mopped his perspiring brow.

'This is a lesson to us that nobody is safe in these violent days,' said Mrs. Belcher. 'How shall we persuade anyone to come to our meetings now, when it seems that even a place of religion provides no sanctuary against those of evil intent?'

'I've said to Mr. Davis before that he really ought to be more careful,' said Mrs. Starkweather. 'I pointed out to him that those side doors seem to be open at all times, and that anyone could come in that way and through the minor hall, but he said he had to leave them unlocked in case of fire. I wonder if that's how the thief got in, since it appears nobody saw him arrive.'

'Oh, but are we sure it was a thief who did it?' said Mr. Hussey significantly.

'Do you incline to the theory that she was put out of the way by the Communists, Mr. Hussey?' said Mrs. Starkweather.

'I could not say, but the whole thing appears rather suspicious to me,' said Mr. Hussey. 'One does not like to be uncharitable, but Trevett in particular strikes me as a most dangerous fellow. He speaks of nothing but revolution and violence, and the overthrow of the state, and altogether uses most unseemly language for a mixed company. I do not know why so many women attend the meetings of this Communist Alliance. If I had a daughter, I assure you that I should never permit her to set foot in that hall on a Tuesday night. Their talk is most unsuitable for female ears.'

'You are quite right,' said Mrs. Belcher, 'and I have had to speak most strongly to some of the lower-class girls about it, for Mr. Trevett has a certain attraction to him that appeals to the weaker sort of person, and they *will* tend to drift into the large hall if not forestalled. I've no doubt at all that he has no compunction in using his great personal magnetism to hypnotize his listeners into doing whatever he wants.'

Mr Hussey looked as though he did not appreciate the idea of anybody's being more personally magnetic than himself, but said nothing.

'I can't see it myself,' said Mrs. Starkweather, who was still considering the original question. 'I mean to say, I should think the Communists had far more to worry about than a harmless old busybody such as Miss Stapleton. I beg your pardon—of course one oughtn't to speak ill of the dead, but you must admit she was very curious by nature. If she thought there was something amiss, then she would not rest until she found out what it was, especially if she suspected some wrongdoing.'

'And she did, didn't she?' said Mildred. 'She was really convinced that the Alliance were up to something. I always thought it was rot, myself, but now she's dead I'm wondering whether there mightn't have been something in it. Perhaps she was right all along.'

'Oh dear,' said Miss Hodges, who had been silent up to now. She was pale and miserable, and was holding a handkerchief in her hand in the expectation that she would cry at any moment, although her eyes had remained stubbornly dry up to now. She felt obliquely guilty about this, and twisted the handkerchief restlessly in her hands, as though by doing so she could wring out a few tears. Mrs. Starkweather regarded her kindly.

'You look done in, Miss Hodges,' she said. 'I believe this has come as a shock to us all.'

Miss Hodges nodded and gave a little sound like a gulp.

'But as Mr. Hussey says, we mustn't allow ourselves to be overwhelmed by it,' went on Mrs. Starkweather.

'No,' agreed Mrs. Belcher, who had got over her moment of weakness and was once again prepared to stand firm against all comers. 'Miss Hodges, we shall need you more than ever. We must all take our share of the duties that poor Miss Stapleton will no longer be able to carry out. The work of the Association must continue.'

'But what about the takings?' said Mildred suddenly. 'Have we any idea how much money was stolen? And why was she carrying the box around with her?'

'The subscriptions were supposed to be counted by the end of the month,' said Mr. Bottle. 'I should have done it myself, but as you know I was indisposed and unable to attend the meeting. I expect Miss Stapleton had taken the box out of the drawer in order to take it home and do it in my stead.'

'I was supposed to do it,' said Miss Hodges in a small voice. 'But what with one thing and another, I—I forgot to take the box with me.'

'By the end of the month?' said Mrs. Starkweather. 'I thought the money was deposited weekly. Wouldn't that make more sense?'

'It is deposited weekly,' said Mr. Bottle. 'Usually I count everything up on Wednesday after the meeting, then take it to the bank. But sometimes we have a little extra money, and I try to make sure it is all deposited by the end of the month, even if it is not my usual day for going to the bank. Some little sum was raised at the jumble sale last Friday, for example.'

'How much?' said Mildred.

'Nearly thirty-five pounds,' said Mrs. Belcher. 'I gave it to Mr. Bottle.'

'Didn't it go to the bank?' said Miss Hodges.

'I am afraid not,' said Mr. Bottle. 'Unfortunately, I put it into the takings box and returned it to the hall, since the bank was closed by the time we had finished. After that I was forced to take to my bed. Of course, at the time I did not know it was pneumonia. Had I been aware of that, I should never have stood out in the rain all that time on Friday. I now wish I had taken the money home with me, for then we should not have lost it, and perhaps Miss Stapleton might not have died at all.'

'Oh, dear me!' said Miss Hodges unhappily.

'Such a small sum to kill someone for,' said Mrs. Starkweather.

'To us, perhaps,' said Mr. Hussey. 'But it would be a great temptation for a poorer man.'

'But if it was someone from the Communist Alliance who killed Miss Stapleton, then presumably they took the money as a blind,' said Mildred. 'To mislead us into thinking they didn't do it, I mean.'

'Perhaps,' said Mr. Hussey, considering. 'Yes, you may be right. I had not thought of that.'

'Goodness me, is that the time?' said Mrs. Belcher suddenly. 'I had no idea we had been talking so long. Shall I see you at Lady Dartington's tomorrow, Nerissa dear?'

'Oh, is that tomorrow?' said Mrs. Starkweather. 'Dear me, I thought it was next week. Yes, I shall be there.'

Mrs. Belcher turned her imperious eye upon Miss Hodges, who quailed slightly.

'Miss Hodges, this is a difficult time for us all, but we must put our chins up and carry on bravely,' she said. 'I am sure I can rely on you to do everything in your power to ensure that the work of the Association continues without interruption. Mildred, dear, do you suppose you can help Miss Hodges with the tea at the next meeting?'

'Of course I can,' said Mildred. 'You and I shall manage, shan't we, Miss Hodges?'

'Oh, yes,' said Miss Hodges, grateful that nobody had shouted at her.

Mrs. Belcher recited a long list of things that needed seeing to, and then sailed out, almost restored to her usual self at the thought of the changes which would now have to be made, and the opportunities this would give her to be even more officious than usual, for it had occurred to her that if the murder *did* turn out to have been motivated by theft, then perhaps they might use Miss Stapleton's death as an object lesson, since the man who had done it must surely have been under the influence of alcohol at the time.

'Poor Marjorie,' said Mrs. Starkweather, once Mrs. Belcher had departed. 'I don't think I've ever seen her so deflated.'

'She'll be all right, you'll see,' said Mildred. 'Just watch—she'll use it as an excuse to fish for pity and get more money out of people.'

'Goodness!' said Mrs. Starkweather. 'I'm not sure I like the sound of that.'

'No, but it makes sense, don't you think? That's what I should do if I were in her shoes.'

'Young people are so pitiless nowadays,' murmured Mrs. Starkweather.

'Has anybody spoken to the police?' said Mr. Bottle. 'What did they say? Are they sure nobody saw anything?'

Everyone shook their heads.

'The police haven't said much at all,' said Mildred. 'They're an impassive lot. They asked me questions for half an hour, but I couldn't understand what they were getting at. They asked where things were kept in the office. They wanted to know who had the keys to the drawer where the takings box was kept, so I said I thought it was you and Miss Stapleton, Mr. Bottle.'

'That is quite right,' said Mr. Bottle. 'I have my key here with me. Then you are sure nobody caught sight of the killer? Which way did he come in, for example? Mrs. Starkweather, you talked of the side entrance that leads into the minor hall. Do you suspect that that is how he got in? It would have taken a matter of minutes to slip in and out that way—with the further advantage that the door is not easily visible from the street. Miss Hodges, Miss Starkweather, I understand you were the last to leave. Are you quite sure you didn't see anyone?'

'Mummy and I left together before Miss Hodges,' said Mildred, 'and I didn't see a thing. Miss Stapleton had gone off somewhere and I didn't even say goodbye to her. I expect she was in the office, digging out the takings box.'

'I saw no-one,' said Miss Hodges, shaking her head vehemently. 'I finished clearing up, then Mr. Pilkington-Soames was kind enough to escort me to the 'bus stop, and I went home.'

'I wonder whether Freddy saw anything,' said Mildred thoughtfully. 'Perhaps we ought to ask him.'

Mr. Bottle was about to say something, but went into another coughing fit.

'Now, Mr. Bottle, I shan't listen to another word about how well you are,' said Mrs. Starkweather. 'You're quite obviously very ill. You must go home and rest.'

'Perhaps you are right,' said Mr. Bottle through his handkerchief.

'And you'd better go in a taxi,' said Mildred, then, as he protested, pointed at the window. 'It's sleeting again. You can't go out in that. I'd send you with Burton but it's his afternoon off.'

Mr. Bottle was duly persuaded and a girl was dispatched to procure a cab. Miss Hodges stood up and prepared to leave too, but as she made her way towards the door she bumped into a large stone reproduction of the Egyptian god Anubis, which was blocking the way to the door most inconveniently, and dropped her bag, which burst open. There was some confusion and not a few bumped heads as everyone darted forward to help her gather her scattered belongings together. Most of them had fallen at Mr. Bottle's feet, and the effort of picking them up brought on another coughing fit in him.

'Miss Hodges, perhaps you would care to come with me,' he said, once he had recovered and she had stammered out her apologies and thanks. 'I believe you live not far from me, and I dare say you would not wish to go out in this inclement weather either.'

Miss Hodges, fearful of putting anybody or everybody out, demurred at first, but was eventually herded into the taxi by the forceful Mildred, and she and Mr. Bottle went off in great state, followed shortly afterwards by Mr. Hussey.

'Well!' said Mildred to her mother, once they had the house to themselves again. 'I suppose you'll tell me off for saying it, but this is all rather thrilling. I've never seen a murder before!'

'Poor Miss Stapleton. I wonder whether we ought to have made more of an effort to be sympathetic,' said her mother doubtfully.

'What do you mean?'

'Why, the only person who seemed sorry she was dead was Marjorie.'

'Oh, of course I'm sorry she was killed,' said Mildred. 'I should never wish this sort of thing upon anybody. I'm not as cold and hard as you seem to think. But you can't deny she was a difficult woman. Some people might even call her a thorn in the side. Not only ours, but the Communists', too. And the only thing to do with a thorn is to pluck it out.'

'Well, somebody has certainly done that,' said Mrs. Stark-weather.

CHAPTER NINE

O N MONDAY FREDDY wandered along to the office of the *Radical*, since he wanted to speak to St. John. The office turned out to be two dingy rooms above an ironmonger's shop near Clerkenwell Green. On climbing the stairs Freddy found that the door to the outer room was open, and he entered without knocking to find two young men in their shirt-sleeves, playing cards with their feet up on the table. They looked up as he came in.

'St. John?' said one of them, and jerked his thumb towards another door which was pulled almost closed, then went back to his game.

St. John was rifling through a stack of documents, frowning. He brightened as Freddy entered.

'Hallo, old chap,' he said. 'Come to see where all the work goes on, have you?'

'I didn't see much work going on out there,' said Freddy. 'Is that what we'll all be doing after the revolution?'

'They're just waiting for the news to come in,' said St. John. 'We hear from the trade unions every week, but they're usually late, and quite often they don't send it in until the last minute. Sometimes they don't send it in at all, in fact.'

'And what do you do then?'

'I write something myself if I happen to know more or less what's been going on that week. If I don't, then I put in last week's news again.'

'Doesn't anybody notice?'

'Not so far,' said St. John. 'There was one week where I accidentally mixed up all the titles, and said the miners' piece had come from the dock-workers' union, and the rail-workers' piece had come from the miners, and so on, and nobody said a thing. I expect no-one reads them, really.'

'Perhaps you ought to make them a little less dry, then,' said Freddy. 'Or, on second thoughts, perhaps not, if you make this sort of mistake often. What day do you go to press?'

'Thursday.'

'Do you expect much news?'

'It depends. I dare say there won't be much this week, unless something unexpected happens. We had rather a thrilling time of it a few weeks ago when John Pettit's house burned down—you know, Rowbotham's deputy at the Labourers' Union—and he narrowly escaped with his life. There was a suspicion of foul play, you see. Obviously we made the most of it, although I dare say it was caused by a spark from his kitchen fire. There's been nothing so exciting since then, though.'

'And what will those two out there do until then if no news comes in?'

'Play cards, I imagine. That's if they turn up. They don't always.'

'Do you pay them?'

'Sometimes,' said St. John. 'When we can afford it.'

There seemed little more to be said on that subject, so Freddy looked around him instead. The room was tiny, only big enough for two desks, some bookshelves, a filing cabinet or two and not much else. St. John's desk was piled high with a jumble of paper, pens, books, periodicals and, somewhat mysteriously, a stuffed owl in a glass jar.

'Oh, someone sent that in,' said St. John in reply to Freddy's questioning look. 'I have no idea why. You'd be surprised at the stuff we get. Some people seem to treat us as a sort of lost property office. They send us things and expect us to put a notice in the paper. But we have a perfectly good lost-and-found column for that, and if they want to advertise then they can jolly well pay us for it.'

'Ah, yes,' said Freddy. 'Do you make much from your small ads?'

'A little,' said St. John. 'We charge two shillings a line, minimum three lines. Cheap, I know, but we're not exactly the *Times*, so we have to charge what we can get.'

'Who takes them down?' said Freddy.

'I do, or Ruth does—if they come in by telephone, that is. Some people deliver them in person, and others send them in by post with payment.'

Freddy picked up a copy of last week's *Radical* and flicked through it casually.

'Hmm—hmm—the usual,' he said. 'People looking for lodgings or work. Requests for false teeth. I can't help thinking there must be quite a shortage of dentures in the world, because I never open a paper without seeing someone asking for them. Perhaps I ought to buy shares in false teeth companies, since they are in such high demand. Now, look at this: someone is prepared to accept twenty-five pounds for a set of ermine. Ermine what, though?'

'I've no idea,' said St. John.

'I shouldn't have thought your readers were the type to wear that sort of thing,' said Freddy. 'Perhaps I've misjudged them.' He glanced down the page again. 'Surprising the nonsense people insist on announcing to the world. I mean to say, look at this: "Leonora: we were so very happy; why must you end it so? It has all been a terrible misunderstanding, and can easily be put right again—Harold."'

'Oh, that's old Harcourt. Poor old chap is about a hundred and six and completely ga-ga. He was considered the future of radical politics in about eighteen seventy, but nothing ever came of it. His wife died ten years ago, but he persists in believing she's left him, and hopes that if he keeps advertising then she'll come back to him. I'd never take his money ordinarily, but he gets so distraught if I try to refuse it that I haven't the heart to turn him down.'

'Do you know everyone who advertises?'

'A good few of them,' said St. John. 'A lot of them are regulars, you see.'

'What about this one, then?' said Freddy. 'It's rather odd. It starts "Daddie Dearest," but the rest is just numbers. What on earth does it mean?'

'What's that?' said St. John, craning his neck to look. 'Oh, those. I don't know who sends those. They come in by post.'

'Where do they come from? And who sends them?'

'I don't know. Does it matter? They come with a postal order, and as long as they're paying we're happy to print whatever they like.'

'But shouldn't you like to know who is sending them?'

'Not especially,' said St. John.

'I don't suppose you have one of the originals, do you? Or one of the envelopes they come in?'

'What? Why should I have kept it?'

'Oh, I often have old envelopes lying around,' said Freddy. 'To scribble notes on, that sort of thing.'

St. John stared, then hunted around on his desk for a few moments.

'No, I don't think I do. Why do you want it?'

'Mere curiosity,' said Freddy. 'You see, I've been reading the most splendid book lately. It tells you all about how to deduce things about a person from their handwriting. And not just the usual stuff, either—you know, whether they're male or female, or whether they're left- or right-handed—but really interesting things. It's quite a science, I understand. Why, there's one chap in Germany who can tell at a glance from your handwriting whether you're married or single, whether you were beaten as a child, and whether you can play the piano—even down to whether you play jazz or classical. It's simply marvellous what science can do these days.'

'It sounds like a lot of tripe to me,' said St. John.

'Oh, but it's not. Anyway, I've always rather fancied myself as a detective, in the manner of Sherlock Holmes or someone of that sort, and I just thought that if you had one of the envelopes I might be able to tell you who was sending the notices.'

'I doubt it,' said St. John. 'If they're the ones I'm thinking of, they're done on a typewriter.'

'Where's Ruth, by the way?' said Freddy, thinking that some change of subject was necessary before he drew any more attention to the coded advertisements.

'She's gone to speak to Trevett,' said St. John. 'We have the big do in Hyde Park coming up, and there are lots of things to see to.'

'What do you mean? Which do?'

'It's to be a sort of rally. The Labourers' Union are organizing it, together with the Communist party. The Alliance is helping, of course, but it would be far too big a thing for us to manage on our own, as we don't have nearly enough people.'

'Oh, the protest, you mean? Yes, I'd heard about that,' said Freddy. 'I dare say the *Clarion* will send me along, and I shall spend the whole day freezing in the mud and catch my death of cold, then you'll print a story about me in your paper and call me a martyr to the cause and my mother will die of shame.'

'But it'll be tremendously good fun,' said St. John. 'They're sending men down from all over the country. It's to be a peaceful thing. And if you're worried about catching cold I shouldn't. There'll be tents and hot food and drink, and people will be speaking, and we have some circus performers coming from Italy and lots of other entertainment. I expect there will be quite a festive atmosphere, in fact. We'll show the police and the powers that be that we workers know how to enjoy ourselves.'

'Who is speaking?'

'Rowbotham of the Labourers' Union, of course. Trevett, naturally. Schuster, perhaps. But there'll be some others, too. And there'll be all sorts of other things going on. It'll be jolly good fun, you'll see.'

'It sounds more like a village fête than a protest against the Government,' said Freddy.

'But that's the idea, don't you see? If we can make them understand the workers are just ordinary people who want to put food on the table for their families, then it ought to go a long way towards making the Government more well-disposed to the thought of meeting our demands. It's Rowbotham's idea. Not everybody likes it, but he's in charge.'

'I see. He wants to give the impression that his workers would rather be skipping about gaily in a meadow full of buttercups than wallowing gleefully in the blood of the bourgeoisie at the barricades, is that it? But what about all that stuff about violent insurrection that you put in your rag?'

'Words,' said St. John dismissively. 'Nobody would really do that sort of thing, would they?'

'I think the Russians might disagree with you,' said Freddy. 'I say, you've changed, haven't you? You used to be all for direct action and blowing up trains.'

St. John sat up straighter.

'Yes, but I'm older now,' he said. 'A man in my position has responsibilities. I can't ask Ruth to marry me if I'm in prison, can I? And by the way, you haven't spoken to her yet.'

'Soon, soon,' said Freddy hurriedly.

'Anyway, this ought to be a splendid rally, and the *Radical* will be there, covering it all. It will be the most thrilling day for news—ought to keep us going for at least a month, in fact—and will be a tremendously good opportunity to get more subscribers. I have plans for the paper, but I can't do anything without money.'

Just then Ruth Chudderley turned up, in company with the Schusters. Despite the wet weather Anton Schuster was dressed as though he were going for a walk along the Promenade des Anglais. His wife seemed to feel the cold more than he did, and was wrapped in a coat with a high fur collar. Together they added a touch of the exotic to the dull grey surroundings.

Ruth looked Freddy up and down in the particular way she had which always made him wonder whether he had dropped half his breakfast down his shirt.

'I haven't seen your article in the paper yet,' she remarked. 'I thought you were going to tell your readers about all the good work the Communist Alliance is doing.'

'I've written the piece,' lied Freddy, 'but I'm afraid it has to get past my editor first. The press are a conservative lot, you know, and there were one or two phrases he wasn't too keen on. He's passed it all the way up to the *Clarion's* owner, Sir Aldridge Featherstone, for approval.'

'Do you think it will be approved?' said Ruth, still with the maddeningly superior expression on her face.

'It's difficult to say. Sir Aldridge is the brother of Mrs. Belcher, the President of the Young Women's Abstinence Association, whom I dare say you know. He consults her in everything that might affect the morals of the man in the street, but as long as your lot haven't offended her recently we might be safe.'

'Hmph,' said Ruth. 'The Y. W. A. A. like nothing better than to take offence at everything we do. I expect we shall never see your piece, in that case.'

'Oh, we might be lucky yet,' said Freddy. 'Sometimes the two of them fall out, and then we ordinary reporters have a few weeks in which to publish as many stories about tragic chorus girls and throat-slashing cocaine gangs as we can possibly pump out before they make it up again and we have to go back to the flower shows and speeches by the Archbishop.'

'I see,' said Ruth, and turned abruptly to St. John. 'Anton has brought his piece for the *Radical*,' she said.

'Oh, jolly good, what?' said St. John.

'Yes,' said Schuster. 'It is a little idea I was working on before I left Vienna. Here I have attempted to give a summary of it in a way that the ordinary man will understand.'

He brought out several folded sheets of paper and handed them to St. John.

'It's rather long,' said St. John doubtfully. 'Eleven sheets of paper. That's twenty-two—no, twenty-one and a half sides. How many words should you say that was?'

'I have not the first idea,' said Schuster blithely.

'About five thousand,' said Freddy, looking at the paper with a practised eye.

'Hmm. We might have to cut it down a bit,' said St. John.

'But no, this I shall not permit,' said Schuster. 'My ideas are not to be chopped about like so many cuts of beef. The force of my argument will be diminished greatly if words are taken away here and there. There are nuances in my thesis that will be lost. No, it must not be. I will not be misrepresented.'

'Well, then, how can we do it?' said St. John. 'It'll have to go onto two pages. Can we afford the extra paper? Can we make it up with advertising?'

'Oh, I forgot to say, the Socialist Book Club have decided not to advertise with us any more,' said Ruth, with supreme unconcern. 'They said they were sick of getting new members from us who never pay.'

'What?' exclaimed St. John in dismay. 'But I thought they were going to start doing the quarter-page displays. I'd already decided where the money was going to go.'

'Well, it seems they changed their mind,' said Ruth.

'Oh,' said St. John. He glanced down at the papers in his hand. 'Well, then, what are we to do with this? It won't all go on page four, as I was planning.'

'Continue it on another page,' said Freddy, flicking through a copy of the *Radical*. 'Look, it'll easily go in place of this—what is it? "Weekly Ruminations From a Communist of the Countryside." It looks fearfully turgid, so I don't suppose anybody reads it. Nobody will miss it for a week if you put the rest of Mr. Schuster's piece there.'

'As a matter of fact, that is my commentary,' said St. John with dignity. 'I have my own little philosophy that I've been developing recently, which I write about in this column. I get a lot of letters in praise of it, and I'll have you know that not one of them has ever used the word "turgid."'

'I expect they were being polite,' said Freddy.

'Am I interrupting?' came a voice, and they all looked up to see Miss Flowers, the elderly lady who had transferred her allegiance from Temperance to Communism, hovering apologetically in the doorway. She saw Ruth and came in.

'Ah, there you are, Ruth, dear,' she said. 'I want to place another announcement in the *Radical*.'

'Where are Warrington and Jessop?' said St. John. 'Didn't they offer to take it down for you?'

Ruth looked into the other room.

'They're not there,' she said impatiently. 'Very well, Miss Flowers, I'll do it for you. We'll use one of the printed forms.'

'Come to put something in the wanteds, Miss F?' said Freddy. 'There's an ermine set going for twenty-five pounds, if that's what you're after.'

'Oh, dear, no,' said Miss Flowers in some amusement. 'Nothing like that. No, I have merely come to advertise some crochet and knitting patterns of my own devising. I find I have a little talent that way, and have recently discovered that I can supplement my meagre income by selling them to others through the pages of Mr. Bagshawe's publication. I offer two patterns for a shilling or five for two, and I am pleased to say that they have been received very favourably.'

She and Ruth went out, followed by Anton Schuster and St. John, who were deep in conversation about Schuster's article. A minute later St. John came back in holding a bundle of letters.

'Here's the post,' he said. 'And here's one of your famous ads. Look.' He tore open an envelope, read the contents and handed it to Freddy. 'What do you make of that? Not much, I expect.'

Freddy looked at the slip of paper inside the envelope just long enough to ascertain that it was indeed one of the 'Daddie Dearest' announcements, then handed it back.

'No,' he said, with a glance towards the window, where Theresa Schuster was standing with her back to them. He hoped she had not heard the exchange, for he had no wish to draw attention to his interest in the matter. St. John put down the advertisement, threw the envelope in the waste-paper basket then went out again, leaving Freddy and Mrs. Schuster alone in the room. She was staring out of the window, seemingly absorbed in something, and Freddy was just musing on how best to approach her with a view to reminding her about his invitation to one of her evening parties, when she turned and beckoned to him with a sly smile. Freddy joined her.

'You see that man?' she said, indicating with a carefully man-icured hand.

Freddy looked and saw a man wearing a flat cap standing at the corner of the street, smoking and apparently watching the antics of a brewery horse that had taken fright at something and was doing its best to rear. There was nothing to distinguish him from any other working man in the street.

'What of him?' he said.

'He is from British Intelligence,' she replied.

'Oh?'

'Yes. They follow us about everywhere. Or at least, they follow Anton. I do not suppose they find me so very interesting.'

'Why do they follow you about?'

She shrugged.

'Anton is a little revolutionary in his ideas,' she said. 'They did the same to us in Vienna. Always there, wherever we went. I find it tiresome, but Anton likes it very much. He says that if they find him threatening enough to shadow him then it must be because his ideas are worth something, and so his life's work has not been in vain.'

'Does he want a revolution, then?'

Again came the shrug.

'Anton is a very clever man,' she said, 'but he is not the practical type, and the idea of violence horrifies him, despite what he preaches. I do not think he would like it.'

'And what about you?'

'I should not mind it,' she said, considering. 'I have lived through one myself and it was not so very bad. You cannot deny that there is much unfairness in your society here. Rich men eat truffles and quails' eggs, while poor ones have no work and their families have no food. Is it so wrong to take just a little from the first and give it to the second?'

'I'm not especially keen on the idea of taking anything from anyone who doesn't want to give it up,' said Freddy. 'Although of course I'd like everybody to have work.'

'I knew you would say that,' she said. 'The English are not the revolutionary sort.' She glanced sideways at him. 'I told you before of our gatherings, I think,' she said. 'I have many friends who like to debate these things, but it is not at all serious or dull. There will be another on Saturday at our house. Will you come? Bring someone if you like.'

'I should be delighted,' said Freddy.

Her face lit up.

'Ah! Excellent,' she said. 'We shall be most pleased to see you, and I know you will enjoy it.'

They were standing together at the window, and she turned and gazed directly into his eyes, and the daylight on her face allowed him to see her properly for the first time. Her eyes were an unusual shade of light brown—almost an amber colour—and he found that she was prettier than he had at first supposed, at least when she smiled. To his surprise, he noticed that she had a small scar running across her cheek, just below her left eye. She was wearing powder, which concealed it to some extent, but it was unmistakably there, and he wondered how he had missed it before, and how she had got it. She was wearing a scent that was unfamiliar to him: not the delicate floral sort that most women of his acquaintance wore, but something that spoke of spices and roses, and made him think of the East. As he breathed it in he began to experience the oddest sensation of light-headedness—even giddiness—almost as though he were drunk, and just for a moment he was glad he had the window-sill for support. She laid a gentle hand on his arm, and he suddenly realized that he must have been staring.

'Come on Saturday,' she said softly.

Then Ruth came in and began talking to Mrs. Schuster as though Freddy were not there. Mrs. Schuster moved away from the window and the two women left the room. Instantly Freddy darted across to St. John's desk and copied down the 'Daddie Dearest' advertisement as quickly as he could, then fished the discarded envelope out of the waste-paper basket and shoved it in his pocket. After that he strolled into the outer office. Warrington and Jessop had returned, and were laughing at something which they had just handed to St. John, who was now reading it and shaking his head. Freddy bade them all goodbye and St. John raised a vague hand.

'Whew!' thought Freddy as he emerged into the street. 'I had no idea Schuster's wife was such a piece of work. She turned her head-lamps on me all right just then. Now, I wonder why. If she's carrying on with Peacock then I don't suppose she was captivated by my handsome face—unless she's the sort who can juggle with a whole menagerie at once. Still, Saturday ought to be interesting.'

Chapter Ten

IT SEEMED A long time to wait until the Schusters' party on Saturday—too long for Freddy, who was anxious to be doing something. He was not the sort of young man to take life seriously as a rule, but he felt uncomfortably as though he were under the watchful eye of Henry Jameson, and sensed that it would be a mistake to let him down. Besides, he was spurred on by his own natural curiosity, and wanted more than anything, first, to solve the mystery of Miss Stapleton's death, and second, to find out whether it had anything to do with the suspected conspiracy among the members of the East London Communist Alliance. He had closely examined the envelope he had retrieved from St. John's waste-paper basket, but had not learnt much from it, for it was a perfectly ordinary envelope of the sort that might be bought at any stationers' shop, and had been addressed using a typewriter, with no handwriting to identify the person who had sent it. The postmark was London, which hardly narrowed it down. Freddy examined the type and saw that the upper-case 'R' was cut off at the top, while the lower-case 'e' was slightly raised. Henry had sent him all the 'Daddie Dearest' messages they had, together with a note that said Freddy might as well try and decipher them too, since their own cryptographers had had no success so far; but without the book which was the key to the cipher, Freddy did not see how he could help.

'All I need to do now is to start hammering out 'r's and 'e's on every typewriter I see,' he muttered to himself. 'I don't suppose there are more than about five thousand of them in London. Still, if I *can* find out who typed these ads, then I might be able to find the book they've been using to write the code.'

In the absence of anything else to do, he decided to attend the Communist Alliance meeting on Tuesday. He arrived early again, as he wanted to scout around the central hall and see whether the police had missed any clues as to the identity of Miss Stapleton's murderer.

'Hallo, Freddy,' said Mildred Starkweather, who was bustling about in the kitchen with Miss Hodges. 'What are you doing here? I should have thought you'd had enough of all this. I do hope you haven't come to be ghoulish and look for horrid things to say about Miss Stapleton in your rag.'

'Far from it,' said Freddy. 'As a matter of fact, I wanted to see whether there was anything I could do to help find out who killed her.'

'Oh, goodness,' said Miss Hodges, who appeared flustered as usual. 'Do the police have any idea who did it?'

'Doesn't look like it,' said Freddy. 'If it was a common thief then I dare say they'll never find him.'

'No,' said Mildred. 'And it looks rather as though that might be the case. Mummy thinks he probably sneaked in through the side door to the minor hall, since there were a few people still in the building and the front door would have been too visible.'

'The side door?' said Freddy, pricking up his ears. 'Show me.'

Mildred cast a doubtful glance at Miss Hodges, who was holding several teaspoons in one hand and a cup in the other and looked as though she were not quite sure what to do with them, then laid down her tea-cloth. She led him into the minor hall, where Mrs. Starkweather was pinning something up on a notice-board.

'There,' said Mildred. 'The door is left unlocked while the hall is in use in case of fire.'

'I see,' said Freddy. 'So anyone in the minor hall can go straight out, while those in the main hall can get to the outer door through those folding doors.'

'That's right,' said Mildred.

Freddy tried the handle of the side door. It opened directly out into a quiet side-street. He glanced up and down, but saw nobody.

'Shut the door, dear, you're letting the cold air in,' said Mrs. Starkweather.

'Sorry, Mrs. S,' said Freddy absently, and did as he was told. He walked out of the minor hall, followed by Mildred, and stood by the door to the committee-room. The doors to this and the minor hall were down a short corridor which was out of sight of the main lobby. If Miss Stapleton had indeed been killed on this spot, then it was little wonder that no-one had seen it happen.

'Is this where she died?' said Mildred suddenly.

'So I understand,' said Freddy.

Mildred looked sober.

'It's pretty awful, really,' she said. 'I know she was a nuisance, but there's no need for that sort of thing.'

'No,' agreed Freddy. He opened the door to the committee-room and glanced inside. It looked exactly the same as it had last week. Then he emerged from the corridor and into the lobby proper. People were starting to arrive for their respective meetings. If the murderer had come in through the front door that night then he might easily have been spotted by anyone who had remained behind in the main hall or the kitchen. The side door through the minor hall was certainly a more discreet route. Freddy remembered the man he had seen leaving the building. Was he the murderer? If he was, then why had he chosen to leave through the front door, when here was a means of escape which was much less visible? Perhaps he was innocent, then, for it would have been much more sensible of him to have left through the side door. Freddy decided to disregard him as a suspect for the present.

'Very well, then,' he said. 'Assuming for a moment that nobody here did it, it looks as though the killer came in through the side door, bumped into Miss Stapleton outside the committee-room, stabbed her and ran off with the money. I understand she was killed with a paper-knife.'

'Yes, I think she was,' said Mildred. 'The police wouldn't tell us officially how she died—I don't know why—but they kept asking questions about this paper-knife, and who it belonged to, so we put two and two together. She must have been carrying it for some reason, and the murderer grabbed it off her. At least, that's the only explanation I can think of as to how he got hold of it.'

'Whom did it belong to?'

'I've no idea. If it's the one I think it is, then it's usually kept in the drawer in the office. All the groups that use the hall have drawers or a cupboard they can use. We only have two drawers, but they're lockable so we can keep money in them and such-like. Not that we do, usually, but Mr. Bottle was ill last week so there was money in the drawer for a few days.'

'Mr. Bottle? He's your treasurer, I believe?'

'Yes. He's had pneumonia, the poor thing. He feels dreadfully guilty about having left the money here for someone to steal and perhaps kill Miss Stapleton for.'

'It was hardly his fault.'

'No, but still,' said Mildred, 'I expect I'd feel the same.'

'The money was kept in a takings box,' said Freddy. 'Did it have a key?'

'Yes,' said Mildred. 'Two keys, in fact. Mr. Bottle has one and Miss Stapleton had the other.'

'Was Miss Stapleton's key missing?'

'I think it must have been,' said Mildred. 'She kept her drawer key and her key to the box on the same ring, you see, but the drawer hadn't been forced, so she must have taken the box out herself shortly before she was murdered. The police asked us if we knew where the drawer key was, so presumably they can't find it, which means the thief must have taken her keys when he took the box.'

Freddy tried to remember what the police had said about the key. Not much, as far as he could recall, for they had said very little about anything.

'Do you think there's a connection between Miss Stapleton's death and the Communists?' said Mildred suddenly.

'I don't know,' said Freddy truthfully.

'She did have a bee in her bonnet, and it was easy to dismiss her suspicions, but sometimes I wonder whether she mightn't have been right. Oh, most of them are harmless enough, I'm sure—I mean, I've known St. John since we were kids, and I know he's all right. But I don't like that girl-friend of his, and there are one or two others I don't think much of either. Peacock and Dyer in particular.'

'Why do you suspect them?' said Freddy.

'Oh, because that Oxford act of theirs is just too much,' said Mildred. 'One can't talk to them without having to listen to one of their interminable anecdotes about how they ducked the Bursar in the river, or left one of the Fellows up a tree without his trousers on. I know that's the sort of thing undergraduates get up to, but there's just a little too much of it in their case.'

'I see,' said Freddy thoughtfully. 'You think they're putting on an act?'

'Don't you see it yourself?'

'They're a hearty pair, certainly,' he conceded. 'What about Sidney Bishop?'

'Is he the one who laughs every time Mr. Trevett says anything, as though it's the funniest joke in the world? He's very polite to us ladies, although Miss Stapleton always spoke to him rather distantly because of his accent. I should say he was a dear.'

'What did Miss Stapleton say about the Communists, exactly? I mean to say, did she have any evidence against them, or was this bee in her bonnet merely a bee?'

'I'm not sure,' said Mildred. 'From what she said, some of the things she saw did sound a little suspicious.'

'What sort of things?'

'Oh, you know—she'd find them in the kitchen before a meeting and they'd stop talking suddenly when she came in. But that's hardly surprising, really, because we all share the kitchen and they might have been talking about private things that were perfectly innocent, but they didn't want her to hear them because they were sick of her snooping around.'

'True,' said Freddy.

'And then there was another time when she saw a book that somebody had left on the table, and she went to pick it up but Peacock snatched it away from her. He did it quite laughingly, and said he didn't think it would be her sort of book at all, but she was offended at his manner.'

'I see. What was the book?'

'No idea,' she said. 'Does it matter?'

'It might,' said Freddy. 'One can pass messages with a book.' She stared at him.

'Of course! Do you mean like in mystery stories, where they cut the pages out of the middle to make a hiding-place?'

'Er—yes, that's one way to do it,' said Freddy. 'But are you sure Miss Stapleton didn't see the name of the book?'

'Yes. She just said it was one of those cheap things in the blue jackets,' said Mildred. She lowered her voice. 'If you ask me, he wasn't passing a message in it at all, but whisked it out of her way because he knew it wasn't the sort of book he ought to leave lying around for the ladies to find.'

'I dare say you're right,' said Freddy, although he seemed doubtful.

Mildred frowned.

'It's all absurd, really, isn't it? The idea that they were passing messages in that way and Miss Stapleton found them and was killed for it. It's too far-fetched for words.'

'I suppose it is,' said Freddy.

'Are you really going to investigate Miss Stapleton's murder?' said Mildred. 'Why? Isn't that the job of the police?'

'Call it curiosity,' said Freddy. 'The police are busy men, so it can't hurt to try and help them, can it? I mean to say, they're outsiders, in a manner of speaking. They don't know the people involved in the case, whereas I do. And a lot of people are naturally suspicious of the police and won't talk to them. I expect most of these Communists aren't too keen on the Law, for example, since they spend half their time throwing bottles at them and getting hauled off to the cells in return.'

'All right, then, when do we start?' said Mildred.

'We?' said Freddy.

'Yes, we. You don't think I'm going to let you leave me out of it, do you?'

'Well, er—' said Freddy. 'I'm not sure your mother would approve of your doing this sort of thing.'

'Probably not,' said Mildred. 'But if we don't tell her she need never know.'

Freddy regarded the usually staid Mildred in surprise, and she flushed slightly.

'I'm tired of being the dull one all the time,' she said. 'All the other girls I know go out and do exciting things. Dancing, and—and—drinking, and all that sort of thing. I should like a little excitement too.'

Freddy was by no means sure that he wanted Mildred Stark-weather tagging along with him in his investigation, since of course he could not tell her his real purpose in trying to find Miss Stapleton's killer. He tried prevarication.

'Very well,' he said. 'I promise I'll let you know what I find out.'

She snorted.

'Oh, no you jolly well won't!' she said. 'If I'm going to do this then I shall do it properly. We must question people and have meetings and compare notes. I'll speak to the members of the Association and you can speak to the Communists, and we can meet afterwards and discuss it and see whether we've made any progress. What do you say to Friday? That ought to give us a bit of time. Oh—' she broke off. 'I can't do Friday, as we're going to the opera. Saturday, then.'

'No, no,' said Freddy in some concern. 'I'm going to the Schusters' on Saturday. Look here, Mildred—'

'To the Schusters'? Why didn't you say so? Then I shall come too.'

'But you can't—'

'Are you already going with someone?'

'No, but—'

'Then it's settled,' said Mildred firmly.

'But Mildred—'

Mildred affected an injured air.

'I see, I'm not pretty or *chic* enough for you, is that it? You don't want to be seen with me. Just because my nose doesn't turn up like Iris Bagshawe's—'

'What's Iris got to do with it?'

'Nothing,' said Mildred.

'Has she been talking to you about me?'

'No, she hasn't said a thing about you. She's getting married, you know.'

'Yes, thank you, I'm perfectly aware of that,' said Freddy a little testily.

'Well, then,' said Mildred, as though she had scored a point. She glared at him, then her mouth began to turn down at the corners and tremble a little. 'You might let me in on it, you know. I don't have an awful lot of fun. Mummy has needed me more than ever since Father died, but I should like to live just a little for once.'

A tear was threatening to form in the corner of her eye, and Freddy gave it up, for once a woman started weeping the argument was lost.

'All right,' he said. 'But you must be discreet. Don't go around telling everybody of our suspicions.'

'Of course I won't! I should think I know how to behave.' She clasped her hands together and beamed. 'Oh, how splendid! Will you really let me come? I was sure you'd say no. Thank you, Freddy. I always thought you must be a darling underneath it all.'

After that there was nothing more to be said, and no further possibility of persuading her to back out. Freddy sighed inwardly and resigned himself to the inevitable.

They had returned to stand outside the kitchen and Mildred was about to pursue the subject further when they were joined by a little man who was wrapped up against the cold in so many coats and scarves that all that could be seen of him was his nose and his moustache.

'Oh, Mr. Bottle!' exclaimed Mildred. 'Ought you to be here? You can't possibly be properly recovered.'

'Thank you, Miss Starkweather, but I am feeling much better,' said Mr. Bottle. 'I have spent four days in bed, but I dislike inactivity, and as soon as I felt well enough I got up. You need not worry about me, for my landlady has been nursing me with great care, and you may be sure that she would not have allowed me to rise from my bed had she not been certain that I was recovered enough to do so.'

'But nobody expected you to come this evening,' said Mildred. 'It's cold outside and it can't be good for you. We don't want you to relapse.'

'I am quite of your opinion,' said Mr. Bottle. 'And I assure you that I shall be very careful not to over-exert myself. However, I cannot in all conscience continue to desert my post after the awful events of last week, for which I cannot but feel I am partly to blame.'

He was removing scarves as he spoke, and Freddy regarded him with sudden attention as his face finally came into view. Mr. Bottle was perhaps in the middle forties, pale and with a thin little nose that was rubbed red from the cold, or possibly from blowing. His eyes were red-rimmed too, and altogether he had the look of someone who was severely under the weather.

Miss Hodges came out of the kitchen just then and gave a squeak when she saw him.

'Oh, dear me!' she said. 'You ought not to be here, Mr. Bottle.'

'Nonsense, I am quite well,' he replied, and glanced past her into the kitchen. 'Might I give you a hand with the preparations?'

Miss Hodges jumped.

'Oh, no, you mustn't exert yourself,' she began, but Mr. Bottle was not to be gainsaid. He ushered her into the kitchen with a firm hand.

'We must all work together now that the excellent Miss Stapleton is no longer with us,' he said. 'It is not to be supposed that we shall prove anything like as efficient as she was, but we have been sent this trial, and we must overcome it. No, no, Miss Starkweather, we can manage perfectly well without your help. I suggest you go and join your mother in the minor hall, for the meeting will soon begin.'

'I'd better go and save a seat for Mrs. Belcher, too,' said Mildred, and departed.

The members of the Communist Alliance were also arriving, and Freddy went to take his seat in the main hall. Miss Flowers was there with her crochet, and he sat next to her again. The meeting went on much as it had done the previous week, although this time there was a lengthy discussion of the plans for the grand rally that was to take place in Hyde Park, followed by a great rattling of tins, since extra funds would be required for its organization. Then St. John stood up and recited a poem of some length, after which Ivor Trevett took to the stage and gave another powerful speech. Freddy listened, his attention caught, and was forced to admit that the man spoke very well, although when he tried to remember afterwards what had been said, he could not. It seemed to Freddy that if there were indeed something afoot, then Trevett must be at the centre of it. He determined that he would keep his eyes open at all costs on Saturday. If there was anything to discover, then he would discover it.

CHAPTER ELEVEN

SO IT WAS that Freddy found himself, against his better
judgment, escorting the very proper Mildred Starkweather
to a private gathering of intellectuals of which he was certain
her mother would never approve. The Schusters lived in a
house in Doughty Street, and as they arrived Freddy could hear
the sounds of voices and music issuing from an open window
upstairs. All the rooms were lit up, and when he rang the bell
there was some little wait before anybody answered it. Despite
her determination to go out and enjoy herself as other young
women did, Mildred was looking a little apprehensive as they
stood on the step. She set her jaw when she saw Freddy looking
at her doubtfully.

'Why does nobody answer the door?' she said, and rang the
bell again.

'Remember, you're not to tell anybody why we're really here,'
said Freddy. 'Just talk about general things and lead the conversation around to the murder if you can, but don't be obvious
about it.'

'Of course I won't be obvious,' said Mildred. 'I can be as subtle as you like. I say, do you think they'll be drinking?'

'Almost certainly.'

'Oh, goodness,' she said. 'Will they expect me to do it too?'

'Not if you don't want to,' said Freddy. In reality he was hoping that Mildred would be tired by half past ten, or so uneasy at the company in which she found herself that she would insist on his taking her home. Then he could return and do some real investigating without being required to act as nursemaid to a young lady who was not accustomed to going to parties of this sort.

At last the door was opened and they were admitted and left to hang their own coats up. They pushed their way through a throng of people and up the stairs, to find themselves in a narrow, dimly-lit hall which was dense with smoke and other, less identifiable scents. A young woman in masculine attire was leaning against a small table, smoking and talking to three men. Suddenly all four burst out laughing. Two foreigners emerged from a nearby room, chattering excitedly, and disappeared towards the back of the house. From one room the sound of a gramophone could be heard, while somewhere else someone was playing the piano and singing.

Since nobody seemed inclined to tell them where to go, Freddy and Mildred entered the nearest room, which turned out to be the drawing-room. It was crowded with people, some standing, others reclining in comfortable chairs, and several more sitting in a group on the floor. Ivor Trevett was standing in the centre of the room, surrounded by a little crowd of admirers, proclaiming at length about something or other. He stood at least a head taller than anyone else, and was altogether an imposing presence. His acolyte Sidney Bishop was one of the group, naturally, as was Ruth Chudderley.

'Hallo, old chap,' said St. John, who had spotted them across the room and now came to join them. 'Mildred, what are you doing here? Shouldn't have thought this was your sort of crowd, what?'

'Of course it's my sort of crowd,' said Mildred. 'I do go out occasionally, you know.'

'But does your mother know you're here?'

'I don't tell her *everything* I do,' she replied loftily. 'Give me a cigarette, Freddy.'

Freddy, who was just in the act of lighting his own, looked up in surprise, but she gave him a meaningful stare and he took the hint and offered her his cigarette-case.

'I didn't know you smoked,' said St. John.

'Didn't you?' said Mildred with affected carelessness.

Freddy lit the gasper for her and watched, fascinated, as she drew on it with great determination. He had to admit she pulled it off rather well and hardly coughed at all, although her eyes watered slightly.

'How does one get a drink here?' she said, once she was able to speak.

'I say, Mildred,' said St. John, as though looking at her in a new light. 'I had no idea you drank, too.'

'I don't *drink*,' she said with dignity. 'But this is a party, and I don't see how one little one can hurt. Freddy, go and get me a—a—cocktail.'

'I don't know about cocktails,' said Freddy, 'but there might be some wine. Let's go and see.'

He took hold of Mildred's arm and conducted her out of the room.

'What do you think you're doing?' he hissed, once they were out of hearing. 'Your mother will string me up by the eyelashes if she finds out you've been smoking and drinking.'

'I'm just trying to fit in,' she said. 'And I'm not *really* going to drink. I'll just hold a glass so I look as though I am.'

In the next room they found the drinks laid out on the dining-table. A cheerful young man was helpfully making cocktails for anyone who asked.

'Gin fizz?' he said to Mildred.

'Yes please,' she said.

'You'd better put lots of ice in it,' said Freddy.

They took their drinks. Mildred sipped hers gingerly and made a face.

'It's horrid,' she whispered. 'Do people really like this stuff?'

'Oh, yes,' said Freddy.

She looked around.

'What do we do now?' she said. 'I expect we ought to go and talk to people we know. Suppose we split up. I'll go and talk to the Chudderley female and see what she has to say. Perhaps you can speak to Mr. Trevett or Mr. Bishop.'

Just then, St. John turned up again, in company with two young women, whom he introduced briefly as members of the East London Communist Alliance's sister organization, the West London Communist Alliance. They immediately fell into conversation with Mildred, and St. John took Freddy aside.

'Come and talk to Ruth,' he said.

'Now?' said Freddy.

'It's as good a time as any,' said St. John.

'But what am I to say?'

'I don't know. Whatever you usually say to women when you're trying to—you know.'

'But I'm not trying to "you know" with Ruth. That's your business. Besides, she looks at me as though I were something the dog chewed up and spat out, then trampled on and buried deep underground for good measure.'

'Rot. She likes you—she told me so.'

'Well, she could do a better job of showing it,' said Freddy. 'Look, I'm not sure this is a good idea.'

But St. John would listen to no protests. He pushed Freddy back into the drawing-room. Ruth Chudderley was not there, and nor was Ivor Trevett.

'Oh,' said St. John, disconcerted. 'She was here a moment ago. I'd better go and find her.'

He disappeared, and Freddy was left on his own, somewhat to his relief. A glance showed him that none of the people in the drawing-room were familiar to him, and so he wandered out again. He had seen no sign of the Schusters so far, but soon found Leonard Peacock talking to Sidney Bishop.

'Ah, it's you again,' said Peacock, in his usual mocking manner. 'The friend of Bagshawe. Tell me, is he really such an ass as he appears? I mean to say, you don't think he's been putting on an act of sorts, and is really some sort of genius in heavy disguise?'

Ordinarily Freddy would have been only too glad to expound upon St. John's asinine tendencies—had done so many times to his face over the years, in fact—but for some reason he found Peacock irritating, and felt uncharacteristically inclined to defend his old school-mate.

'Oh, he's not all that bad,' he said. 'In fact, I should say he was rather decent at heart. A serious type, but sincere enough.'

'You disappoint me,' said Peacock. 'I was hoping you'd have some juicy stories to tell us about his younger days. Someone told me he used to be quite the agitator, but I can hardly believe it myself. Very well, I suppose I shall have to go elsewhere for my fun.'

'Where's your friend Dyer?' said Freddy.

'Somewhere about,' said Peacock with a shrug.

'I rather thought the two of you were inseparable.'

'Really? I don't know where you got that idea. We were thrown together at university, so I tolerate him, but that's all. He's not exactly the thing, you see. Nothing but a jumped-up tradesman's son.'

'Is he?' said Freddy, wondering why this ought to matter to an avowed Communist.

'We can't all be born into the aristocracy,' said Sidney Bishop with a laugh. 'Some of us must work our way up, and even then we'll only get so far.'

'I dare say,' said Peacock idly.

'But of course, in future none of this sort of thing will matter,' went on Bishop.

Peacock seemed to have lost interest in the subject, and shortly afterwards wandered off, leaving Freddy to study

Sidney Bishop curiously. It was almost the first time he had seen him out of the company of Ivor Trevett, and he wanted to find out more about him. Bishop was a rubicund little man whose face wore an almost permanent expression of cheeriness. Freddy would have guessed him to be a butcher, but he was wrong as it turned out, for Bishop soon informed him that he had been engaged in the sartorial trade for many years, and had dressed many gentlemen in the business line—although he had never been fortunate enough to tailor for the highest ranks of society, he added.

'Now this is beautiful work, if you don't mind my saying so,' he said, regarding Freddy's suit with a practised eye. 'I should say from the cut you've had it four or five years—but look at this! Begging your pardon, sir.' He reached out and felt the lapel of Freddy's jacket, then took a step back and stared hard at the left sleeve. 'There's no mistaking the quality of that stitch. If you were to press me, I should say Dunnings on Conduit Street.'

'That's right,' said Freddy in surprise, and Bishop gave a sigh of satisfaction.

'I knew it!' he said.

'You're an expert, I see,' said Freddy.

'Not to say expert,' said Bishop modestly. 'But I like to think I have an eye for these things. It comes with experience. I can tell a lot about a man from his dress.'

'Can you, now? What should you say about me, then?'

'I should say you're used to the best, but your valet is careless, if you'll excuse my saying so, sir.'

'Yes, he's quite atrocious,' said Freddy, who had no valet. 'I caught him using one of my best shirts to clean the windows the other day. I beat him soundly, of course, but I don't think he's learned his lesson.'

'Oh—ah,' said Bishop, unsure as to whether he might be permitted to laugh.

'I like this game,' said Freddy. 'Now, what should you say about Trevett from his clothes?'

'Ah, now Mr. Trevett I do know about, because I used to dress him myself, back in his acting days,' said Bishop, looking pleased and drawing himself up.

'Really? You've known him for a long time, I gather.'

'Oh, yes,' said Bishop, nodding. 'I had a passion for the theatre for many years, and came to know Mr. Trevett that way, when he saw some of my work and was kind enough to say he liked it. I made many of his suits over the years, although I do less for him nowadays, as he prefers to dress in more Bohemian fashion. A splendid actor, he was—still is, in fact. I'd say it was a pity that he gave it up, except that he took up a far greater cause, so the theatre's loss is the country's gain.'

'Do you think he is destined for greatness?'

'Oh, without a doubt,' said Bishop. 'He's the sort who could lead men into battle whether they wanted to go or not. If anyone can rouse the country, I reckon he can.'

'Has he always been a Communist?' said Freddy. 'And what about you, for that matter? When did you join the Alliance?'

'Over two years I've been coming now,' said Bishop proudly. 'I never miss a meeting.'

'Did you join because of Trevett?'

'I did. I'm flattered to say he asked me to come along one evening, because he thought I might find it interesting. It was shortly after he was elected President of the Alliance, and I went along—just to please him, since I didn't know much about the cause at the time. But it's such a privilege to hear him speak that I've kept on coming ever since.'

'I've heard him speak myself,' said Freddy. 'I was at your last two meetings. Terribly unfortunate what happened to Miss Stapleton, don't you think?'

'Who?' said Bishop.

'Didn't you hear about the murder? The Temperance lady.'

'Ah, yes,' said Bishop. 'I'd forgotten. Remiss of me. Yes, it was a dreadful thing to happen.'

'Have the police spoken to you about it?' said Freddy.

'Yes, they did, but only briefly. I didn't have much to tell them, I'm afraid. I was there that evening but I didn't see who killed her.'

'An odd sort, Miss Stapleton was,' went on Freddy. 'You know how these middle-aged women get when they have nothing else to do. You'll think it funny, I dare say, but she seemed to think you lot were up to something.'

'Up to something?' said Bishop, with a laugh. 'Such as what?'

'I couldn't tell you. Of course, everybody knew it was just one of her fancies, but I suppose that sort of thing is only to be expected. They're a conventional lot in general in the Temperance movement, and I expect they find the Communist ideal a little frightening. I hear she was something of a nuisance to you.'

'Oh, I shouldn't say that, exactly,' said Bishop, his head on one side. 'She used to complain about the noise, sometimes. And she didn't like the fact that we had three drawers in the office and they had only two. But we could hardly do anything about that, could we? We've been there longer and it's first come first served.'

'I wonder who killed her,' said Freddy.

'I thought they said it was a thief,' said Bishop.

'I dare say it was. I'm sure the police will find him sooner or later. I know they're looking into it very carefully.'

'I'm glad to hear it,' said Bishop. He spoke politely, but he seemed uninterested in the subject, and Freddy could only suppose that he was so caught up with his hero-worship of Ivor Trevett that he had no attention to spare for anything else. As if in confirmation of this, Trevett happened to walk past just at that moment. Bishop immediately excused himself and went to follow his idol, leaving Freddy standing by himself, wondering what to do next. Mildred was still talking to the two girls, so he decided to get himself another drink. He had still seen no sign of the Schusters, and was curious to see how they would behave while in their own element. In the hall he bumped into Ronald Dyer, who had been described by Leonard Peacock as a jumped-up tradesman's son. Dyer seemed to be troubled by no inkling of his friend's opinion of him.

'Hallo,' he said cheerily. 'Rather a jolly do, what?'

'Rather,' agreed Freddy. 'I must say I was expecting something a bit more pursed-lipped than this. Less carousing and more earnest conversation, that sort of thing.'

'Oh, we know how to shake a leg just as well as anybody,' said Dyer. 'All work and no play makes Jack a dull boy, don't you think? Why are you really here, by the way?'

The change of manner was so sudden that Freddy was caught by surprise.

'What do you mean?' he said after a moment. 'I'm here because Mrs. Schuster invited me.'

'You're not one of us, though.'

'No. Does that matter?'

'It might,' said Dyer.

They regarded one another for a moment, then Dyer said:

'I should be very careful if I were you.'

'Careful? Of what?' said Freddy.

'They don't like interlopers here. If they suspect you've come to snoop around—for a story, perhaps—they won't be best pleased.'

'But I'm a press-man,' said Freddy lightly. 'We can't help looking as though we're snooping around, even when we're not. It's terribly unfortunate.'

'Is that so?' said Dyer. He glanced about and leaned forward. Freddy thought he was about to say something confidentially when Ivor Trevett, with Sidney Bishop once again in tow, swept up to them and clapped Dyer on the shoulder.

'There you are, my boy,' he said. 'Erskine has arrived at last. You'd better come and speak to him. I fear he is still smarting over that unfortunate mix-up with the union money, and he won't listen to me when I tell him nobody suspects him of being deliberately underhanded.'

He and Bishop bore Dyer away with them, much to Freddy's annoyance, for he was sure Dyer had been on the point of telling him something important. Did Dyer suspect his real purpose in coming here tonight? And what had he meant by his suggestion that Freddy be careful? Was it a friendly warning or a threat? Freddy could not tell, but whatever the case, he intended to be on his guard that evening.

He went in search of the Schusters again, and eventually found Anton Schuster at the back of the house in his study, with a small crowd of people. Here the real intellectual discussion was taking place. There was no music in this room, and Schuster was ensconced in a tall winged armchair, a glass of whisky in one hand and a foreign-looking cigar in the other, holding forth at length to a rapt circle of people who were crowded around him on chairs and tables and the floor, hanging on his every word. The opposite wall was lined with bookshelves, but the room was too full for Freddy to pick his way across and get a good look at them, to see if there were any books in blue jackets. He came out and glanced into another room that was obviously used as a sort of second parlour. This was where the sound of the piano had been coming from. An earnest young man in horn-rimmed spectacles, his shirt-sleeves rolled up to the elbows, was playing a mazurka on the instrument and making heavy weather of it, while a loud card game was going on at a table by the window. Theresa Schuster was standing with Leonard Peacock, watching the players. Suddenly there was a cheer, and one player scooped up all the money that had been thrown in with great satisfaction. Mrs. Schuster clapped and laughed, and made some congratulatory remark. Then the lucky winner vacated his seat and Peacock took his place. Mrs. Schuster stood by him, her hand on his shoulder, and prepared to watch him play.

Nobody had seen Freddy, and he withdrew silently. He found himself standing next to a flight of stairs and went up it. The landing at the top was illuminated by a single light above the door to the lavatory, while the rest of the floor was in shadow. He went along the landing and looked into one or two rooms, but saw nothing of note. Mrs. Schuster's room was easily identifiable from the jewellery and paints and hair-brushes scattered around the dressing-table. A diaphanous wisp of something was draped over the back of a chair. Freddy glanced into a few drawers, conscious that someone might come up the stairs at any minute, but found nothing of interest, and certainly no books. The room next door was evidently occupied by Anton Schuster. It smelt strongly of tobacco, and was strewn with papers, books and periodicals, although again none of them seemed to be what Freddy was looking for. He was frustrated at the fact that Miss Stapleton had not told Mildred the title of the book she had seen. He felt as though he were looking for a needle in a haystack, for not only did he not know the name of the book, neither did he have any evidence that it was the one he wanted—the book that was presumably the key to the coded advertisements placed in the *Radical*.

He slipped out of the room and along to the end of the landing, where there was a cupboard. He opened the door and found it was not a cupboard at all but a box-room of sorts. With a glance behind him he entered and turned on the light. The floor was uncarpeted and the walls and window bare. Here a mish-mash of old furniture was stored, but one corner of the room was clear, and held a table and chair. By it was a small bookshelf, and the first thing Freddy spotted on it was a typewriter with its cover on. His heart leapt. He paused to listen at the door in case anybody was coming, then brought down the machine and uncovered it. There was no paper that he could see, so he tore out a page from his notebook and inserted it. He typed an 'e,' then, as that told him nothing on its own, added 'ggs.' The top of the 'e' was a little higher than the tops of the other letters. He tapped out one or two more words for confirmation, then typed an upper-case 'R,' and was not at all surprised to see that the top of it was sliced off.

There were some books on the shelf, too, and he was just about to turn his attention to them when he heard the sound of voices coming up the stairs. Quick as a flash, he turned off the light and listened. Instead of pausing by the lavatory, however, the voices came closer. Freddy looked around in panic and darted behind a large, antique wardrobe with a cracked and splintered front—just as the door opened and someone came in, turning on the light as they did so. It was at that moment that Freddy made two unwelcome discoveries: first, that he had left the paper in the typewriter; and second, that with the light switched on, his presence behind the wardrobe was clearly reflected in the window for anyone to see.

CHAPTER TWELVE

FREDDY FROZE AND shut his eyes for a second as the sound of footsteps crossed the room. He expected to be hauled out and at the very least forced to explain why he had made the unforgivable *faux pas* of snooping around the Schusters' private apartments. To his surprise, however, the footsteps did not pause, but crossed the room and passed through a door. He opened his eyes and saw from the reflection in the window that the room was empty. Whoever it was must not have seen him. He emerged cautiously from behind the wardrobe and noticed for the first time that there was a door in the far wall, partially concealed behind a large heap of boxes. Breathing a silent sigh of relief, he tiptoed across to the typewriter and carefully removed the paper from it, but did not dare risk putting the machine back where he had found it. He was about to leave the room before he was caught, but the sound of voices from the other side of the inner door aroused his curiosity. He silently moved towards it, and, after a moment's hesitation, applied his ear to the crack. He recognized Leonard Peacock's loud voice immediately, but the person to whom he was talking spoke more quietly and Freddy was unable to identify who it was, although it was certainly a man. He chided himself for his own cowardice in having closed his eyes as the newcomers had crossed the room, for had he kept them open he might have seen who the other person was.

'—simply won't work,' Peacock was saying. 'I told you it was no good, and that he can't be trusted. I've had my suspicions about him for some time. He's going to blow the whole thing wide open, I tell you.'

There came the muffled sound of the other speaker, then Peacock replied:

'You'd better take care of it, then. Not I—it would be too obvious. Tonight, preferably. Or soon, at any rate.'

The other speaker talked for a few moments, but Freddy could hear none of it, then:

'I've thought of a way round that,' said Peacock. 'I was speaking to that ass Bagshawe—'

His voice fell, and Freddy strained to hear, but could distinguish nothing more than the sound of murmuring.

'Oh, there's no doubt of it,' came Peacock's voice, raised again. 'He was spotted, you see. He'll be easy enough to fool. I know the type—will say yes to anything. No—not just yet; we'll leave it till closer to the time, I think. We don't want him to suspect anything. Now, about the other thing—'

The other man spoke, then Peacock's voice came again:

'What about Thursday night? Is this fellow square? Can we be sure he won't talk out of turn? Very well, I'll get it, then. You'd better give me his name—oh, and some money, too. All right—I'll see you at Russell Square at seven o'clock. I'll wait on the corner opposite the hotel.'

There came the sound of footsteps and Freddy darted back from the door and out onto the landing. He was just in time to lock himself in the lavatory before Peacock and his unidentified companion walked past and down the stairs. Freddy had intended to wait a moment or two then come out in time to see who the second man was. Unfortunately for him, however, he found that the bolt on the door had stuck, and by the time he got it undone the two of them had disappeared. Freddy dashed downstairs and looked around. In the doorway of the dining-room Peacock was talking to Trevett, whom he was almost sure was not the owner of the second voice. Where was Anton Schuster? Freddy glanced into the study and saw that Schuster was no longer there. He kicked himself at his bad luck at having missed his chance to see the second man, although he was almost certain it was the Austrian, for who else but he would know of the existence of the inner box-room? At that, it occurred to Freddy that perhaps the two speakers had left some clue in the second room. Glancing around to make sure nobody was watching, he returned upstairs to the box-room and peered cautiously through the inner door. The second room was little more than a large cupboard, and contained nothing but boxes, a wooden stool and a lamp. Freddy wondered at the stool until he looked inside one or two of the boxes and found they were all full of books. Perhaps Schuster came up here now and again to look through his collection in peace and quiet. Freddy was about to turn and leave when his eye fell on a little stack of books which had been left on top of a pile of boxes. One of them was a cheap novel, wrapped in a bright blue jacket, such as one buys at a railway station. The title was *The Secret of the Black Veil*, and its author was unknown to Freddy, although a quick glance inside showed the novel to be of the sensational type. Freddy quickly noted down the edition number and the date of publication, and put the book back where he had found it. If this was indeed the book he was looking for, then it was better not to alert the conspirators to the fact that their code had been broken.

There was little else to be seen here, so he switched off the lamp and came out into the main box-room. A glance at the shelves next to the table revealed nothing of interest either. He replaced the typewriter, then with a last look around the room turned off the light and emerged onto the landing, where he almost jumped out of his skin, for there before him stood Theresa Schuster.

'Hallo,' he said as casually as he could manage. 'I was just— er—looking for someone, but I see she's not here.'

'Nobody is up here except ourselves,' said Mrs. Schuster. She was wearing an evening-gown in a soft greenish-gold which shimmered as she moved, and set off the amber of her eyes to perfection. Around her neck was a choker of jade green glass beads in a bronze-coloured setting, and she wore earrings to match. She was standing near him, and again he caught the faint scent of roses and spices.

'I—' he began, intending to launch into a further explanation as to why he was snooping around in his hostess's house, but something about the satisfied little smile that turned up the corners of her mouth as she looked at him told him that she was not interested—or perhaps had noticed nothing out of the ordinary—and he was unable to continue. It was most unusual for him to find himself dumb-struck, and he wondered at it.

'I'm sorry I did not see you arrive,' she said. 'But you see, it is true what I told you—that Anton and I like to enjoy ourselves.'

'Er—yes,' said Freddy.

'Myself, I like it particularly,' she said, and her tone was full of meaning.

It was most odd. He was perfectly conscious that she was deliberately exercising her powers of mesmerism on him—could feel the force of it from where he stood—and yet despite that knowledge, he could not turn his gaze away from those amber eyes of hers. Close up, he could once again see the faint scar that ran across her left cheekbone. She saw him looking at it.

'Feel it,' she said, and before he could stop her she caught up his hand, put it to her face, and ran his fingers gently across it. Had she kissed him it could not have felt more intimate.

'How did you get it?' he said.

Her brows drew together as though she were in momentary pain.

'From my first husband,' she said. 'He was a bad man, a violent man.'

'What happened to him?'

'He died,' she replied shortly. 'Then Anton came, and was kind to me. But he is old, and I wonder sometimes whether he is strong enough to protect me. What about you?' She turned her eyes to his left ear-lobe, which was ragged and half-missing. 'I see you have known violence too. But I know you are not the sort to be frightened by it. Should you protect me if I were in danger?'

'Are you in danger?'

'I know we have enemies,' she said with sudden intensity. 'And I know they would like nothing more than to see me dead.' Then her face cleared and she smiled. 'But I feel I can trust you. If something should happen, then I am sure you will not turn me away if I come to you for help.'

'Certainly not, what?' he said stupidly.

She was still holding his hand, and she laid it against her lips.

'Thank you,' she said. 'I will remember your words. I feel a sympathy with you, and know you would not let me come to harm. But you must say nothing of this to anyone, or you, too, will be in danger.'

'Oh—er—rather,' said Freddy.

Someone was coming up the stairs, and she let go of his hand and moved away from him.

'Remember,' she said, then turned and went downstairs.

Freddy remained where he was, for she had left him feeling a little dazed. After a few minutes he shook himself, took a deep breath, and forced himself to consider the encounter dispassionately. To his surprise, he found that the hand she had taken in hers was tingling, and that his heart was racing as though he had been running. He had to admit that whatever power she had exercised on him, she had done it very effectively.

'I wonder if they learn hypnotism at school in Austria,' he said musingly to himself. 'And what exactly does she want of me? Does she really have enemies, as she said? Or is she trying to draw me in for some other purpose?'

He had no answers to his questions at present, so there was nothing to do but go downstairs and look for Mildred, for he was starting to think that this was a suitable moment in which to leave. He had found out a number of interesting things that evening, but it was probably best to stop now, before his activities began to arouse suspicion. Besides, he realized with a sudden shock as he glanced at his watch, it was already after midnight, and Mildred had promised her mother that she would not be home late. But Mildred was nowhere to be found. Freddy put his head into the dining-room. She was not there, but two other people he recognized were: Ruth Chudderley and Ivor Trevett, who to judge from their current attitude were on much friendlier terms than anyone had supposed. Freddy withdrew his head hurriedly and gave a silent whistle.

'Well, there's a turn-up!' he said to himself. 'So much for St. John's hopes, although I don't suppose there was ever much chance for him anyway. Odd, though. I should have said she was a cold fish, but it seems not.'

Eventually he found Mildred in the drawing-room. She was sitting on the floor among a group of people, giggling uncontrollably.

'Freddy!' she cried gaily when she caught sight of him. 'Look, everyone, this is Freddy. Move up so he can sit down. We're playing the most marvellous game,' she said to him. 'It's called "Hobbes and Descartes Took the 'Bus." Everyone has to add a famous philosopher to the list and you have to remember them all, and if you miss one out or get them in the wrong order you have to take a drink.' She gave a sorrowful hiccup. 'I've an awful memory, so I'm losing rather badly.'

Freddy noticed that she was speaking very carefully and deliberately, and he looked at the glass beside her in dismay.

'Mildred, you idiot,' he said 'How much have you had?'

She waved a hand.

'I don't know,' she said. 'It can't be much, though. These drinks are only small. I mean to say, three of them would barely fill a teacup. And there was rather a nice cigarette, too. It tasted much better than that horrid one of yours, and gave me a lovely floaty feeling, just like being on a cloud.'

'Good God!' exclaimed Freddy. He had the sinking sensation that he was about to get into trouble for this.

'There's no need for that,' said Mildred primly. 'I say, you're not going to tell Mummy, are you?'

'Of course I'm not going to tell her. As a matter of fact, at this moment I'm considering emigration. Look here, my girl, I'm taking you home this minute.'

'But I don't want to go home,' said Mildred, pouting.

'Have you any idea what time it is?'

'No,' said Mildred. 'I lost my watch in a card game.'

Freddy raised his eyes and forced himself to remain calm.

'Well, I can tell you,' he said. 'It's nearly one o'clock, and you promised your mother you'd be home before midnight.'

'I'm sure she won't mind,' said Mildred. 'In fact, I dare say she won't even find out. She's probably asleep by now.'

'I thought you said she was going to wait up for you.'

'Then she'll have to wait a bit longer, won't she?' said Mildred. She beamed around at her new friends. 'We're having fun, aren't we? Someone get me another drink. Hi! What do you think you're doing?'

This last exclamation came as Freddy hauled her to her feet by the elbows and marched her out of the room without ceremony.

'We're going home,' he said.

'Do you treat all your women like this?' she said indignantly, as Freddy fetched her coat and hat and threw them at her.

'Only the fatheaded ones,' he replied.

'That's jolly rude,' she said.

'I thought you weren't going to drink?'

'But I didn't—at least, not very much. There's no harm in one or two, is there?'

'One or two? Nine or ten, more like, from the looks of you,' said Freddy.

'Nonsense,' said Mildred. 'If I'd had that many I'd be drunk, and as you can see, I'm perfectly sober. Oh! How did that happen?'

She had slid down the wall, and was now sitting on the floor, looking about her in surprise.

'Up you get,' said Freddy, and hauled her upright again. Between them they got her coat and hat on. Mildred wanted to say goodbye to her friends, but Freddy propelled her out through the front door, ignoring her protests, then hurried her down the street. After a few yards, however, it became clear that the cold night air was having an unfortunate effect on

Mildred's ability to remain standing. She clung to his arm and began to stagger, laughing hysterically as she did so.

'I want to go to a night-club,' she slurred.

'You want to go to bed,' he said. 'We'd better find a taxi.' He stopped and let go of Mildred's arm while he tried to flag down an approaching cab. 'Damn, it's taken,' he said, then turned back to find that she had once again sunk to the ground. He picked her up again, but she could barely keep to her feet. She was evidently completely incapable. She suddenly seemed to realize that all was not well.

'Why can't I stand up?' she said.

'Because you're roaring drunk, you idiot,' he said.

'Oh, goodness me!' she exclaimed in dismay. 'What am I to do? I can't go home, or Mummy will kill me. Where can I go?'

'The best place for you is in bed,' said Freddy. 'Can you pretend to be sober, do you think? You might manage it if you don't stop to chat when you get in.'

But one look at her was enough to tell him that that was impossible. His heart sank. Mrs. Starkweather was an upright and unsuspicious sort, and would be most unamused to find that the young man to whom she had entrusted the safety of her only daughter had taken her out and brought her home three sheets in the wind. Even though he was not at fault in this instance, he sensed he was in for the most terrific wigging.

'I can't go home,' she repeated with a hiccup. 'Freddy, you must let me stay at your place tonight.'

Freddy tried to calculate by what factor his offence would be compounded in Mrs. Starkweather's eyes if he took Mildred back to his flat for the night, but decided it was beyond the power of mathematics.

'Oh, no you don't,' he said. 'You'll go home and face up to it, just as everybody else has to. And anyway, it won't be you who gets into trouble,' he went on sourly. 'It'll be me, as usual. She'll say I put you up to it.'

'Why would she say that? You don't think I told her I was coming out with you, do you?'

'Didn't you?'

'Of course not. Why, the very idea! She'd have locked me up in my room rather than let me go if she knew I was with you.'

'Really? I thought she liked me.'

'She does like you. But *trusting* you is quite a different thing. Your reputation goes before you, you see,' said Mildred darkly. 'I know lots of girls who aren't allowed to go out if their mothers hear that you're going to be one of the party.'

'Good Lord!' said Freddy. It had never occurred to him that fearful mamas across London might be taking steps to shield their daughters from his pernicious influence, and he could not decide whether to be insulted or flattered.

'So you see, it will be all the worse if you take me home now, because she'll know I was with you tonight,' said Mildred. 'You're in the clear as long as she never finds out. I'll go home in the morning and think of some excuse in the meantime.'

'But—' said Freddy.

'You'd better do as I say if you don't want to get us both into trouble,' she said.

'But—' said Freddy again. He did not like this at all.

Just then a taxi arrived. Mildred was still leaning heavily against him, and he shovelled her into the cab with more efficiency than good manners. She immediately fell asleep.

'Where to?' said the driver.

Freddy looked at Mildred and tried to picture Mrs. Starkweather's face if he arrived at Upper Montagu Street with her unconscious daughter slung over his shoulder.

'Fleet Street,' he said.

The driver smirked.

'Right you are, sir,' he said, and they set off. In a very few minutes they arrived at Freddy's place, and Freddy, with some difficulty and a little assistance from the taxi-driver, at last managed to get Mildred out of the car and up the stairs. He then put her into his bed and went into the sitting-room, there to spend an uncomfortable night curled up on the sofa.

CHAPTER THIRTEEN

H E WAS AWOKEN at just after eight by someone shaking him by the shoulder. It was Mildred.

'Mph? What's that?' he said groggily, and tried to sit up.

'You do sleep late,' she said. 'I've been awake for hours. Listen, I've been thinking: we'll have to tell Mummy I stayed at Iris's last night.'

'What?'

'I told her I was going out with Iris anyway, so it'll be easy enough to convince her. I'll just say Iris was taken ill, or something, so I didn't want to leave her.'

'Taken—ill?' said Freddy. He was not at his best first thing in the morning, and it took a little while for new ideas to register in his brain.

'I'm going to telephone her now,' said Mildred.

'Who, your mother?'

'Well, Iris first. I'd better make sure she'll back me up. Then I'll call Mummy and explain.'

Freddy had now woken up properly and was regarding Mildred in something like wonder.

'Mildred, aren't you feeling awfully sick?' he said.

'No,' said Mildred in surprise.

'No headache, or anything like that?'

'Well, perhaps a slight one,' she said, as though she had only just noticed it. 'But I always wake up with a bit of a headache when I go to bed late. Why?'

Freddy stared.

'No reason,' he said at last.

'I am rather hungry, though. I don't suppose you have anything for breakfast?'

'Breakfast?' said Freddy, as though this were an alien concept. It was rare that he rose early enough to indulge in breakfast.

'Oh, never mind,' said Mildred. 'We can go out somewhere once I've telephoned Iris and Mummy.'

Two long telephone-calls later, they went out to a little eating-place near Charlotte Street. Mildred ate with a hearty relish, and Freddy could do nothing but watch in amazement as she polished off a large plate of kippers, then followed it up with two boiled eggs and finally several crumpets with butter and honey. At last she pushed her plate away and gave a sigh of satisfaction.

'I don't think I've enjoyed a meal so much in ages,' she said. A worried look flitted across her face. 'I drank rather a lot last night, didn't I?'

'I think you did, yes,' said Freddy.

'I know I must have, because I don't remember much about it. I didn't make a fool of myself, did I? I mean to say, I didn't do anything *too* dreadful? I remember losing my watch playing cards, but there wasn't anything worse than that, was there?'

'I don't think so,' said Freddy, who was feeling slightly guilty at having abandoned her for almost the entire evening.

'I didn't find out anything about Miss Stapleton,' she said sadly. 'Or if I did, I don't remember it. Perhaps I'm not cut out to be a detective.'

'Never mind,' said Freddy. 'You had fun, at any rate. That's what you wanted, isn't it?'

'Yes, I did,' she said, brightening up. 'It was fun. I can say I've tried all that sort of thing now, although once was enough, I think. I shan't do it again.' She looked up as a smartly-dressed young woman with a head of golden-brown curls came in and joined them. 'Oh, hallo, Iris. There was no need to come out, you know. I'm quite all right.'

'What on earth have you been doing, Mildred?' said Iris Bagshawe, sitting down at their table and removing her gloves in a business-like fashion. 'I didn't understand half of what you said just now on the telephone. Of course I'll say whatever you like, but tell me what you meant. Have you really been drinking?' She glared at Freddy. 'What have you been doing now?' she said accusingly. 'You know Mildred doesn't drink.'

'I haven't done anything,' said Freddy. 'We went to a party last night and Mildred found out, just as thousands have done before her, that gin cocktails are best taken in moderation. It was nothing to do with me.'

'I don't believe that for a second,' said Iris. She had a very pretty nose of which she was rather proud, but she was now wrinkling it up as she looked at Freddy, as though he were something distasteful. 'I know exactly what you're like. I'll bet you told her it was soda water or something, just for a joke.'

'Oh, no he didn't,' said Mildred. 'I did drink too much, but it wasn't really his fault.'

'It wasn't my fault at all,' said Freddy, stung by the 'really.' 'It's not as though I forced the stuff down your throat, is it? As a matter of fact, I seem to recall warning you off it several times.'

'Hmm,' said Iris sceptically. 'Where exactly did you take her?'

'To a party at the house of some friends of your brother's,' said Freddy. 'It was meant to be a sort of salon of Communist intellectuals, but it turns out that Communist intellectuals like to drink just as much as the rest of us, and they wanted Mildred to join in.'

'Oh, they're the worst for that sort of thing,' said Iris. 'We had to have words with St. John when he brought a couple of them home to Tewkesbury at Christmas. They drank the house dry and were quite ill-mannered. I mean to say, one can ignore an uneducated accent, but they were rude to the servants—which one doesn't exactly expect from people who are supposed to be trying to improve the lot of the working man—and they took liberties with the supplies. And on top of all that, one of them got rather over-familiar with me.'

'Did he, indeed?' said Freddy, more indignantly than he had intended.

'Yes. Ralph had to speak to him about it. He soon stopped after that.'

'I should think so. How is old Ralph, by the way?'

'Oh, all right, I expect,' said Iris, dismissing her intended with magnificent indifference. 'Did you see St. John last night, then? I haven't seen him for weeks. Is he still chasing after that horrid girl who always looks as though she's chewing a lemon?'

'Ah, yes,' said Freddy. 'He is, but I don't think you need worry about ending up with her for a sister-in-law. When I saw her last night she was—er—demonstrating an enthusiastic admiration for another man's political convictions.'

'What? Who?' said Mildred, open-mouthed.

'Ivor Trevett.'

'Goodness!' said Mildred. 'Poor St. John. He'll be awfully upset.'

'I dare say he will, but I'm glad of it,' said Iris. 'He's an ass, but the Chudderley would have made him miserable. And the rest of us, too,' she added. 'Imagine having to make polite conversation with someone who can't understand a joke.'

As it happened, this was exactly Freddy's opinion of Iris's fiancé, but he said nothing.

'Oh, that man at the next table's forgotten his umbrella,' said Mildred suddenly. She picked up the article in question and went after him, and Iris Bagshawe immediately turned to Freddy, eyes narrowed.

'What are you up to?' she hissed. 'Why did you take Mildred out? She's far too innocent for you—not your type at all.'

'She talked me into it,' he replied. 'If you must know, I was there looking for a story, and she insisted on coming.'

'You didn't—you didn't—do anything *awful*, did you?' she said, with a note of fear in her voice.

'Of course I didn't do anything awful,' he said stiffly. 'I took her to the party, then I took her home and tucked her up in bed as though she were a new-born babe, while I spent the night freezing on the sofa.'

'Hmm. Well, if you say so, I suppose I ought to believe it,' she said. 'But you'd better be telling the truth.'

'I am, I swear it,' said Freddy.

She regarded him with something akin to sorrow.

'It really is time you grew up, you know,' she said.

Freddy was nettled at this, for he felt he had been behaving well lately, and that he was being unfairly attacked. He had no opportunity to say this, however, before Mildred came back in. Iris rose and put on her gloves.

'Come on, Mildred,' she said. 'We'll go home together and concoct something for your mother on the way. I'm sure we can think of something convincing.'

'All right,' agreed Mildred. They prepared to depart. 'Thank you, Freddy,' she said. 'I had a splendid evening. Let me know if you find anything out,' she added in a whisper as Iris straightened her hat.

Freddy nodded, and the two girls left, Iris casting a doubtful glance back at him as she did so, and leaving him in no very cheerful frame of mind. There was nothing to do now but settle the bill and head back home, where he fell into bed and slept until the early afternoon.

Chapter Fourteen

FREDDY'S NEXT CONCERN was to tell Henry Jameson all he had learnt at the Schusters' party, but he quickly found that even Intelligence men take Sundays off, for nobody answered when he called. It would have to wait until Monday, he decided, but in the meantime there was no harm in trying to track down a copy of *The Secret of the Black Veil*, the book he had found in the second box-room at the Schusters' house. He eventually found a slightly dog-eared copy tucked behind all the other books on a shelf outside a dingy bookseller's shop at Waterloo, and bore his prize triumphantly back home, where he brought out all the coded advertisements Henry had given him and set to work with the most recent message, hoping against hope that he was on the right path. After a few minutes he pulled at his ear in disappointment and looked at the string of gibberish in front of him. Unless he had been reading the code incorrectly, this was the wrong book. He tried again, just to be sure that he was doing it properly, but no—the message which came out made no sense at all. The advertisement from the previous week produced equally unsatisfactory results, as did the one from the week before that. This was a blow, and Freddy was ready to give up, annoyed that he had seemingly been so close to solving the coded messages only to be disappointed. He decided to have one last attempt, this time taking the oldest of the advertisements and trying with that, and immediately sat up in excitement as a message began to form before his eyes.

'Ah!' he said, and regarded his handiwork. Now this was certainly a communication of sorts, although Freddy had little idea what it meant. As far as he could tell, the purpose of the message was to call a meeting of a particular group of people, but he was unable to understand anything beyond that, for the people and places referred to had been given code-names. From what he could see, however, it did not refer directly to any of the members of the East London Communist Alliance. He took another advertisement, and for the next two or three hours absorbed himself in the task of deciphering the coded announcements. When he had finished he gazed at the results thoughtfully. He had managed to decipher twenty-four messages, all of which were much the same as the first one and made little sense to him, although Henry Jameson might understand them better. There was nothing to be done until he could speak to Henry, so Freddy put the papers away and spent the rest of Sunday in idle pursuits.

The next day he took the book and the advertisements to the *Clarion*'s offices with him when he went in to work. His colleague Jolliffe saw him poring over the three messages he had been unable to decipher, and looked on with interest as Freddy scratched his head.

'Is it a new game?' he said.

'You might say that,' said Freddy. 'It's one of those codes that you crack by referring to pages in a book. Just a silly thing, you know. Mungo bet me I couldn't decipher it. I've got all except three of them, but I can't understand these ones at all.'

'Are you sure you're using the right book?' said Jolliffe, coming to look.

'I think so,' said Freddy. 'It worked for the other messages.'

'Perhaps they've tried to make these ones more difficult,' said Jolliffe. 'Have you tried counting the pages backwards?'

'I didn't think of that,' said Freddy, and tried it. 'No go,' he said at length.

'Let me try,' said Jolliffe. He pored over the book for some minutes with a pencil, then frowned. 'I think it must be a different book,' he said. 'I mean to say, look here: page twenty-one has nothing but an illustration on it. And this one, too: it says page thirteen, but the word that comes out is 'inflatable.' That doesn't make sense. And page four is the copyright page and doesn't have enough lines. This can't be the right book.'

'Yes, I think you must be right,' said Freddy.

'It looks as though the book you want is a short one, too,' observed Jolliffe. 'All the pages given are low numbers. Isn't there a clue in one of the other messages as to what it is?'

'No, and it's a damned nuisance,' said Freddy. He was disappointed, for he had hoped to turn up triumphantly at Henry's office with the codes all deciphered. Still, he had made a start, and he was anxious to report what he had found so far.

Henry was looking distracted and worried when they met, but cheered up a little when Freddy placed the book and the messages on his desk.

'Oh, well done!' he said. 'How did you find it?'

'It was at the Schusters' house,' replied Freddy.

'You didn't take it from there?' said Henry, in some alarm.

'No, I left it and bought my own copy.'

'I'm glad to see you have some sense,' said Henry, relieved. 'Best not to draw attention to ourselves if possible. What else did you find?'

'Well, it appears that Anton Schuster is the one who is writing and posting the advertisements,' said Freddy. He felt in his pocket and brought out the envelope he had taken from St. John's waste-paper basket. 'This is how they arrive,' he said. 'The typewriter which was used to type that address was at the Schusters' house.'

'Is that so?' said Henry. He read carefully through the messages Freddy had written down from the codes. 'Hmm,' he said at last. 'Code-names within a code, I see, and it's a pity you couldn't crack the last few, but look at these seven messages here. I don't suppose you remember what happened on the dates mentioned?'

'Not offhand,' said Freddy politely.

'No, you wouldn't,' said Henry. 'Last year we had a certain amount of trouble with unofficial strikes in several places at once by some of the more excitable members of the Labourers' Union. Rowbotham hadn't approved them, and there wasn't a vote, but somehow several small groups managed to organize themselves efficiently enough to walk out all at the same time. Each of the strikes was preceded—and supposedly caused— by the sacking of a shop steward, and we strongly suspect the dismissals were deliberately orchestrated in order to foment unrest. We believed John Pettit and his group of agitators were behind it, but he denied it absolutely—condemned the strikers, in fact—and we couldn't find any evidence that he was lying. But now it looks as though Schuster had a hand in it, too. He must have been communicating with the activists in the North by means of these advertisements. I dare say if we search Pettit's house we'll find he, too, owns a copy of *The Secret of the Black Veil*.'

'I doubt it,' said Freddy. 'I understand his house burned down a few weeks ago—oh!'

He stopped and laughed suddenly.

'What?' said Henry.

'Of course! That's why the last three messages make no sense,' said Freddy. 'Pettit lost his copy of the book in the fire and they had to change to a new one quickly.'

'Ah, yes,' said Henry. 'I wonder why he didn't just buy a new copy, though.'

'They don't print many copies of these penny-dreadfuls,' said Freddy. 'I expect once they've all sold out they don't bother printing any more. I had trouble finding it myself.'

'Yes, that makes sense,' said Henry. He looked at the papers before him. 'So, then, thanks to you, we now have a firm connection between the East London Communist Alliance and what is going on elsewhere. I knew there was *something*. It's just a pity we don't have the messages for the last three weeks.

I'd like very much to know what they say, as I have the feeling they are planning something very soon, and I suspect it has something to do with this march and rally on the fifteenth.'

'Yes, they're all getting very excited about that,' said Freddy. 'What do you think it is, then? Do you expect all the workers to descend on London for a day's fun, and then refuse to go back to work afterwards, spurred on by their leaders? Surely you'd have heard something to that effect if that were the case.'

'No, I don't think it's anything as obvious as that,' said Henry. 'I know I said it might be possible to organize a general strike in secret, but I do rather think we'd have got wind of it somehow— and in any case, the majority of workers like to have a say in these matters. I can't imagine their being at all keen to walk out without being asked to vote on it first. No, whatever it is, it must be known only to a small number of people. But who is behind it, in your opinion? Are they all in on it, do you think?'

'I can't say for certain,' said Freddy, 'but I know Leonard Peacock, at least, is plotting something.'

'Oh?' said Henry, and listened as Freddy related the conversation he had overheard between Peacock and the other unidentified person.

'That's interesting,' he said at last. 'It looks as though they suspect someone of being a traitor.'

'Yes,' said Freddy. 'I don't know who it is, but I shouldn't like to be in his shoes at present. They seemed to be considering a replacement for him, but they thought Trevett wouldn't be suitable.'

'I wonder whether that means Trevett isn't part of all this,' said Henry musingly.

'Perhaps it does. For my part, if I were brewing up a secret plot I shouldn't ask him to take part in it. He's so fond of talking at the top of his voice to anyone who will listen that I'm not sure one could trust him to keep it quiet. Still, he and Schuster do seem prone to disappearing into corners to confer together, so I suppose we oughtn't to discount him completely.'

'Then I shan't cross him off the list just yet,' said Henry. 'Who was Peacock talking to, do you think?'

'I don't know. I thought it might have been Schuster, but I couldn't say for sure. The voice was too quiet to make anything out.'

'What about your friend Bagshawe? Might he have been the second person? Do you think he knows anything?'

'It wasn't St. John,' said Freddy, 'because they were talking about him. They said he would be easy enough to fool, although I have no idea what they meant by that. I assume it has something to do with the *Radical*. No, I know he's done one or two queer things in the past, but I think we may have to accept that he isn't concerned in this particular business.'

'Well, you know him best, so I suppose I ought to trust your judgment,' said Henry. He sighed. 'It's all very frustrating. I was hoping we'd find some evidence against Anton Schuster, but it appears he's too discreet for us.'

'But are you sure he's the one behind all this?'

'Of course one can't be sure of anything,' said Henry. 'But he has a history of stirring things up while keeping in the background. Words can be just as dangerous as guns, and the Austrians certainly considered him a threat. If he hadn't left Vienna when he did he would most likely have been arrested for sedition. Now we've got him, and I'd much rather we hadn't. Very well; did you find out anything else?'

'No—at least, not exactly. But Mrs. Schuster seems to think someone wants to kill her,' said Freddy slowly.

'Oh? Did she say who?'

'No. To be perfectly truthful I couldn't decide whether to believe her or not. I rather thought at the time she had other intentions, and was using the story as a means to get my sympathy.'

'I see. And did she—er—get your sympathy?'

'I'm not sure. I can't quite make her out. She's something of a vamp, so it's difficult to tell whether she's sincere or whether she merely likes collecting men.'

'She might be useful, though. Do you think you might allow yourself to be collected?' said Henry.

'Oh, I never refuse an appeal from a lady,' said Freddy lightly. 'Although I have the feeling that this one might be a little more dangerous than most.'

'I have every faith in you,' said Henry with a smile.

'I should like to know what Peacock is planning,' went on Freddy. 'Whatever it is, he's doing it on Thursday night.'

'Can you find out?' said Henry. 'You might follow him.'

'I could try, I suppose,' said Freddy. 'But wouldn't it be better if one of your people did it? What about your man on the spot? I haven't heard anything from him.'

'Nor have we,' said Henry, half to himself. 'I was expecting a report this morning. No, I think it would be better if you did it. You don't mind that sort of thing, do you?'

'Not at all,' said Freddy. 'I'm as curious as you are to find out what this mysterious plot is. Do you think Miss Stapleton found out about it and was silenced for her pains? I don't suppose you've made any progress on that case, by the way?'

'Not much,' admitted Henry. 'The problem is we have very little evidence apart from a dead body and a missing takings box. Nobody will admit to having seen her after half past nine that evening. I'm beginning to think there's no connection at all between Olive Stapleton's death and the Communist Alliance.'

'Oh, but there must be,' said Freddy. 'Tell the police to keep digging. They'll find something, you'll see.'

Chapter Fifteen

THE POLICE *HAD* been digging, it seemed, for news soon got out that Ronald Dyer had gone missing. The first Freddy heard about it was from Mildred Starkweather, who telephoned him at the office on Tuesday. He was out on a story, and so did not receive the message until almost lunch-time.

'I tried you at home but you weren't there,' she said. 'Then I remembered you work sometimes.'

'Yes, I do work sometimes,' said Freddy in some distraction. He was at that moment frowning over three stories which had been put on his desk at once, and wondering which one to look at first.

'Anyway,' Mildred went on, 'I dare say you've heard about Ronald Dyer.'

'No,' said Freddy, his attention snapping back to her at once. 'What about him?'

'He's run off!' she said.

'What do you mean, he's run off? Do you mean he's disappeared?'

'Yes. We heard it from the police this morning. They wanted to know whether Miss Stapleton had ever mentioned having any suspicions about him. Well, Mummy and I couldn't remember anything in particular—I mean to say, she was suspicious of all of them, but never mentioned Dyer in particular, as far as I know—so we said no. They weren't going to tell us anything else, but I got it out of them that he's vanished from his flat and nobody knows where he's gone.'

'Who reported it?' said Freddy. 'Peacock, I suppose?'

'Yes. Apparently they share rooms. Peacock says that Dyer went out on Sunday and didn't come back. He thought nothing of it at first, but then Sunday night went by and Monday, and still he didn't turn up. Peacock called the bank where Dyer works, and they hadn't seen him either, and wanted to know when he'd be coming in. Then Peacock got a bit worried and went into Dyer's bedroom, and found he'd left a note to say that he was sorry for what he'd done, and that he was going away for a while, and that nobody was to look for him.'

'Sorry for what he'd done?' repeated Freddy. 'What had he done?'

'He didn't say, but it's perfectly obvious, isn't it? Why, he must have been talking about Miss Stapleton. The note was a sort of confession to the killing.'

'Good Lord!' said Freddy. 'Is that what the police said?'

'Well, no,' admitted Mildred. 'They didn't say much at all really, but what else could it possibly be?'

'I don't know,' said Freddy. He was thinking. Ronald Dyer might conceivably have murdered Miss Stapleton—he had certainly been at the central hall that night, at around the time Miss Stapleton had died. But it seemed very odd. Freddy did not know Dyer at all well, of course, but he should never have thought of him as the type to stab an elderly woman to death for a relatively small amount of money. It had been a petty sort of crime, he thought. Yes—that was the word: petty. Even if the takings box had been stolen purely to divert attention away from the Communist Alliance, this was not a *grand* sort of murder. It did not seem to fit with the kind of conspiracy he was now investigating, which was supposedly founded on great causes and the class struggle. There was no doubt that Dyer's disappearance and the note he had left did look very suspicious, but Freddy was not convinced.

Mildred was still talking.

'By the way, Mummy didn't suspect a thing about the party,' she said. 'Iris and I came up with a beautiful story about her having been taken ill, and told her Iris's 'phone hadn't been working, so we couldn't call, and she fell for it.'

'Oh—ah—jolly good,' said Freddy.

'I put in a good word for you with Iris,' she went on. 'She seemed to think it was all your fault, so I told her it wasn't. I think I managed to convince her.'

'Splendid,' said Freddy.

'You might talk her round if you tried, you know.'

'I don't want to talk her round.'

'Oh, but Ralph is the limit. I don't know what she sees in him. You don't really want her to marry him, do you?'

'It's none of my business whom she chooses to marry,' said Freddy coldly. 'Look, I'd better go. You will tell me if you hear anything else, won't you?'

Mildred promised to do so and hung up, leaving Freddy to ponder what he had heard. At length he picked up the telephone again and made a call to the police. He soon found out that the Communist Alliance were now claiming that some of their money had gone missing too. It looked, in fact, as though Ronald Dyer had been stealing funds from them for some time. The police were non-committal about their suspicions, but it was impossible not to draw the conclusion that here was the murderer of Olive Stapleton. For many months Dyer had contented himself with taking money only from his own organization, but on that Tuesday night, when confronted with a defenceless woman holding a box full of cash, he had been unable to resist temptation, and had struck. For some days he had sat tight, sure that there was no evidence to link him with the crime, but eventually he had been overcome by guilt, or fear, or something else, and had vanished, leaving a note of confession. It all seemed perfectly clear. Freddy drummed his fingers on the desk for some minutes, for he did not believe a word of it. He called Henry Jameson and proposed a walk in St. James's park.

'I have rather a foreboding about this,' said Henry Jameson, as they strolled around the lake. 'Dyer was our man, in a manner of speaking, and I don't mind telling you I'm not a little concerned about him. We haven't heard from him since last week.'

'What do you mean, "in a manner of speaking?"' said Freddy.

'You might call him a turncoat of sorts,' replied Henry. 'He was an avowed Communist—still is, as far as I know—but he became uneasy when Schuster arrived, as he suspected the man of being some sort of agitator, out to cause trouble. Dyer's the kind of moderate who would rather see a Communist government brought about by peaceful means, and he became alarmed at the change in direction at the Alliance once Schuster got his feet under the table. We got wind of this through another of our agents, and persuaded Dyer to let us know if he found out about anything illegal. He was wary of us at first, but he didn't like what was happening and so eventually agreed to send us along a report every so often. I was never certain whether or not to trust him, so we didn't tell him too much about what we knew at this end, but the information he gave was usually sound enough.'

'What did he tell you?'

'Precious little, as it happens. He knew Leonard Peacock from Oxford, but he didn't think Peacock trusted him, and told me quite frankly that he didn't expect to gain admittance to the group's inner circle. Dyer was on the Committee, but he knew he wasn't fully accepted by the leaders of the Alliance. He told me they were holding secret meetings without him, and that they withheld information from him. They never mentioned the coded advertisements in his presence, for example, although we'd charged him with trying to find out what they were. Was he at the Schusters' on Saturday?'

'Yes,' said Freddy. 'And I wonder whether his disappearance mightn't be partly to do with me. I got the impression he was trying to tell me something that night. He wanted to know why I was really there, and said I ought to be careful. I couldn't find out any more because just then Trevett came along and swept him away, and I rather think he overheard what we were saying. Then later in the box-room Peacock said that *somebody* couldn't be trusted. Perhaps he was talking about Dyer.'

'Hmm. It would make sense,' said Henry.

'Peacock said some disparaging things about Dyer on Saturday,' said Freddy. 'He told me he'd never liked him.'

'They shared rooms, you know,' said Henry. 'It was at Peacock's suggestion, apparently. We thought it would be a good way for Dyer to find out more, but of course it also enabled Peacock to keep an eye on him.'

'Did they know he was in communication with you?'

'I didn't think so until now. He always assured me he was very careful and that they had no reason to find out.'

'He didn't really steal the Communists' money, did he?'

Henry was silent for a moment.

'I don't know,' he said at last. 'He *might* have. His motives in working for us weren't purely disinterested, since we had to pay him for the information he gave us. He was short of funds, he said, and wasn't about to betray anybody unless we made it worth his while. So if that's the case, then it's also possible he wasn't above helping himself to the takings whenever he felt like it.'

'And what about Olive Stapleton?'

'He might have done that, too, yes.'

'But you don't really believe it, do you?'

'No.'

'What about the note he left? Was it written or typed?' said Freddy, although he could already guess the answer.

'It was typed.'

'On a machine with a raised lower-case "e" and a sliced-off upper-case "R," I expect.'

'Why, yes. However did you guess?' said Henry dryly.

'It's a good thing they don't know we know about the type-writer,' said Freddy.

'Yes, that was a good find of yours. Of course, there's no proof that Dyer didn't type the note himself. He might easily have done it while he was at the Schusters' on Saturday.'

'But it's suggestive, don't you think? Why should a man type a letter of that kind at a party? I mean to say, it's not the sort of thing one normally does on these occasions. Surely if he really was having an attack of remorse, he'd have gone home and written the note by hand afterwards, once he had some peace and quiet and time to think about it.'

'Yes,' said Henry. 'But from the point of view of someone planning something underhand, it's much easier to type a letter than to copy someone's handwriting.'

'Look here,' said Freddy. 'Can't you arrest Anton Schuster now? After all, thanks to the typewriter you have proof that he was at least partly responsible for the unofficial strikes. He's evidently a danger. Wouldn't it make sense to put him out of the way so he can't cause any more trouble?'

'It might,' conceded Henry. 'But he's only one man, and we'd like to catch all of them. From what you say, Leonard Peacock at least is also involved in the conspiracy, and most likely some of the other members of the Alliance too. But we don't have any evidence against them, and who's to say they won't simply carry on without Schuster if we arrest him? Besides, the man I'd really like to get is John Pettit. As far as I'm concerned he's the most dangerous man in Britain. He's a radical, yes, but he's also a union man through and through, and he has many loyal supporters who won't hesitate to follow him wherever he leads. If he were to become leader of the Labourers' Union, then I don't mind telling you that I fear for the stability of the country.'

'Do you still think Miss Stapleton's death is connected with all this?'

'I don't know. It's a facer, all right. One doesn't wish to be unsympathetic to the dead, but this murder has rather thrown a monkey-wrench into the machinery. The whole thing would be much simpler if Miss Stapleton had kept her nose out of matters that didn't concern her. I expect the Communists would be relieved if we'd take it as read that Dyer did it, but I don't think it's that simple.'

'What do you think has happened to Dyer?' said Freddy. 'Is he dead or has he done a bunk?'

'I don't know, but I fear the worst,' said Henry soberly.

'They must find him sooner or later, surely, even if the worst *has* happened. I mean to say, it's not all that easy to hide a fully-grown man. Where could they have put him?'

'Personally speaking,' said Henry carefully, 'if I had a bulky object I wanted to dispose of, I'd drop it into the Thames at Greenhithe or Gravesend just as the tide was going out.'

They fell silent, thinking of the implications of this, then Henry looked up.

'So now we must rely on you,' he said. 'The police are going to put it about that they believe Dyer was a thief, if not a murderer, so there's no reason to suppose the plotters have any suspicion that we're on to them. That means you can continue to investigate freely as you have been doing. You don't think they suspect you?'

'Not as far as I can tell. I've done my best to look as affably idiotic as possible. I had a close shave on Saturday when they nearly found me in the box-room, but other than that, nobody's given any indication that they think I'm anything other than what I claim to be: that is, a press-man sniffing around—not too hard—for a story.'

'Good,' said Henry. 'Go on as you have, then, and see what you can unearth. You'll go to the meeting tonight, won't you?'

'Try and stop me,' said Freddy. 'I want to see what Peacock has to say about all this. I never liked the fellow, and I like him even less now.'

'Don't arouse his suspicions,' warned Henry.

'I won't. Don't forget, I'm supposed to be shadowing him tomorrow, so I shall have to keep him happy until then. I don't want to put the wind up him and frighten him into changing his arrangements. I wonder where he's going, though. He said he was going to need money for whatever it was. Presumably that means he's going to buy something.'

'Just be careful,' said Henry. 'I feel bad enough about Dyer already. I don't want to lose another man.'

'Don't worry, you won't,' said Freddy.

CHAPTER SIXTEEN

IN THE LITTLE kitchen of Clerkenwell Central Hall, the Temperance ladies were wondering among themselves at the latest developments in the case.

'I knew it!' said Mrs. Belcher. 'Didn't I always say, Nerissa, that that young man was up to no good? I could see it in his eyes. There was a sort of evil light in them. I never trusted him, and I said so, didn't I?'

'Really? I can't say I remember your mentioning it,' said Mrs. Starkweather doubtfully. 'And I'm afraid you have the advantage of me. I always thought him a very polite young man, if a little inclined towards rowdy jokes.'

'Drink!' exclaimed Mrs. Belcher. 'That is what it always comes back to. I have no doubt Dyer had been drinking before he killed poor Miss Stapleton.'

'He seemed sober enough to me that night,' said Mildred.

'They know how to hide it,' said Mrs. Belcher ominously. 'Oh, yes, they learn all the tricks. I am quite sure that while

Dyer was greeting you all so politely, his belly was full of the demon, and his eyes were darting this way and that, avidly seeking a weapon with which to dispatch our poor Miss Stapleton. I expect all that evening he was rubbing his hands together with glee at the idea of wreaking chaos and misery among our virtuous little family. How he must have cackled as he drove the knife home!'

Miss Hodges, counting teaspoons, jumped and squeaked in distress.

'Such a pity I was struck down by one of my heads that evening,' went on Mrs. Belcher, unheeding. 'I wish I had been there, as I am sure I should have noticed what Dyer was about. I know the signs to look out for, you see. They are quite unmistakable. A man under the influence has rolling eyes and a tendency to slaver. If he is practised enough, then he will be able to suppress the compulsion in company for the most part, but I have many years' experience in battling the scourge, and can spot it with ease.'

'Oh, my goodness!' said Miss Hodges. 'But—but are they sure Mr. Dyer did it? What is it that makes them suspect him?'

'Why, the confession, of course,' said Mrs. Belcher. 'He left a note saying he was sorry for what he had done, then made his escape. I imagine he has gone to the Continent—France, perhaps. If that is the case, then I dare say he will never be caught. The French are hardened drinkers themselves, and think nothing of killing people who happen to offend them, so they will not be interested in bringing Dyer to justice.'

'But are they really sure?' said Miss Hodges. 'I should hate to think they had got the wrong person.'

'Well, since he has disappeared, I think we must assume that he did it,' said Mr. Bottle, who had been watching the ladies work. 'Who else could it have been? None of us, naturally. And if he has any sense, then he won't return. Murder is an ugly business, and whoever did it will certainly be hanged for it, don't you agree, Miss Hodges?'

Miss Hodges went white and said, 'Oh, my goodness!' again.

'Ah, good evening, Mr. Pilkington-Soames,' said Mrs. Belcher, as Freddy arrived. 'I expect you've heard the news.'

'What's that?' said Freddy. 'Do you mean about Ronald Dyer? Has he turned up yet?'

'No,' said Mildred. 'And I don't suppose he will, either.'

'I tell you now, he's innocent,' came a voice, and they turned to see the elderly Miss Flowers standing in the doorway of the kitchen, wearing a sober expression that was quite unlike her normal cheerful demeanour.

'Oh, I didn't see you there, Miss Flowers,' said Mrs. Starkweather. 'It's all very dreadful, of course, but one doesn't know what to think. I mean to say, his disappearance looks so very suspicious.'

'Suspicious or not, it's ridiculous,' said Miss Flowers with a snort. 'Why, you might as well accuse me of having done it.'

'The police didn't say anything for certain,' said Mildred. 'You know they never like to give anything away, but they hinted at it pretty strongly. It seems he'd been taking money from your lot for months.'

'Well, I won't believe it,' said Miss Flowers. 'I knew his mother, you see. He's not the type.'

'Now, do we have everything?' said Mrs. Belcher, who had not heard the exchange. 'Miss Hodges, take the teacups through to the hall, please.'

'Allow me,' said Freddy, for Miss Hodges was looking even more distressed than usual, and he feared for the safety of so much crockery in her hands all at once. He picked up a tray and Mildred took another, and they went through into the minor hall. When they came out they found that Ruth Chudderley had arrived, in company with Ivor Trevett. Ruth threw Mildred a look of disdainful amusement.

'Back on duty today, Mildred?' she said. 'I must say, I had no idea Temperance was a part-time undertaking. Perhaps you might teach your friends how to play "Hobbes and Descartes Took the 'Bus" at your meeting this evening. It's much easier to remember things when you're sober.'

She passed on, and Mildred flushed.

'Horrid cat!' she said. 'I don't know what St. John sees in her. She's beastly superior and unkind.'

'Hmm?' said Freddy, who was staring absent-mindedly after Ruth. 'Now, what the devil—?'

'She'll only make him unhappy—that is, if she ever accepts him. I don't suppose she will, now. Lucky for him, I say.'

Freddy glanced at Mildred. She was looking hot and cross, and he nudged her in friendly fashion.

'Buck up, old girl,' he said. 'I shouldn't waste time worrying about the Chudderley if I were you. You're worth ten of her.'

'Do you think so?' said Mildred. 'That's very kind of you.'

'Not kind at all,' said Freddy. 'I abhor the very name of kindness and never speak anything but the plain, unvarnished truth, regardless of the consequences. Remind me to tell you what I said to the Prince of Wales when I bumped into him at Ascot last year. It nearly ended in my arrest, but you'll notice he's been wearing purple and parting his hair on the left ever since.'

'Idiot,' said Mildred more cheerfully.

'No, but look,' said Freddy.

St. John had just arrived, and they watched as he spotted Ruth and Trevett standing together and stopped dead. His brows lowered and a furious look descended upon his features. For a second it looked as though he were about to pass them by without speaking, but then he seemed to change his mind and went up to talk to them. An unmistakable *froideur* had developed between the three of them, and the conversation was a short one, then Ruth and Trevett smiled stiffly and went into the main hall, while St. John came across to where Freddy and Mildred were standing.

'Hallo, St. John,' said Mildred in some trepidation. 'Are you all right? You look a little cross this evening.'

'Why do you say that? I'm not cross at all,' said St. John crossly, and stalked off. Freddy and Mildred glanced at one another.

'Oh dear,' said Mildred. 'He must have found out what's been going on.'

'Looks like it, doesn't it?' said Freddy.

'I hate it when everyone's out of sorts,' said Mildred. 'Our ladies are all in a bad mood at the moment too. I suppose it's only to be expected, after what's happened. Mrs. Belcher has been complaining that she can't get the girls to do what she tells them, because they were used to Miss Stapleton. Miss Hodges is upset because she feels guilty that she forgot to take the takings box home with her that evening, and she thinks Miss Stapleton wouldn't have been killed if she'd remembered. And Mummy is even vaguer than usual—but I'm used to that.'

The Temperance meeting was about to begin, and Mildred disappeared into the minor hall, leaving Freddy frowning in thought. After a moment he shook himself and went to join the Communists in the main hall. He had intended to take his usual seat by Miss Flowers, but she was standing at the front of the room, talking to Sidney Bishop and Leonard Peacock, so he sat down on a seat at the back and prepared to observe proceedings closely. However, there was little to observe this week. Much of the meeting was dedicated once again to preparations for the march and rally that was to take place in Hyde Park the coming Saturday. Leaflets were handed out showing the expected order of events, and there was a call for volunteers to man the Communist Alliance stall throughout the day. There was an air of excitement about the whole thing, and it appeared as though everybody was expecting to enjoy themselves. Nobody mentioned Ronald Dyer or his disappearance. Presumably the leaders of the Alliance had decided to pretend nothing was wrong—perhaps so as not to divert attention away from this most important event. Freddy looked around the hall. There was no sign of the Schusters today, and he wondered where they were.

At last the meeting broke up, and everybody filed out slowly. In the lobby Freddy bumped into Sidney Bishop.

'Hallo, hallo,' said Bishop, with an attempt at his usual cheery manner, but Freddy could see that something was bothering him, and remembered that Bishop was the group's treasurer.

'I hear one of your members has skipped with the cash,' he said, not unsympathetically.

'Everybody's heard about it, it seems,' said Bishop with a sigh. 'I don't mind saying I feel a fool, Mr. Pilkington-Soames. I can't think how I didn't spot what he was doing, but I let him take it as easy as winking. I trusted him, you see. Didn't see any reason not to. One doesn't expect that kind of behaviour from your sort.'

'Oh, our sort are the worst,' said Freddy. 'I don't even leave any money lying around if my family are in the house. I had an aunt who used to steal half the silver whenever she came to visit. Naturally, it wasn't the done thing to mention it, but she positively clanked as she kissed us goodbye, and one had much ado to pretend not to hear it.'

'I wish I could laugh about it,' said Bishop glumly. 'The money was my responsibility and I failed in my duty. Why, I shouldn't be a bit surprised if they voted me off the Committee as soon as may be. They won't do it just now, with the rally coming up, but I expect someone will put forward a motion soon enough, and then I'll be out on my ear.'

He went off, shaking his head. Freddy watched him go and wondered what had happened to the Alliance's money. Had Dyer taken it? If not he, then who? Freddy wanted to find out more, and so offered his services in the matter of tidying up.

'Hallo, are you here again?' said Peacock jovially. 'Yes, help if you like.'

They stacked chairs for a few minutes, then Freddy said:

'I understand you've lost a member.'

'Oh, is that it? I thought you couldn't be here for the fun of it. You're sniffing about for a story again. Well, don't look at me,' said Peacock in his usual careless manner. 'That ass ought to have been more careful if he didn't want to be caught with his hand in the money-box. But once you start stabbing old ladies—well, then there's an end to it. The police don't look too kindly on that sort of thing, as I expect you know.'

'Was he really stealing money from you too?'

'Pots of the stuff, it seems. I don't know why Bishop didn't notice, as a matter of fact. You'd think as treasurer he might have kept at least half an eye on the goods. But you'll have to ask him about all that. I don't know anything.'

'Where do you think Dyer has gone?' said Freddy.

'I couldn't tell you,' said Peacock, with an easy shrug. 'And I don't care much, either. It's good riddance, as far as I'm concerned. I don't suppose he'll dare show his face here again.'

'But aren't you worried he might have come to harm?'

'Not particularly. As I think I told you, I never liked him much, and if he's been going around murdering people, then he deserves everything he gets.'

'But you shared rooms, didn't you?'

'Only because it was cheaper that way, and I was a little short of the ready,' said Peacock. 'If I'd had a choice, I should never have agreed to it.'

He strolled off, looking quite at ease with himself and the world, and Freddy watched him go thoughtfully. To look at him and Dyer only two weeks ago, one would have thought they had been the best of friends, but now Peacock was insisting that there had been no friendship at all, even though they had lived together, and was doing his best to dissociate himself from his old Oxford pal. But where had Dyer disappeared to? Whether he had taken the money or not, he had certainly been playing a dangerous game, and it looked rather as though he had paid the price for it.

Freddy was recalled from his musings by the sound of raised voices out in the lobby. He went out to see what was going on, and was confronted by the sight of St. John and Trevett standing nose to nose—or as near as possible, given the disparity in their heights—glaring at one another, while various ladies looked on with hands clasped and eyes wide. Ruth Chudderley was one of them.

'I don't know what you're talking about,' said Trevett, eyeing St. John loftily. 'Ruth is perfectly entitled to do as she pleases.'

'I know your sort,' said St. John. He was breathing heavily through his nostrils, and looked not unlike an angry bull. 'You talk and talk until a woman doesn't know which way is up and which way is down, and she's so blinded she falls for your rot. You oughtn't to take advantage like that.'

'Nobody has taken advantage of me, St. John,' said Ruth with dignity. 'That's just like you, to assume a woman has no brain of her own or ability to think. I assure you I'm quite as rational as you are, and I know my ups from my downs perfectly well.'

'But you let this—this—*bearded caperer*—' (he spat out the phrase) '—talk you into who knows what. You can't possibly be thinking straight.'

'I beg your pardon,' replied Ruth. 'I will not be accused of lacking reason. My actions are based upon wholly logical foundations. I find Ivor's company more congenial than yours, and his mental endowments more worthy of my admiration. Furthermore, Ivor has the good manners to listen to what I have to say, and to engage me in vigorous debate, instead of regarding me as though I were some kind of performing animal—a sort of trick to show off to people—just because I am a woman who happens to be interested in politics. Ivor and I have been talking about starting our own newspaper together, and he has assured me that I won't be confined to the women's page this time. I shall get to write pieces more befitting my intellectual capacity, and be treated as an equal.'

'But I do treat you as an equal,' said St. John. 'And what's wrong with the women's page? I can hardly write that myself, can I? What do I know about croup and that sort of thing?'

'About as much as I do, I imagine,' said Ruth. 'Or possibly more, since I grew up an only child and have spent little time in the company of babies.'

'But—' said St. John, but Ruth was not listening. She went on calmly:

'Why should you assume that I have any more interest in the subject than you, just because I am a woman? It is precisely this sort of fallacy which has prevented the development of the truly egalitarian society towards which we are all supposed to be working. Perhaps my ideas are more revolutionary than yours, St. John, as I see you have trouble in accepting them. However, Ivor has no such difficulty. He is as committed to the concepts of equality between the sexes and free love as I am, and as such I believe is more deserving of my affection.'

At the mention of free love, Trevett directed a leer of the utmost complacency at St. John which Ruth did not see. Its meaning was unmistakable, and it provoked St. John beyond measure. With a roar, he lunged at Trevett's throat, and there was a chorus of shrieks as the ladies all fell over themselves to get out of the way. The two men grappled for a few moments, then Trevett managed to shove St. John away from him. The two of them glared at one another, panting.

'What?' said Trevett. 'You don't think I'm going to fight you, do you? Why, I should as soon fight my grandmother. And I expect she'd put up a better show than you anyway,' he added.

'We'll see about that,' said St. John. He began dancing about, fists in the air. 'Your grandmother's not here to protect you now, you weaselly Welsh poltroon. You don't want to fight because it will spoil your hair. Why, you're nothing but a coward!'

'Oh, a coward, am I?' snapped Trevett, and threw a punch unexpectedly which glanced off St. John's jaw. St. John staggered back briefly, then landed a blow in Trevett's midriff that caused him to double up. After that the real fight began. The two men backed into the main hall and squared up to each other. From his stance, it looked as though Trevett had done some boxing in his time, and he certainly had the advantage of height; however, St. John was stockier and more compact, and by now was in a fine temper. They circled around one another warily, then began to exchange blows.

'Oh, goodness, what shall we do?' said Mrs. Starkweather, looking about her. Ruth was shouting at the two men to stop, while Mildred watched, rapt, her fists held up unconsciously, as St. John and Trevett continued their fight, oblivious to everybody and everything around them. It seemed they would not stop until one of them had beaten the other to a pulp—and it was very soon clear which of them would come off worst. St. John's rage had served him well up to now, but he was evidently unused to fighting, and his method was undisciplined, while Trevett's height and superior technique gave him a distinct advantage. Freddy could see that this was unlikely to end well for St. John.

'Now, look here—' he began, but nobody was listening, for St. John had now given up any idea of fighting with his fists, and had launched himself at Trevett and begun to wrestle with him. The two men fell to the floor and started rolling around. Trevett grabbed hold of St. John's nose and began to twist it. St. John gave an agonized cry.

'I say,' said Freddy, and started forward, with some idea of pulling the two of them apart, but just as he bent down St. John pushed Trevett off him and lashed out wildly with a fist, which hit Freddy hard in the eye and knocked him backwards onto the floor. He lay there, stars dancing about in front of his eyes, as Leonard Peacock, Sidney Bishop and Mr. Davis the caretaker came forward to separate the fighting men. Trevett staggered to his feet, glowered around and left the hall without another word, followed by Ruth, while Mildred and Mrs. Starkweather rushed forward to see to St. John, whose face was a bloody mess.

'We'd better clean you up,' said Mrs. Starkweather, once it had been established that his demise was not imminent. 'I'll get some water.'

She hurried off to the kitchen, leaving Mildred with St. John. He was sitting slumped on the floor, the picture of defeated misery, as far as one could see under the remains of his face.

'You'd better go home and get some sleep, I think,' she said. 'Do you need a doctor?'

'Why does nothing ever go right?' he said glumly, ignoring her question. 'Why do I never win at anything?'

'What do you mean?' she said. 'Why, I thought you were splendid just then. You're nowhere near his size but you gave as good as you got, and very nearly beat him, too!'

'He'd have killed me if they hadn't dragged him off,' said St. John. 'I never was any good at fighting.'

'Nonsense,' she said stoutly. 'He is rather a Goliath, I'll admit, but you were David and had right on your side, so good for you.'

'Did I have right on my side?'

'Why, of course!' she said. 'You were defending the woman you loved, and there's something very fine about that. It's a pity she's not worth defending, but that can't be helped.'

'I always believed she was too good for me,' he said. 'But I thought if I was patient enough then she'd come around eventually.'

'Too good for you?' said Mildred with a snort of disgust. 'She's not fit to lick your boots. She led you by the nose, and all the while she was misbehaving with someone else. I should forget her if I were you.'

'I can never forget her,' said St. John tragically. 'I shall retire to the country to live a quiet life and think about her until I die.'

'Don't be silly,' said Mildred. 'You'll get over her soon enough. Now, can you stand up? Come to the kitchen and we'll see to that face of yours.'

They left the room, St. John limping slightly, leaving Freddy alone in the hall, lying with a hand across his eyes. Eventually he sat up and felt the damage gingerly, wincing.

'You ought to have left them to it,' said a voice, and he started and squinted up to see Theresa Schuster gazing down at him with a half-smile.

'I didn't know you were here,' he said stupidly.

'No, I came towards the end,' she said. She knelt down beside him and touched a finger gently to his sore eye. 'You see Ivor has his Ruth and St. John has his Mildred,' she said. 'Who is to look after you?'

'It's only a bruise,' he said.

'Still, I will bathe it. I have only a wet handkerchief, but it will be enough.'

He sat obediently as she dabbed the handkerchief carefully over his eye.

'There,' she said at last. 'You will have a black eye, and all the women will look at you and think to themselves what a fine man you are.'

'Oh, I see you've got Freddy,' said Mrs. Starkweather, who just then came into the hall. 'Thank you, Mrs. Schuster. That was very brave of you, Freddy, although perhaps just a little foolish, too.'

'He has a kind heart, and did not want to see his friend killed,' said Theresa Schuster. She stood up. 'Keep the handkerchief,' she said to Freddy, then turned on her heels and left as quickly as she had arrived. Freddy watched her go.

'I wonder where she sprang from,' said Mrs. Starkweather. 'I didn't see her earlier.'

Freddy did not reply, for he was thinking about his eye. It had stopped hurting, and all he could feel now was a kind of tingling sensation. That might certainly be the effect of the punch, although he was at a loss to explain the additional tingling in his hand where Theresa Schuster had brushed her fingers against it.

CHAPTER SEVENTEEN

FREDDY FOUND IT very hard to concentrate on Thursday, for he was thinking about his intention to follow Leonard Peacock that night. What was the thing Peacock had mentioned that cost money and could not be traced? Freddy was determined to find out, and was irritated when his editor, Mr. Bickerstaffe, sent him out to cover a story about a prisoner who had escaped from Wormwood Scrubs dressed as a woman. By two o'clock Freddy had informed himself of the salient facts of the case and was on his way back to the office, composing the piece in his head (not exactly difficult, for it was the sort of story which almost wrote itself), when he remembered he had one or two things to buy, and so alighted at Oxford Circus. After concluding his errands to his satisfaction, he was about to resume his journey when he was struck by a sudden thought and came to a halt. Turning back, he headed for a certain draper's shop and went inside. He emerged a little while later, whistling, then glanced at his watch and returned to the office and spent an hour or so digging through some back issues of the *Clarion*. After that he stared out of the window and drummed his pencil loudly on the desk until told to lay off it by Jolliffe, who was trying to work. By four o'clock he was beginning to worry that he was too late, and that Peacock had already left on his journey to wherever he was going. What if Freddy had missed him? Peacock had arranged to meet the unidentified person from the Schusters' box-room at Russell Square at seven o'clock, in order to receive some money, but what if they had changed their plans in the meantime and had decided to meet at an earlier hour?

In the end, Freddy gave up all pretence at working and left the *Clarion*'s offices at five, intending to spend the next two hours waiting at Russell Square for Peacock to turn up. It was a cold, damp evening, and he did not wish to be spotted, so he went into the Hotel Russell itself and sat in the bar, nursing a whisky and watching the passing traffic through the window. Nothing happened for some time, and he began to grow impatient, even though the appointed hour had not yet arrived. At last, at about five to seven he spotted Leonard Peacock crossing the road to Russell Square, having presumably just emerged from the Underground station. Peacock bought a newspaper and stood on the corner of the square, apparently absorbed in reading it. Freddy watched carefully. Who was going to meet him? He was almost sure it would be Anton Schuster, and he craned his neck to glance up and down the street, looking for the familiar dapper figure. The traffic had become heavier now, as everybody headed home, and the cars were moving sluggishly forward. Just then, to Freddy's great annoyance, an omnibus came to a halt in front of the window of the hotel bar, blocking his view of the other side of the street. He was suddenly alarmed. What if Peacock were to meet his correspondent and disappear before the 'bus had moved on? Throwing some money down, he dashed out of the hotel and saw that his fears were partly correct, for Peacock had walked a little way down the street and was looking about, seemingly in search of a taxi. The other person must have already come and gone. Freddy clicked his tongue in exasperation as a cab stopped and Peacock jumped in. He cast about desperately and saw another cab approaching in the other direction. He waved frantically to stop it.

'Follow that taxi!' he said, pointing.

'But it's going the other way,' objected the driver.

'Then you'll just have to turn around,' said Freddy. 'Do it and I'll double your fare.'

The man needed no further urging. With a shout and several honks of his horn he described a full turn in the middle of the road and set off in the direction of Euston, leaving behind him an answering cacophony of horns as drivers expressed their indignation at this flagrant disregard for the rules of the road.

'I was rather hoping we wouldn't be spotted,' said Freddy, wincing at the racket.

'Well you should've mentioned that before, shouldn't you?' said the taxi-driver.

The traffic was moving slowly, so they had no difficulty in keeping their quarry in sight. The first taxi passed King's Cross, then turned up the Caledonian Road. On it continued, heading away from the centre of town and North-East up Seven Sisters Road as far as Finsbury Park, where it stopped. A hundred yards behind, Freddy's cab did likewise.

'Finsbury Park,' said the driver. 'Want me to wait?'

'Yes, I suppose you'd better,' said Freddy, and got out. It was dark, but he could see the figure of Peacock under the street-lamps as he disappeared through the gates into the park. Freddy followed. There was less light here, but Freddy could just glimpse Peacock heading in the direction of the lake. Freddy crept quietly after him, keeping in the shadow of the trees to his left—a good thing, too, for after fifty yards or so he suddenly became aware of the sound of footsteps walking briskly behind him. Quick as lightning he slipped further into the trees and stood, heart beating fast, as whoever it was hurried past him along the path. The sound of motor-cars could be heard faintly in the distance, but other than that all was quiet. Then Freddy heard voices close by. Taking a deep breath he peered out cautiously from behind a tree. Two men were standing a little way away on the path. If he could only get nearer, then he should be able to hear what they were saying. Silently, keeping to the grass, he tiptoed closer, using the trees as cover. A dim light shone from somewhere—perhaps the boating-lake— and in the dull blue glow he could see Peacock standing with a rough-looking man he did not know.

'You're sure it hasn't been used for anything that will get us into trouble?' Peacock was saying. 'It's rather important and I want to be sure. This must all seem wholly above the board.'

'It will,' said the other man. 'I got it off an old mate of mine what died, and he took it off a dead German in the war. It ain't killed anyone in this country, anyhow.'

'Good,' said Peacock. 'I don't want the police looking too deeply into our story. Now, I dare say you want paying.'

He handed over a note or two, and the other counted the money and put it in his pocket.

'Don't forget, there's more where that came from if you'll say what I tell you to afterwards,' said Peacock. 'Just sit tight and you'll hear from me soon enough.'

'Right you are,' said the man. 'You working on something big, then?'

'I should say so,' said Peacock. 'We've had something of a set-back this week, and had to change our plans at the last minute, but as it happens I think this way will be much more effective. Now, not a word. We know where you are if we hear you've been talking out of turn.'

'I know how to keep quiet,' said the other. 'You take care of your business and I'll take care of mine.'

The two men nodded their goodbyes at one another, then the second one departed, Peacock following shortly afterwards. Freddy gave them five minutes then returned to his taxi and went home, there to think about what he had learned. Like Henry Jameson, he had assumed the conspiracy related to some sort of widespread and illegal strike action, but this was far more serious than he had imagined, for if the plotters were buying guns, then that could only mean one thing—they were planning to kill someone. But who? And why? And what did Peacock mean when he told the man in Finsbury Park that he would be called upon to say something afterwards? Say something to whom? None of it was clear, and Freddy did not like it one bit. It was a pity they had been unable to decipher the last of the coded announcements. What book were the conspirators using now to pass on their messages? The copies of the advertisements were lying on a table nearby, and he picked them up and gazed at them in frustration, as though hoping that the answer would somehow present itself to him. Had he missed something obvious? He remembered Jolliffe's observation that the new key to the cipher must be a short book, since the page numbers given for the last three messages had been low ones. But what sort of book had so few pages? Freddy tried to look at the question from the conspirators' point of view. After John Pettit's house had burned down, they must have had to think of a new key which could be obtained at short notice. Freddy's eye fell on a dog-eared copy of the *Radical* which had fallen down beside the sofa, and his eyebrows rose. It could not be that easy, could it? But of course it would make sense! Why, what could be more likely than that all of them would have a copy of the *Radical*, and that they would decide to use that publication temporarily, just until they had decided upon a new one?

He took the newspaper and flicked through it. It was last week's edition, and contained the coded message which had arrived at the *Radical*'s office while Freddy was there. The sender could not possibly have known what was to be in the paper that week, so the key to the cipher must be an earlier edition—perhaps the one from the week before. Freddy rummaged around until he found the previous week's copy, then pulled out his notebook and set to work. He saw almost immediately that his guess had been a good one, and in a very few minutes he was looking at the decoded message before him. It referred to some event in the near future, and gave urgent instructions to a number of people who were referred to only by code-names. It took no great leap of deduction to guess that the event in question was the march and rally that were going to take place that Saturday coming, but there was much that remained a mystery.

'Who are all these people?' he murmured to himself. 'I only wish I knew. Silly names they've given everybody. Daisy and Marigold and Hollyhock. All very pretty, but not exactly helpful. And who are the Tumblers? I don't like this at all.'

Freddy stared straight ahead and his expression became grim. It was clear now that there was a murder planned for Saturday, and it was also beginning to be clear to him who the intended victim was. He did not know exactly how the killers planned to get away with it, but he did know that if they succeeded, then the country was likely to be plunged into turmoil for some weeks. It was a daring plot, right enough, but would it come off?

He turned to the remaining two messages, but found he could not decipher those, as he did not have the relevant copies of the *Radical*. He would have to leave that to Henry Jameson and his men—but how fortunate that the plotters had not decided upon a new key yet, and had kept on using St. John's newspaper. It was careless of them, but perhaps they had considered it unnecessary, given that they had remained undiscovered up to now. Whatever the case, it was vitally important to communicate this latest message to Henry, and without delay. It was now ten o'clock, and Freddy dialled Henry's number, but without much hope. There was no answer, but he determined he should take what he had learned to the Intelligence man first thing the next day, for there was no time to lose.

Freddy suspected that tomorrow would be a busy day, and was contemplating whether or not to turn in, despite the earliness of the hour, when the door-bell rang. He answered it and to his surprise saw Theresa Schuster standing before him. She had pulled her hat down low over her head, and her fur collar up around her face, and he knew immediately that something was very wrong.

'Please help me,' she said, almost in a whisper. There was an appeal in her amber eyes that Freddy could not refuse.

'What is it?' he said. He allowed her to pass, then looked up and down the hall outside, but saw nobody. He closed the door and turned to look at her. She had removed her hat and pulled down her collar, and Freddy drew in his breath, for her face was almost unrecognizable. One eye was half-closed and red, while her lip was swollen, and there were ugly purplish marks all down one side of her face.

'Good God! Who did this?' he exclaimed. 'Sit down and I'll get you a drink. No, don't argue.'

He conducted her gently but firmly to a seat and pressed a large glass of brandy on her, then sat down by her and regarded her in the greatest concern as she took a sip. She was trembling, he noticed.

'What happened?' he said.

'I have been a fool,' she replied.

'What do you mean?'

She looked down at her drink, then back up at him.

'You are kind, I know. I will tell you all, even though it will make you think badly of me.'

'I don't think badly of you,' he said.

'But you will,' she said. 'I am a very wicked woman. I have betrayed my husband and paid the price for it.'

'Did he do this to you?'

'Oh, no, no! Of course not. Anton knows nothing of this— and besides, he would never do anything so terrible. He is the most gentle of husbands and would never raise his hand to a woman.'

'Then who was it?'

Again she hesitated.

'You must understand, I thought he loved me,' she said. 'And I thought I loved him. But it was all a lie, I realize that now. He is young and handsome, and he makes me laugh. And I— well, I am only a woman, and we women are weak. We fall for the lies men tell us, and we do bad things. But I found out that he is not all he appeared to be. He is just the same as my first husband, who tried to kill me. I swore then that I should never again love such a man, but you see I have made exactly the same mistake this time. I tried to please him but somehow I made him angry, and he punished me for it. Perhaps I deserved it, I do not know.'

'Are you talking about Leonard Peacock?' said Freddy.

There was a pause, then she nodded.

'Now you have heard all,' she said. 'I know you must feel contempt for me, but still I demand your kindness. Please take me home. I ran away but he followed me, and he is waiting outside for me somewhere, I know it. I am so terribly frightened that he will find me and harm me even more than he already has—perhaps even kill me. Anton goes to bed early, and his heart is not strong, so I dare not telephone and ask him to come and fetch me, for the shock of it would do him no good at all. I will think of some story to tell him later, but for now will you take pity on me? Will you protect me?'

She gazed into his face, and he saw tears starting in her eyes.

'Of course I will,' he said firmly. 'He shan't touch you again if I can help it.'

She gave something that sounded like a sob.

'Thank you,' she said. She put down her unfinished drink then stood up and waited as he went to throw on his coat and hat. Then they left the flat together and went down the stairs into the street. The entrance to Freddy's place was in a little side-road off Fleet Street. Here all was dark and in shadow.

'We'd better look for a taxi,' said Freddy. Or, rather, that is what he intended to say, but before he could utter the words he received the shock of his life as he was grabbed around the neck from behind and an odd-smelling handkerchief was clamped across his nose. He struggled and tried to shout, but his attacker was stronger than he, and had the element of surprise. Within a minute or two Freddy felt himself becoming weaker as his arms and legs grew heavy. Then he heard the voice of Theresa Schuster.

'It was too easy,' she said, and that was the last thing he knew before everything went dark.

CHAPTER EIGHTEEN

H E DRIFTED GRADUALLY back into consciousness a little while later—although it took several minutes longer than that for his brain to resume its usual functions with any degree of efficiency—and for some time he lay there, puzzling over the question of why his normally comfortable bed had suddenly become cold, hard and uneven. By degrees his memory returned, although he was still by no means sure that he was not in the middle of a particularly unpleasant dream. At last his ringing headache, the humming noise that filled his ears, and the jolting he felt at intervals forced him to conclude that he had indeed been lured into a trap by Theresa Schuster, and that he was now lying in the foot-well of a car which was conducting him to some unknown destination. Someone had thrown a rough blanket over him—probably to hide him from view—and the hairs prickled at him disagreeably. From the sound of muttered voices nearby he sensed that this was not the moment to jump up and attempt an escape—and in any case, he still felt horribly weak and queasy, and was fairly certain he lacked the strength to run more than a few yards before they caught him again. Instead he concentrated as far as he could on lying still so they did not know he was awake, and listening to what was being said. Who were his attackers? Mrs. Schuster was one, of course, and he winced at the thought of how she had taken him for a fool so easily. He ought to have been on his guard when she had turned up at his door, but he had been blinded by her apparent injuries—no doubt the result of artfully-applied rouge—and the appeal in those mesmerizing eyes of hers. He had also been spurred on by his dislike of Leonard Peacock, whose voice he could hear talking now. It must have been Peacock who had grabbed him and knocked him out with the chloroform. Now he finally understood whom Peacock had been talking about in the box-room that night at the Schusters'. Freddy had assumed that St. John was the man who was easily fooled and would say yes to anything, but in fact it was Freddy himself Peacock had been referring to. What an idiot he had been! But who else was concerned in the plot? As far as Freddy could tell, Peacock was driving and Theresa Schuster was sitting in the front with him, but there was another person in the car, too. Freddy could feel a foot by his head, and knew somebody was sitting in the back seat. Where were they taking him, and why? There was one cause for relief, at least—they had not killed him immediately, so presumably they had attacked and kidnapped him for some other reason, and not merely to put him out of the way. He had thought himself discreet, but evidently he had aroused their suspicions in some way—perhaps when St. John had drawn attention to the coded advertisements that day in the *Radical's* office. Theresa Schuster had been there at the time, and Freddy had been almost sure she had noticed nothing, but it looked as though he had been mistaken. He strained his ears to try and hear what his captors were saying, but they were mostly silent. The car drove on, and Freddy closed his eyes, willing the pain in his head to go away. He was just starting to drift off again when he felt the car slow and come to a stop. The door opened and he felt himself being hauled roughly out onto the pavement. He made a half-hearted attempt to pretend to be still unconscious, but Peacock gave him a shove that made him stagger and almost fall, and said:

'I know you're awake. Don't try any funny stuff or it'll be the worse for you.'

They were in a dingy street that Freddy did not recognize, but he did not have time for more than a quick glance around before he was bundled through a door and down some stairs. He was too groggy to put up more than a feeble show of resistance as Peacock threw him onto a hard chair and bound him to it by his hands, then blindfolded him and left the room without a word. Now Freddy was well and truly caught, and it would be untruthful to say that he was not afraid, for he feared greatly that the plotters wanted him for some purpose that would not turn out well for him. He sat quietly for some minutes, listening. In the next room he could hear the sound of muffled voices—one of them that of Theresa Schuster. He strained his ears but could not hear what they were saying. He had no idea of the identity of the third person who had been in the car with them, for whoever it was had stayed inside while the others had brought Freddy into the house, and the voices were too quiet to identify them with any certainty. Freddy waited, since there was nothing else to do. After a while Peacock came back in, untied him from the chair, then retied his hands behind his back.

'There's a bed here,' he said. 'You can thank Theresa for that. I'd have left you on the chair.'

Then, before Freddy could say a word, he went out again. There was the sound of a key turning in a lock, then silence. Freddy was still wearing his blindfold. He stood up and took a few uncertain and stumbling steps forward until he felt the edge of the bed. He lowered himself onto it carefully and lay down. His head was throbbing and his thoughts were in a whirl, and he thought he should never sleep, but eventually he fell into an uncomfortable doze filled with strange, unsettling dreams. Some hours later he awoke, and lay thinking until a grey light began to filter through his blindfold and he judged it to be about eight o'clock. He had been listening for movement, and at last he heard the sound of footsteps descending the creaky wooden stairs, followed by a key turning in the lock.

'Pleasant night, I hope?' came Peacock's sardonic voice.

'Could have been better,' said Freddy. 'You'll pardon me if I don't get up just yet. Tell them I'll have breakfast in bed. I've a fancy for sausages and bacon. Are the muffins fresh?'

'Funny, aren't you?'

'No, I'm stiff and tired, and I've one or two things that need seeing to, but it's a little difficult with my hands tied,' said Freddy.

He felt himself being hauled into a sitting position, then the bonds on his hands were removed. Freddy pulled off the blindfold and winced at the daylight which filtered through the window. Peacock was standing before him. There was not a trace of his usual complacent expression; instead he looked deadly serious.

'Under the bed,' he said. 'I'll be back in fifteen minutes. Don't try anything smart.'

He went out and Freddy was left to flex his fingers and try to restore some feeling into his hands, which were numb and painful after having been tied for so long. A plate of something unappetizing had been left on a table by the bed. Freddy attended to his needs and then, still slightly unsteady on his feet, went over to the window to look out into the tiny area in front of the house. The glass was clouded with the grime of years, and the window was barred, leaving no possibility of escape that way. Above him, all he could see was a small patch of sky, dull and grey.

After a while he heard footsteps again—more than one set this time—then the door opened and Freddy turned to see Peacock's large frame filling the doorway, blocking someone else from view. Peacock was holding a gun and entered cautiously.

'I was almost sure you'd be waiting behind the door to try and brain me with a chair,' he said.

'Sorry, I didn't realize that was the done thing in this establishment,' said Freddy politely. 'I can do it now, if you like.'

'No need,' said Peacock. He moved into the room and Freddy caught sight of his companion. He raised his eyebrows.

'Oh, it's you, is it?' he said as Sidney Bishop came to stand before him. 'I must admit, you had me fooled.'

'I don't look like much, do I?' agreed Sidney Bishop. 'It's useful sometimes. You'd better tie his hands again.'

Peacock started forward but Freddy said quickly:

'Look here, is that necessary? It hurts, and you've got a gun, and there are bars on the windows and a lock on the door. I'm not entirely stupid; I should think I know when I'm beaten.'

'You've some sense, then,' said Bishop. He stood and regarded Freddy appraisingly. 'Keep the gun on him,' he said to Peacock. 'Shoot him if he stirs.'

The change in him was remarkable. Gone was the cheerful little man with the apologetic air who lived for the praise of his betters. In its place was something altogether more ominous—frightening, even, for Freddy had no doubt that he had meant exactly what he said about using the gun.

'Are you in charge of all this—whatever it is?' he said.

'Not to say "in charge,"' said Bishop, considering. 'Who can claim to have authority over his fellow man? But someone has to do the thinking, and I'm good at that.'

'You mean to say the others aren't?' said Freddy, and put his hands up hurriedly as he saw Peacock's gun hand twitch. 'I'm just asking,' he said. 'I mean to say, I can hardly boast of being a prize intellect myself, can I? Not after I fell into your trap so easily. Where is Mrs. Schuster, by the way? Upstairs, gloating over the rest of her collection of trussed-up pigeons? Is Dyer one of them?'

Peacock gave a mirthless laugh.

'Dyer's floating somewhere off Sheerness, I imagine,' he said. 'He had an attack of remorse. They'll find his clothes eventually, where he left them on the beach. Couldn't live with himself any longer, they'll say at the inquest. Such a dreadful pity.'

'You don't think anybody believes that, do you?' said Freddy. Peacock shrugged.

'They'll have to, in the absence of any other evidence,' he said.

'You killed him because you were frightened he'd give you away. And I expect you're going to do the same to me,' said Freddy, looking at the gun warily. It seemed fairly obvious that he would not get out of his predicament alive, but there was no harm in trying to find out as much as he could in the meantime, just in case. 'Is that the gun you bought last night?' he said.

'Oh, so you know about that,' said Bishop. 'Perhaps you are cleverer than you look, after all. Suppose you tell us what else you know, and who else you've told about it.'

'Why should I do that if you're going to kill me anyway?' said Freddy.

'No reason at all,' said Peacock. He stepped forward and placed the gun against Freddy's temple. Freddy decided he was not ready to die quite yet.

'I don't *know* anything,' he said quickly, 'but if you'd like me to guess, I should say you're planning to assassinate old Rowbotham tomorrow at the rally, so that John Pettit can take over as leader of the Labourers' Union. I don't know exactly what you have planned after that, but I imagine it's a series of small, unofficial strikes that are intended to grow into larger ones, until half the country has walked out. I dare say there'll be mass demonstrations, too, and much blaming of the whole situation on the mine-owners and the factory-owners. You did a dummy run last year in a few places, just to make sure it was possible to stir up a strike at short notice. I expect you're hoping for something like a general strike, but of a more spontaneous nature than the last one.'

'Not a bad guess,' said Bishop. 'We've a good many men all set to mobilize around the country. I reckon we ought to get a good showing.'

'But look here, I don't see how it can work,' said Freddy. 'I know Rowbotham's a dull old stick, but he's hardly offensive enough to require doing away with, and he has many supporters on the moderate side of things. If the idea is to allow Pettit to take over the union and wreak his nonsense on the country, then there are all sorts of flaws in your plan. I mean to say, you can't just shoot someone in a public place without the police looking sideways at you. Do you really mean to kill Rowbotham in Hyde Park, in front of several thousand witnesses? Why, everybody will know who did it. You'll be caught, and then Pettit will never become union leader. He'll be arrested for being part of the plot—or at the very least public opinion will turn against him. After all, they're hardly going to let him run the union if they know he persuaded his friends to nobble the opposition, are they? How do you propose to get around that?'

'Oh, we have our little ideas,' said Bishop. The pleased smiles on his and Peacock's faces did not lessen in the slightest, and Freddy felt that he was missing something.

'Good morning,' said a voice from the doorway. It was Theresa Schuster. She entered, her face showing no trace of the injuries Freddy had seen the night before, and regarded Freddy with an expression he might almost have described as mischievous.

'Found some soap, did you?' he said, and she let out a laugh that contained genuine humour.

'I am sorry,' she said, 'but it was necessary. You do not mind so very much, do you?'

There was no sensible answer to this, so Freddy said nothing. Theresa approached the three of them.

'Put the gun down, Leonard,' she said. 'There is no need for it.'

'Don't believe it,' said Peacock sharply. 'This one's a slippery character. He followed me to Finsbury Park last night—at least, I assume he did. That's right, isn't it?'

He glanced at Freddy, who nodded reluctantly.

'The question is: why? Oh, it's easy enough to guess that you overheard us on Saturday—Theresa said she caught you snooping about upstairs—but why were you doing it?'

'I was looking for a story,' said Freddy. 'It was all because of Miss Stapleton, you see.'

'Who?' said Theresa. 'Ah, the woman who was killed. What of her?'

'She suspected you were all up to something, and told Mrs. Belcher,' said Freddy. 'Mrs. Belcher then told her brother, Sir Aldridge Featherstone, who owns my paper, the *Clarion*. They sent me along to see if there was anything in it, and it seems there was, because that very night Miss Stapleton was murdered.'

'That was nothing to do with us,' said Peacock. 'Unless Dyer did it after all.'

'No, I don't think he did,' said Freddy. 'Anyway, I started to nose about a bit—just out of curiosity, you know—and discovered more than I expected to. We reporters like to get to a story before everybody else, and I'd say I've certainly done that. Something like this could keep the paper going for weeks. But look here: I'm not interested in giving you away for something you haven't done yet. Instead of all this assassination stuff, shouldn't you prefer to have a little positive publicity for your organization? I can arrange for the publication of a series of articles about John Pettit, and the East London Communist Alliance, and anything else you care to name. Surely that's a better way of getting converts to your cause than shooting dead a harmless old wind-bag? That sort of thing will only frighten everyone into thinking that society's about to collapse, and cause them to turn to the Government to protect them.'

'Turn to this sorry excuse for a Government?' exclaimed Sidney Bishop with sudden vehemence. 'No they won't—not when they find out the whole thing was a conspiracy by the Government itself to discredit the unions and thereby the working man. Once they know the Government has been plotting against them, they'll soon understand where their loyalty lies, and then we've got 'em!'

'What do you mean, the Government has been plotting against them?' said Freddy.

Peacock gave an unpleasant smile.

'Can't you guess?' he said. 'You don't think you fooled us with that lie of yours about looking for a scoop, do you? We know perfectly well whom you're working for. You gave yourself away when Theresa saw you were far too interested in our little messages, and after that we had you followed—all the way to Whitehall. You're in the Government's pay, aren't you?'

'No,' replied Freddy truthfully, as he realized with a stab of indignation that Henry had never offered him any money for the job.

'Oh, don't bother pretending. I tell you, you were seen. But we don't mind, do we, Bishop?'

'Not at all,' said Bishop, with something like his old cheery manner. 'As a matter of fact we're rather pleased. We've a use for you now. And to think they say the upper classes are worthless good-for-nothings! Why, you're going to be a great help to us.'

'What do you mean?' said Freddy fearfully.

'You don't think we want people getting the idea that *we* killed old Rowbotham, do you?' said Peacock. 'As you so rightly say, the police aren't keen on that sort of thing, and nor is it the best way to get votes. None of us would ever dream of doing anything like that.'

'Certainly not,' agreed Bishop. 'But British Intelligence, now—there's a different matter. Everybody knows they've been spying on us, looking for a way to destroy the Communist movement, and with it the hopes of the working-class man. When we show them evidence that Rowbotham was done in by one of them, then you'll soon see what happens. The man in the street doesn't like being lied to, Mr. Pilkington-Soames. If he suspects the Government has been trying to pull the wool over his eyes, then he'll turn to people who can be trusted to tell the truth. And we'll be ready for them. We'll get them to rise up, all right. It'll be glorious!'

There was a fervent gleam in his eye as he said it. Freddy stared at him, hardly believing his ears.

'Do I understand you correctly?' he said at last. 'Are you saying that you're going to get *me* to kill him?'

CHAPTER NINETEEN

THERESA SCHUSTER CAME to stand directly before him. A thin beam of watery sunlight edged its way through the window behind him and threw her scar into sharp relief.

'Would you?' she said. 'Would you do it for me?'

'No,' he said.

She laughed, not at all offended.

'No, I did not think so,' she said. 'You are not so weak, or so stupid. I knew I should fool you only once, so I waited carefully for my moment, as I did not want to waste it.'

'I suppose I ought to thank you for the compliment,' he said. 'Then I take it you're going to pin the blame on me? How do you propose to do that?'

'Oh, there's plenty of evidence against you,' said Peacock. 'Or there will be, at any rate. We have a good few photographs of you and that mandarin sitting in the park together. But not only that: we also have a man in East London who has a most interesting tale to tell about a chap who approached him while he was cleaning a gun on his back step a few months ago, and asked to buy the gun off him. Being a law-abiding citizen, he refused, but later found the gun had gone missing.'

'I expect this chap who wanted to buy the gun looked like me, did he?' said Freddy.

'I expect he did,' said Peacock. 'Then there are the documents that Theresa planted in your flat last night. Lots of letters with official letterheads, instructing you to do all sorts of things. They don't mention murder in so many words, but the inference is clear. The Government will probably claim they're forgeries, but that doesn't matter, as the doubt will have been planted in people's minds. Then you'll be found with the gun, of course.'

'Won't they notice my death wasn't natural?' inquired Freddy. There was an air of unreality about the whole conversation that made him almost inclined to laugh.

'A terrible car smash, it was,' said Bishop. 'Nobody could possibly have survived it.'

'I see you've thought of everything,' said Freddy.

Theresa Schuster gazed at him affectionately.

'It is a glorious thing you are doing,' she said.

'Perhaps, but I'd prefer to have the choice,' said Freddy. 'Where's your husband, by the way? What does he think of this little hobby of yours?'

'Anton is a darling,' she replied. 'He was proud to marry a daughter of the revolution, and he supports me in everything, but he is old, and prefers to live more quietly than I. He is very rich, and gives me money when I need it.'

'What do you mean, a daughter of the revolution?'

'My father was a Bolshevik and a Commander in the Red Army,' she said. 'He was killed in the civil war, but I preserve his memory with care. The battle has been all but won in Russia, but we must not stop there, and so I continue the struggle elsewhere.'

Freddy suddenly remembered something she had said once, about having lived through a revolution, and wondered why her meaning had not struck him at the time.

'You're Russian?' he said in surprise.

'Of course. Did you not know?'

'No, I thought you were Austrian. Don't tell me you're Russian too,' he said to Peacock.

'Don't be ridiculous,' said Peacock. 'I'm as English as you are.'

'Then what do you get out of all this?'

'Why, the chance to change things. Everything's too deadly dull these days. I missed the war, but that doesn't mean I can't stir the country up a bit, eh?'

'Do you mean you're doing it purely for the fun of it?'

Peacock shrugged.

'Why not?' he said.

Freddy had no reply to this. He, too, had done many things for the fun of it, but it had never occurred to him to murder someone or foment social unrest as a means to relieve his ennui. It struck him now that Peacock was a very dangerous man— perhaps the most dangerous of all of them, in fact—and he resolved to be very careful in his dealings with him.

'Does Trevett know about all this?' he said.

'No,' said Bishop. 'As a matter of fact, we originally meant to give him the—er—credit for doing the job, but then you came along and we changed our plans. It's probably for the best. If he'd got wind of it he'd have been bound to give us away. Can't hold his tongue, you see. He has to be the centre of attention.'

'I thought you were an admirer of his.'

'Perhaps I was, once,' said Bishop. 'But that was a long time ago. Just because a man has a talent for speaking doesn't mean he's any good to the cause. Trevett's a feather-brain, Mr. Pilkington-Soames. We won't need his sort when the revolution comes. We need people with brains and strength, and the sense to shut up at the right time. I hope you don't mind staying with us a while longer, by the way. Today might be a bit dull, but there'll be plenty of excitement tomorrow. Tie him up now,' he said to Peacock, then turned and left the room.

Peacock handed the gun to Theresa Schuster, who levelled it at Freddy as his hands were bound once again.

'There's no point in that, is there?' said Freddy, as Peacock made to put the blindfold back on. Peacock glanced at Theresa, who shrugged.

'Let him see,' she said. 'After all, it is his last day.'

Freddy suppressed a shiver at her careless tone, then the door was shut and the key turned in the lock, and he was left alone in the room once more to make himself as comfortable as he could. He sat down on the bed and set himself to thinking hard. Now that he knew what Bishop and Peacock had planned for him, his future looked gloomy, to say the least. To be murdered was bad enough, but to be used ignominiously as a pawn in a political game after his death was even worse. He brooded glumly over this for a while, but could see no way out for himself, for there seemed no escape from that dingy room—and even supposing he managed to untie himself and pass through a locked door, how could he creep past his captors, who were dangerous men, and would clearly not baulk at killing him in cold blood if necessary? Besides, more people had begun to arrive at the house now; three or four times Freddy heard a knock at the front door, and then footsteps and the creaking of stairs as a newcomer was admitted and brought downstairs into the next room. It was only to be expected, given that such a conspiracy would be difficult to execute by only three people, but from his point of view it made the prospect of escape look even more remote. Still, if Freddy was about to meet his end, he was certainly not about to go along with it like a lamb—in that, at least, his captors had made a mistake, for by telling him of his fate in advance, they had left him with nothing to lose. It was not exactly a cheerful thought, but Freddy, who was by nature a generally accommodating sort, had a streak of obstinacy in him which rose to the surface once in a while, and which was now demanding satisfaction.

'If this is the end, then I'm damned if I'll go quietly,' he said to himself. 'Never let it be said that a Pilkington-Soames died a coward's death. If Rowbotham *can* be saved then I'll do it by hook or by crook even if I have to take a bullet in the back to do it.'

Fine words, but it was easier said than done, and Freddy was not at all sure of how he was to go about it, stuck in his prison as he was. The first thing to do, it seemed, was to find out the exact details of what was planned for the next day. Would the plotters take Freddy with them to Hyde Park? Surely they would have to, for how could they get away with pinning the assassination on him if he were not present that day? Of course, there was always the danger that he would try to escape or attract attention, but it was a risk they must take if their plan were to work. But what *was* the plan? Freddy grimaced in frustration. He could hear the sound of scraping chairs and muttered voices in the next room, and wanted to know what they were saying. Was there any way in which he could listen to their conversation? The walls of the house were thin, and to judge by the sound of footsteps, there were no coverings on any of the floors. Freddy's eye fell on the cast-iron fireplace, which was cold and bare, for no fire had been lit there. He moved over to it, then knelt down in the thin carpet of ashes which had not been swept up. He poked his head inside the fireplace, being careful not to overbalance, since his hands were still tied behind his back, and listened. Now he could hear some of the voices much more clearly.

'—stand outside if it's raining,' said someone, although the rough-sounding voice was not one he recognized.

'Well you'll just have to,' came Bishop's voice. 'We'll need you to move as quickly as possible, so it's no good your sitting there all cosy-like in your van when we'll need you to take a hand. Now, you park where we told you, keep the engine running and wait just outside.'

The first man grumbled, but he had evidently walked away from the chimney, for he could no longer be heard clearly. Freddy set himself to listen. The floor was cold and grubby, and with his hands behind his back he could not find a way to get comfortable, but this was his only chance of hearing what the conspirators were saying, and so he settled down to find out as much as he could. At midday he had to move away from the fireplace when Peacock came in, a plate of cold food in one hand and a gun in the other. Freddy was untied and allowed a few minutes to eat. He was not at all hungry, but judged it was better not to arouse suspicion—and besides, he wanted to keep his strength up. Afterwards, Peacock tied him up and left the room without having said a word, and Freddy returned to his station in front of the fire. By the end of the day, he thought he had heard enough to understand what was intended. After Mr. Rowbotham had finished his speech, he was to leave the stage and enter a tent which had been set up next to it for the benefit of the speakers, for the weather was expected to be wet. At that moment, somebody—Freddy did not know who—was to create some sort of diversion outside. While it was going on, Rowbotham would be set upon and knocked out with chloroform, then thrown into a motor-van parked at the back of the tent, and driven away before anybody had time to realize what was going on. Once he was in the van his fate would be sealed, for presumably he was to be shot dead there—perhaps while still unconscious. Nobody would witness his death, making it all the easier for the plotters to set the scene and place the blame for the crime on Freddy's shoulders.

'There'll be thousands of people there tomorrow, and in all the confusion nobody will be able to say for certain what's the truth,' he said to himself. 'But rumours spread like wildfire, and if they can produce a witness or two—as I'm sure they will— then I've no doubt they can convince plenty of people that I was the one who did it, on the orders of Intelligence. That will set the cat among the pigeons, all right! I shouldn't wonder if it were to cause a fearful scandal. I suppose the intention is to drive the workers into the arms of the Communists and whip up unrest. At least, that's what Bishop wants, and Theresa Schuster too. But Peacock, now; he's not a Communist—I'd bet my life on it. I've seen the type often enough. He's an out-and-out trouble-maker, who's doing it for the fun of the thing. I must try and stop them somehow, but I can't do that if I'm stuck here. Are they going to take me with them? I only hope so. I must get to Hyde Park tomorrow one way or another.'

With this and other reflections the day passed slowly and the shadows lengthened, and at last, long after darkness had fallen, Freddy lay down on the bed and eventually fell asleep.

CHAPTER TWENTY

THE FEBRUARY MARCH, as it later became jocularly known, was an event which many hoped would go down in history as a spectacular demonstration of solidarity among the honest working people of Great Britain. Despite St. John Bagshawe's description of it as being likely to prove an enjoyable outing for many, most of the participants arrived in a spirit of grim determination, bent upon showing that the ordinary man would no longer consent to being ignored by the Government in his quest for fairer pay and conditions. Little by little, wages had been cut and working hours lengthened, and the unions wanted an end to it. No more would men be unable to feed their families or afford to aspire to a civilized existence. The people would speak and the Government would have no choice but to listen. It was time to protest in the mass—and protest they did. From Camberwell, Sutton and East Grinstead they came; from Bolton, Wrexham and Durham; from Huddersfield, Wigan and Glasgow. From all over the country men and women descended on London, resolute in their desire to make their voices heard. They gathered in Trafalgar Square, a sea of flat caps and bowler hats, carrying oilskins against the rain that threatened at every minute, for the sky was lowering and black. They played concertinas, mouth-organs and drums. They sang and shouted slogans, and held aloft banners—some printed expensively, others hand-painted—bearing the names of their respective trade associations. Coal-miners, shipwrights, dock-workers, factory-workers, train-drivers, 'bus-drivers, brewers, bakers, steel-workers and more—all were represented that day among the teeming crowds. The noise was deafening. They gathered, and then they marched. Along Pall Mall they went and up Regent Street. Into Piccadilly they poured in their thousands, chanting, shouting and singing, accompanied by hundreds of policemen on horseback and thousands more on foot—for there were fears that what had started out as a march would turn into a riot without the heavy presence of the authorities. Londoners might have grumbled at the slowness of the traffic and the closure of many of the more expensive shops along the route (for who knew whether the provincial lower classes might not take it into their heads to engage in a spot of looting as they passed?), but for the most part the march went on peacefully—indeed, it was noted that many visitors from further afield were taking the opportunity to admire the landmarks of the capital city as they proceeded, and were turning their heads this way and that, pointing out one famous building or another to their companions.

By three o'clock most of the marchers had reached Hyde Park Corner and were spilling into the park itself and up towards Speakers' Corner. Here the atmosphere was noticeably more festive, for a brass band had set up and was playing the marchers through the park with a succession of rousing tunes. As the protesters continued into the park they were handed leaflets and pamphlets by representatives of a number of organizations, while farther on still stalls had been set up, many offering hot and cold food and drink to weary travellers. Near Speakers' Corner itself a stage had been set up, upon which various important personages were to take turns in addressing the crowd. It was currently occupied by a man whose diminutive stature belied his impressive vocal projection, and who was striding back and forth, expounding upon the subject of the day and punctuating his words rhythmically with a forefinger. Here, too, many policemen stood by on foot or horseback, keeping a sharp eye out for any signs of trouble—although, of course, they could have no idea of the real danger which threatened the event at that moment, but were merely looking out for pick-pockets and any indication of violence among the protesters.

Near the park, on a little side-street just off the Bayswater Road, a car stood. Inside it, Theresa Schuster and Freddy sat in silence. They had arrived nearly two hours ago with Peacock and Bishop, and another silent man whom Freddy did not know, then the three men had gone away, leaving Mrs. Schuster to watch the prisoner. Freddy was fighting a feeling of grogginess, for he suspected that his captors had put something into his food or drink in order to render him docile for the day's events. He ought to have expected it, he supposed, since he had been wondering how they intended to show their prisoner to witnesses in Hyde Park without his showing signs of unwillingness. But even had he not been feeling woolly-headed, he could not have tried to escape, for Mrs. Schuster was sitting close by him in the back seat, pressing a tiny derringer to his ribs under the cover of a brightly-coloured silk scarf. The gun prodded uncomfortably, but Freddy dared not wriggle.

'I say, you're going to give me a bruise with that thing,' he said at last. 'I know it's there. Is it really necessary to poke me so hard with it?'

She moved the gun away very slightly, but said nothing. Freddy sighed inwardly, and stared out of the window. The street was quiet, but people passed by on foot occasionally, on their way to the rally.

'Whose car is this?' he said suddenly. 'Is this how you're planning to get away? Aren't you worried someone will see it and the police will trace it?'

'No,' she said. 'This is your car.'

'My car?'

'Yes. Sidney hired it in your name, and we had them bring it to Fleet Street.'

'You've thought of everything, I see.'

'Yes,' she said simply.

'Might we have the window open? I'm feeling rather sick,' said Freddy, not untruthfully. 'You don't want me making a mess all over the place, now, do you? Don't worry, I won't shout,' he went on, as he saw her regarding him closely.

'You will not have the chance,' she said. 'Very well. You do it.'

He moved away carefully and opened the window slightly. A cold draught came in and revived him a little. He was beginning to think more clearly now.

'Who was that other man who came with us?' he said.

'It is not important,' she replied. 'You will never see him again.'

'How many people are in on this?'

She was silent. Freddy tried again.

'Who is actually going to do the deed?' he said. 'This isn't the gun you bought for the purpose, is it?'

'No,' she said. 'Leonard has taken that.'

'I do hope he has the sense not to leave any finger-prints on it.'

She merely smiled. He looked at her.

'I believe you're enjoying this,' he said. 'You are, aren't you? I don't believe it's the politics at all. You're in it for the fun of it, like Peacock. That's why you and he get along so well. Oh, perhaps you were a revolutionary once, but that's not what drives you now, is it? You like trouble. You like to have men under your thumb, doing dangerous things at your command.'

She laughed, not at all disconcerted.

'Do you think so?' she said. 'Perhaps you are right. I do like to have men in my power. Leonard will do anything I tell him, and so will Sidney, and Anton. And so will you, is that not so?'

'I might have, before I knew what you were,' said Freddy. 'But I hope I'm not quite so easily cowed as to walk blindly to my own doom just because you ask me to.'

'True. I have not so much power,' she said. 'But I do not need it, for I have this. This gun is your mistress now, and you will do as she tells you.'

She raised the pistol and caressed his cheek gently with it, then placed it against his right ear-lobe. Freddy froze, and swallowed.

'You have already lost one ear,' she said smoothly. 'Perhaps we can shoot this other one to match it.'

'I'd far rather you didn't,' he managed eventually.

She smiled and lowered the gun, pressing it into his ribs again.

'Of course I shall not,' she said. 'You did not really believe I should do such a thing, did you? As long as you are good I am to keep you safe and unharmed. It will not do for the police to find bullet-holes in you. Then how shall we convince everybody?'

'I don't know how you expect anyone to believe you at all,' he said. His heart was still racing, but he hoped his tone was casual. 'I mean to say, it's a pretty thin story, don't you think? To start with, you may have noticed that we're not at the rally. If we sit here all day in the car then there will be no witnesses to place me on the spot for Rowbotham's killing. Of course, you can still claim I did it if you plant enough evidence, but it's a fantastic story you're asking people to believe, and there'll always be a doubt in people's minds unless you can prove I was actually there. Aren't you planning to parade me about in front of some convenient eye-witnesses?'

'Yes,' she said. 'But not until closer to the time. The longer we are outside, the more likely you are to try and escape, is it not so? Here in the car I can look after you alone, but outside it is a different matter. Have patience. We shall wait until one of the men comes back, and then we shall all go out together.'

Freddy's heart sank. He might have been able to overpower Theresa Schuster alone, but against two of them he would have no chance. His captors were not as foolish as he had hoped. Mrs. Schuster still had the gun pressed firmly against him, and evidently had no intention of lowering her guard. In this confined space, with the pistol sticking into his ribs, he dared not attempt to try and wrest the gun from her.

They sat in silence for a while, then Mrs. Schuster suddenly stiffened and gave an exclamation of impatience. Freddy looked up and saw what she had seen: the elderly Miss Flowers, walking down the street towards them, in the direction of the park, holding an umbrella. She was presumably on her way to the rally.

'Be silent,' hissed Mrs. Schuster.

But Miss Flowers had already glanced into the car and seen them. An expression of surprise and pleasure spread across her face and she stopped.

'We had better get out,' said Mrs. Schuster quietly. 'I warn you—if you try to say a word I shall shoot you without hesitation. Open the door.'

Freddy did so, and stepped out onto the pavement, followed quickly by Mrs. Schuster, who took his arm as though to steady herself, then held onto it firmly and stood close to him. He could feel the derringer against his right side, still hidden under the scarf.

'Hallo, Miss F,' he said as jovially as he could manage. His mind was racing as he tried to think of a way to attract her attention. A significant glance was out of the question, for Theresa was watching him like a hawk—and besides, he was sure a glance would not be enough to convey the message.

'Oh, Mr. Pilkington-Soames,' said Miss Flowers, lowering her umbrella and folding it up. 'And Mrs. Schuster. How delightful! I was worried I should not see anybody I knew today. There are so many people that it is only too easy to get lost in the crowd, but here you are!'

Freddy quickly saw that he was not to be allowed to speak, for Mrs. Schuster immediately launched into conversation with Miss Flowers. They talked of the rally and the march, and of the speeches that were to be made that day, and of people they had seen. Then Mrs. Schuster was telling Miss Flowers that Anton was somewhere about, as he was to address the crowd, and that Mr. Pilkington-Soames had kindly agreed to look after her that day, for she did not like being alone.

'Did you go to the march, Miss Flowers?' she said.

'I was there at the start,' said Miss Flowers, 'but I fear the crowds are a little too much for me these days, so I crept away home and had some tea—I live near Paddington, so it's easy enough—then decided to walk to the park for the speeches. I am very much looking forward to seeing your husband speak, Mrs. Schuster. And what about you, Mr. Pilkington-Soames? Are you finding plenty of—er—material for your paper today?'

Freddy did not have a chance to reply, because Mrs. Schuster said:

'Oh, I have promised to introduce him to all the most important people, and I am sure he will find many things to write about. We could not have dreamed that the march would be such a success, do you not agree?'

'Oh, quite,' said Miss Flowers. 'It is just a pity the weather is so damp.'

Mrs. Schuster shivered.

'Indeed, it is true. And so cold! I am glad I put on my thickest coat.' She glanced at the vivid pink woollen scarf—almost a shawl—which Miss Flowers was wearing. 'But you will be warm too, in this thick scarf. It is very beautiful. Did you make it yourself?'

'Why, yes, I did,' said Miss Flowers, flushing with pleasure. 'It is one of my own, from my own pattern. There is a matching pair of mittens, which I have not quite finished yet. I have done them in purple, as a sort of contrast, you know.'

Freddy had been looking up and down the street, wondering whether he dared try and attract the attention of someone less vague than Miss Flowers, and had not been listening carefully to the conversation, so nearly missed this last remark. Almost too late the familiar words registered, and he turned to her, hiding his astonishment.

'Purple mittens?' he said. 'I should have thought green would be more practical.'

Mrs. Schuster wrinkled her nose at him and laughed.

'Men, they know nothing of colour,' she said confidentially to Miss Flowers. She gazed down complacently at her own pretty scarf, and Freddy immediately took the opportunity to mouth the words 'help me' at Miss Flowers. She made no sign that she had seen, but said:

'Yes, perhaps green would go better with brown or grey. Green is more of a masculine colour, I think. Perhaps I shall make you a pair, Mr. Pilkington-Soames.'

The two ladies laughed.

'Are you coming to the park now?' inquired Miss Flowers.

'In a little while,' said Mrs. Schuster. 'We are waiting for someone.'

'Then I shall see you later,' said Miss Flowers. She held out a hand, palm upward, and gave an exclamation of impatience. 'Oh, I thought it had stopped raining. You had better sit in the car if you don't want to get wet.'

She made as if to open her umbrella, and Mrs. Schuster and Freddy turned to get back into the car. At that moment Miss Flowers struck, hooking Mrs. Schuster's right arm with the umbrella, and pulling it backwards with a sharp jerk. Mrs. Schuster let out a shriek as the gun went off, firing harmlessly into the pavement. She dropped the pistol with a clatter, but before she could bend to pick it up, Freddy opened the car door wide, shoved her roughly inside, then slammed it shut, ignoring her cry of rage. He picked up the derringer and stuck it in his pocket.

'Quick!' he said, grabbing Miss Flowers by the arm. 'Let's go!'

CHAPTER TWENTY-ONE

THEY RAN AS fast as they could to the end of the street, Freddy hustling Miss Flowers along and not stopping to look behind him. Fortunately, Miss Flowers was more nimble than one might have supposed, and got up quite a turn of speed without Freddy's help. When they reached Bayswater Road they turned left and ran across the road into the park. Once among the crowds they stopped to catch their breath.

'I do hope you're not hurt,' said Miss Flowers.

'I don't think so,' said Freddy. 'I've no time for it, anyway. We have to stop Peacock and Bishop. They're going to kidnap Rowbotham and shoot him.'

'Oh, dear me!' said Miss Flowers in dismay. 'Is that what they're doing? I had no idea of it.'

'They kept it very quiet, as you can imagine. But they're going to do it soon, and I have to find a way to stop them.'

'But how?'

'I'm not sure. I shall think of something in a minute. Now, you'd better go and telephone Henry Jameson. After that, talk to the police. There are enough of them here to stop an army of assassins. In the meantime, I'll try and warn old Rowbotham.'

'I'll do what I can,' said the old woman.

'When all this is over I shall kiss you, Miss F,' said Freddy. 'I had no idea you were working for Intelligence. It's just lucky you turned up when you did.'

'Not lucky at all,' said Miss Flowers. 'Mr. Jameson was looking for you all yesterday and had a watch kept on your flat as he suspected something had gone wrong. When the motor-car turned up he had it followed and sent me along to find out whether you were inside it. With any luck they'll have arrested Mrs. Schuster by now.'

'Good Lord!' said Freddy, who had begun in recent days to doubt the competence of his masters. 'Jolly good show, what?'

'At any rate, there ought to be someone I can speak to hereabouts,' she went on. 'Mr. Jameson has a few men standing by, as he suspected there would be trouble—although as far as I know nobody expected anything like this. I only hope we can stop it.'

'So do I,' said Freddy grimly. He glanced at his watch. 'It's nearly four. Rowbotham's due to speak about now, I think. There's no time to wait until we've managed to find your chaps, as they might put the plan into action at any moment. I think I shall just have to risk going in there myself. At any rate, I might be able to waylay Rowbotham and stop him from falling into the trap.'

'I shall find someone and return as quickly as I can,' promised Miss Flowers.

She departed with celerity and Freddy looked across at the stage. There was no-one up there at that moment, but in front of the stage three circus performers dressed in yellow were keeping the crowd entertained with somersaults and feats of agility. St. John had mentioned that there was to be something of the kind, Freddy remembered. By the stage was the small tent in which Rowbotham was to be attacked. Were Peacock and Bishop waiting there even now? How did they intend to stop anybody else from entering? By their authority as Committee members of the East London Communist Alliance, he supposed—for nobody would expect official representatives of the rally's organizing body to have any nefarious purpose in mind, and most people would be quite likely to do as instructed if turned away from the tent. Freddy was wondering how best to proceed when he noticed that a small group of men were now standing on the stage. One of them was heavy-set, with lugubrious features and a red nose. Freddy recognized him as Mr. Rowbotham himself. The union man conferred with the other two men, who appeared to be assistants or secretaries, then moved forward, to a smattering of cheers and applause, and began to speak. The crowd, including the circus performers, fell quiet and listened. Rowbotham was not a natural orator, but he had a simple, no-nonsense way of expressing himself which endeared him to his many supporters. Freddy had listened to his speeches often enough, and in any case had no time to listen, for there was not a second to lose. He began to push his way through the crowd towards the stage. Unfor-

CLARA BENSON

tunately, his attention was on his objective and he was not looking where he was going, and as he went he trod heavily on the foot of a man who was eating a pork pie, causing him to drop it on the ground.

'Sorry, I'm in a terrible hurry,' said Freddy, and attempted to push on. But the man was not in a mood to let the offence pass without redress, for he was tired, wet and hungry, and his corns were paining him, and this young fool had not only aggravated his existing affliction, but had also done him out of his dinner.

'Oh, no you don't,' he said, moving to block Freddy's way. 'What d'you think you're playing at? You can't just run off and leave a man's pie in the mud. What are you going to do about it?'

To judge from the smell of him, he had been drinking, and he was clearly in a bad temper. Ordinarily, Freddy would have bestowed his most ingratiating smile upon the man and pressed a few shillings into his hand, but he had no money on him—presumably his note-case had fallen out of his pocket at some point while he was unconscious on Thursday night—and so he had nothing to offer by way of recompense.

'Why, I—er—' he said. 'I'm dreadfully sorry. I'd stump up if I could, but owing to certain unfortunate contingencies I'm afraid I'm a little embarrassed for the necessary at present.'

'What?' said the man suspiciously.

'He means he's got no money,' said a sharp-looking fellow standing nearby.

'Well, that ain't good enough,' said the offended party, and made a grab for Freddy's collar. Freddy stepped back hurriedly, but in his haste slipped on a patch of mud and fell over. He

233

struggled to his feet and prepared to flee. With the queer sort of sixth sense which often prevails in such cases, the people in the vicinity had begun to anticipate an entertainment, and a small crowd was now gathering. This drew the attention of two constables, who pushed their way through with a view to forestalling any disturbance.

'What's all this, then?' said one of them, regarding Freddy as he attempted ineffectually to brush the dirt off his coat.

'Trouble,' said the sharp-looking fellow briefly.

'Well, then, you two had better come along with us,' said the policeman.

'Oh, but I can't,' said Freddy in some dismay. 'I must get to that tent over there. It's dreadfully important.'

'What's so important?' said the policeman.

Freddy lowered his voice, aware that many ears were listening.

'I'm with Intelligence,' he said. 'There's a plot to shoot Rowbotham, and I have to stop them.'

The two policemen eyed him—dishevelled, covered in mud, and still sporting the black eye he had received on Tuesday during the fight between Trevett and St. John—and quickly drew their own conclusions as to the extent of his grasp upon reality. Freddy saw that he was unlikely to win this argument, and decided not to waste time in pleading his case. He turned and made a dash for it, treading once again on the foot of the man he had bereft of his pie as he scrambled through the crowd towards the front. The two policemen followed, but by taking a turn to the left and doubling back on himself he succeeded in shaking them off. He hoped they would give up the search, but he could not spare the time to worry about them, for on the stage Rowbotham was showing signs of coming to the end of his speech. Freddy was about to head towards the steps at the side of the stage, when he heard a voice calling his name and he turned to see St. John and Mildred Starkweather coming towards him.

'Hallo, old chap,' said St. John. 'Pretty-looking shiner you've got there. Not as good as mine, of course.' Indeed, St. John's face was a riot of colour, although he seemed cheerful enough. 'Mildred put some stuff on my bruises and they're clearing up nicely.'

Freddy reached a decision.

'Never mind that,' he said. 'I need your help. It's urgent.'

'What's up?' said St. John in surprise.

Freddy explained as briefly as possible, to exclamations of astonishment.

'Look here, you're joking, aren't you?' said St. John at last.

'I'm deadly serious. Peacock's in there with a gun, and if we don't hurry it'll be too late.'

Freddy's face was so grim that they had no choice but to believe him.

'But what are you going to do?' said St. John.

'I'm going to try and stop them, but I need you to get Rowbotham out of the way. Go onto the stage and get him as far away as you can. I was going to do it myself, but he doesn't know me, and he'll be more likely to do as you say. I'm expecting reinforcements at any minute, but if we don't do something soon it might be too late.'

'You'll do it, won't you?' said Mildred to St. John.

St. John looked at Mildred, then set his jaw.

'Of course I will. Rowbotham's a good chap. You can rely on me, Freddy.'

'Splendid,' said Freddy. 'Just remember, whatever you do, *don't let him go into the tent.*'

'You wait here,' said St. John to Mildred. 'I won't have you getting hurt.'

She nodded, wide-eyed, and watched as St. John and Freddy departed. Four policemen were standing near the tent, watching Rowbotham and scanning the crowd, looking out for trouble. At the door of the tent stood a stony-faced man whom Freddy recognized immediately as the one who had come in the car with them. His heart beat fast. The plan was going ahead, then. It looked as though Miss Flowers had been right when she said that Theresa Schuster was likely to have been arrested, for evidently she had not been able to get to her co-conspirators and warn them of the danger. But where were the Intelligence men? Where was Special Branch? They must surely arrive at any moment. Until then, Freddy would have to shift for himself or disaster might occur.

On the stage Rowbotham coughed and moved on to his concluding remarks, as his two assistants took notes. St. John stood by the steps and awaited his moment, while Freddy went around to the back of the tent. Here there was another flap, outside which a motor-van bearing the name of a bakery firm was parked, its engine running. A man was sitting in the van, smoking, sheltering from the drizzling rain. This must be the van into which the conspirators planned to bundle the unconscious Rowbotham, after which he would be shot dead. Then the van, with Rowbotham's body in it, was to be abandoned, and the killers would drive away in the hired car. After that, they had planned to stage Freddy's death and put it about that he was the assassin, acting on the orders of Intelligence. It looked as though the man in the motor-van was supposed to be keeping watch on the back of the tent, to ensure that nobody got in, although he was not exactly doing his job properly. Freddy decided to take the direct approach. He sauntered up to the van and knocked on the window. The man opened the door and regarded him suspiciously.

'I say,' said Freddy. 'If I were you I'd make myself scarce nowish.'

'What d'you mean?' said the man.

'Why, the game's up,' said Freddy. 'The police will be here at any moment, and if they find you then you're quite likely to find yourself on the receiving end of twenty years' hard labour. That's if they don't hang you, of course. I haven't read up on sentencing rules lately, but I seem to remember it doesn't matter whether you fired the gun or not; if they think you had anything to do with it then they'll send you to the gallows just as cheerfully as they will the murderer himself.'

The man regarded him blankly, confirming Freddy in his initial impression that the conspirators' driver was not the most quick-thinking of men. He sighed and brought out the pistol he had taken from Mrs. Schuster.

'I see you're having a little trouble. Does this make things any clearer?' he said, pointing the gun at the man's chest. 'To be perfectly honest with you, I have the most awful aim, but it ought to be easy enough from this distance, I should think.'

'Gawd!' exclaimed the man. 'All right, there's no need for that. I can take a hint.'

'Hardly,' said Freddy, watching as the man drove off. He turned back to the tent. 'Now what?' he said to himself. His original vague idea had been to intercept the men as they came out with Rowbotham, using Mrs. Schuster's unloaded gun as a threat. It was hardly the best plan, but it was the only one he had. But since Rowbotham ought to be quite safe thanks to St. John, there seemed no sense in Freddy's putting himself in danger. Perhaps the best thing to do would be to stand outside the tent, wait for Miss Flowers to arrive with help, and only bring out the pistol if necessary. He peered in through the flap cautiously. It was dark inside, but he could just make out Peacock standing by the front entrance with the stony-faced man. There was no sign of Bishop. Freddy withdrew his head and pondered what to do. He looked about him, and to his dismay saw the two constables from whom he had just run away heading in his direction. At any moment they would see him. There was nothing for it: he slipped silently inside the tent and stood in the shadows. Much to his relief, Peacock and the stony-faced man were looking the other way, out through the front flap, and did not hear him come in. He stole forward a foot or two and stared out through the front opening, which was a large one. He could just make out Rowbotham's feet on the raised stage. St. John was there, watching intently and awaiting his moment. Freddy waited a minute, then sidled away quietly, intending to see whether the policemen had gone. He turned, and bumped straight into Sidney Bishop, who was just then coming in through the back entrance.

'Here, what's all this?' said Bishop in astonishment. His eyebrows drew together in cold displeasure, as Freddy inwardly cursed his bad luck. 'How did you get here? Peacock!'

Peacock turned, saw Freddy and brought out a revolver—presumably the one with which they were intending to kill Rowbotham. Freddy backed away, but stumbled against a pile of ropes which had been left on the floor. There was no chance of making his escape now.

'Judson,' snapped Bishop to the stony-faced man. 'Stand by with the chloroform. Watch out for Rowbotham. You,' he said to Freddy. 'How did you get away? Where's Theresa?'

'Somewhere outside,' lied Freddy. 'She thought it wasn't safe in the car so brought me out. I shook her off.'

'And came here?' said Peacock.

'I thought I might be able to persuade you not to go ahead with it,' said Freddy. He knew it was the thinnest of thin stories, but he did not want the men to get the idea that they had nothing to lose, for then they might start shooting.

'I don't believe a word of it,' said Bishop. 'What have you done with Theresa? Peacock, search him.'

Peacock grabbed hold of Freddy and patted his pockets. He brought out the derringer and handed it to Bishop. They both looked grim. Peacock placed his own gun against Freddy's heart and pulled back the safety-catch.

'Where is she?' he said.

'I left her in the car,' said Freddy hurriedly. 'Truly I did. Look, you can't shoot that thing in here. It'll make the most frightful noise and ruin your plan to pin the blame on me.'

'Don't shoot him yet,' said Bishop. 'He's right. We need to get Rowbotham first. Don't worry—Theresa can look after herself. She won't say a word if she's caught.'

Peacock threw a disgusted look at Freddy and lowered the revolver.

'I'll keep an eye on him,' said Bishop, raising the derringer. 'You go and help Judson.'

Peacock reluctantly put the revolver back into his pocket and returned to the tent entrance to watch. Now was Freddy's moment to escape from Bishop, who was evidently unaware that the derringer was unloaded, but he did not do so, for just then there was a burst of applause outside as Rowbotham's speech came to an end. Freddy watched, holding his breath, as Rowbotham turned and began to walk towards the steps which led down to the tent, in company with his two secretaries. At that moment, through the tent flap Freddy saw three pairs of legs clad in yellow jump onto the stage, brightly-coloured streamers waving and fluttering behind them. The three acrobats began to skip around the two secretaries, winding the streamers around them playfully. There was a ripple of laughter from the crowd. Rowbotham had not noticed, and continued towards the steps. Just then Freddy remembered something: the coded advertisements had referred to 'tumblers.' Could this be what they meant? Yes, of course! The acrobats had been employed to create the distraction and keep Rowbotham's assistants on the stage, giving the conspirators a valuable few extra seconds in which to execute their plan. But where was St. John? Freddy watched anxiously, and breathed a silent sigh of relief as he saw his friend rush up to Rowbotham and accost him before he could begin to descend the steps. Peacock, standing by the front flap, shifted and clicked his tongue.

'Damn!' he said.

Freddy was just contemplating whether to seize the moment to make his escape when to his consternation he heard a booming voice ring out, and saw the familiar figure of Ivor Trevett ascend the steps to the stage two at a time.

'Rowbotham, old chap,' said Trevett familiarly, and clapped the union man on the shoulder. 'Marvellous speech. Now, I want to speak to you. I'm on in a minute, but let's get out of this filthy rain.'

Before St. John could say a word, Trevett turned and conducted Mr. Rowbotham down the steps, talking all the while. Rowbotham had completely forgotten St. John, who could do nothing but hurry after them. The three of them entered the tent at the same time. Freddy lifted his eyes to heaven in exasperation.

'No time for that now,' said Peacock smoothly, stepping forward. 'Trevett, you'd better get back on the stage. They're running late and you don't want to keep them waiting. Bagshawe, what are you doing here? Get off with you. You know you're not allowed in here.'

But St. John was unable to contain his indignation at Trevett's unwitting destruction of the rescue plan.

'You fathead!' he said crossly to Trevett. 'Don't you know what's going on?' He turned to Rowbotham. 'You'd better come outside, sir. It's not safe here.'

'What?' said Rowbotham.

Trevett cast the briefest of contemptuous glances at St. John, and turned his back on his rival.

'I don't know who this fellow is,' he said to Rowbotham. 'Now—'

This was the moment in which the conspirators had intended to strike, but this unexpected intervention by Trevett and St. John had thrown the whole thing up into the air. Judson was taken aback, and was looking to Peacock for direction. Surely they would abandon the plan now? But Freddy had reckoned without Peacock's audacity. He saw Peacock put his hand into his pocket, and instantly understood what he meant to do. He ran forward and threw himself at Peacock.

'Oh, no you don't,' he said. 'St. John, help me!'

St. John ran to assist. Trevett, still not understanding what was going on, and seeing his friend Peacock apparently being attacked two against one, strode forward and pulled St. John away, leaving Freddy to grapple with Peacock alone.

'What the devil are you up to now?' said Trevett to St. John.

'You ass!' exclaimed St. John, attempting to free himself from Trevett's grasp, but Trevett held him firmly, and so St. John could do nothing but watch as Freddy and Peacock struggled together and Freddy did his best to prevent his opponent from shooting anybody. But Peacock was taller and stronger than Freddy, and at last succeeded in bringing the revolver out of his pocket. He levelled it at Rowbotham and pulled the trigger, just as Freddy seized his arm again. There was a ringing report which caused several people to cry out, and the shot went wide. The jolt caused Peacock and Freddy to overbalance, and they fell to the ground, Freddy still trying to get hold of the gun. Trevett in his shock had let go of St. John, who now ran forward to assist. Between them they managed to wrench the gun from Peacock's hand. St. John gave a grunt of triumph, but they had reckoned without Bishop, who just then moved forward and fired the little derringer at Freddy. The trigger clicked harmlessly, and Bishop gave an exclamation of anger and instead cuffed Freddy across the head with it, knocking him sideways and causing him to drop Peacock's revolver. Peacock had just made a dive for it when suddenly the tent was full of police and men with guns, who laid hands on Peacock, Bishop and Judson with great efficiency, disarmed them and placed them in handcuffs.

Freddy lay, dazed, on the ground, as the men swarmed around him, barking orders and asking questions.

'Are you all right, sir?' said a voice above him.

'Bit of a headache,' he managed. 'You won't mind if I don't help clear up, will you? I'm rather comfortable down here.'

'Concussion, by the looks of it,' said someone else. 'Better get him to a doctor.'

Freddy let them talk. He had no intention of moving. If they wanted a doctor to see him, then that was entirely their affair. Just then someone came and stood over him, and he squinted up and saw a pair of round spectacles. It was Henry Jameson.

'Good work,' said Henry. 'But if you're going to do this sort of thing in future, perhaps you'd better let me know first.'

Then he went away and began giving quiet orders, as Freddy lay on the cold ground and waited for the doctor to come.

CHAPTER TWENTY-TWO

TEN DAYS LATER Freddy arrived at Clerkenwell Central Hall to find Mildred Starkweather and St. John Bagshawe in the kitchen, stacking cups and saucers on trays and talking comfortably in the manner of old friends. Miss Hodges was there too, crossing things off a list.

'Hallo, Freddy, old chap,' said St. John. 'Should have thought you'd have had enough of this place by now, what?'

'Not at all,' said Freddy. 'I came along to make sure the Temperance ladies were behaving themselves. But what are you doing here? I thought they'd forcibly disbanded the Communist Alliance, or proscribed you, or something.'

'Oh, I'm here to help Mildred,' said St. John. 'Yes, the police have shut us down. Rather unfortunate, really. They've been crawling all over the *Radical*'s offices too, looking for evidence that we knew about the plot. Of course I told them I didn't suspect a thing, and how could I help it if people wanted to pass secret messages through the small ads? I think I've convinced them now, but it hasn't helped business. Ruth's left, you know. A good thing when all's said and done, I suppose, but she left me short-handed. It's just lucky I thought to ask Mildred.'

'Are you going to work for the *Radical*?' said Freddy to Mildred in surprise. 'How did you get permission?'

'As a matter of fact, Mummy doesn't mind at all,' said Mildred. 'At least, she didn't once I told her that I'd made it a condition that St. John must give the Association two pages every week. I hope you're quite recovered now, by the way. That was a nasty knock on the head you got.'

'Oh, it takes more than a clip over the ear to keep me down, as my mother will tell you,' said Freddy airily.

'The two of you were terribly brave,' said Mildred, with a glance at St. John. 'You might have been killed!'

'We'd have been perfectly safe had it not been for that ass Trevett,' said St. John. 'I always knew he had more beard than brains.'

'Ah, yes,' said Freddy. 'I understand he's feeling let down by Schuster.'

'He is,' said St. John. 'They'd been in secret talks about forming a new political party, with Trevett as the leader. But this plot to assassinate Rowbotham has put paid to that once and for all. I expect you've heard that the police have found enough evidence to charge Pettit. After his house burned down he moved to his sister's, and they discovered a lot of incriminating documents there. Old Rowbotham is breathing fire and brimstone, and says he's determined to root out any militancy he finds. Any supporters of Pettit are going to be chucked out of the union, apparently.'

'But then presumably they'll mobilize elsewhere,' said Freddy.

'Oh, no doubt,' said St. John. 'Still, that's not Rowbotham's problem, is it? And I can quite understand his point of view. I mean to say, it doesn't do to have one's own associates plotting to put a bullet in one's head, does it?'

'I haven't seen much about it in the papers,' said Mildred. 'I expect they've asked you to keep quiet about it, have they?'

'Yes,' said Freddy. 'They didn't want to stir things up any more than necessary. And I think they're a little worried about possible attempts to whip up public sympathy for Theresa Schuster. Beauty in distress, and all that. Unfortunately, it seems she's decided to claim that Peacock forced her into taking part in the plot, and there's no saying that a jury might not believe her. She's rather good at convincing people to take her view of things.'

Mildred snorted.

'I say she deserves everything she gets. She's nothing but a trouble-maker. But what about Mr. Schuster? I can't believe he didn't know what his wife was getting up to.'

'Oh, I'm sure he knew perfectly well what was going on,' said Freddy. 'The police can't prove it, but they've arrested him anyway. I dare say they'll find something to charge him with. He always said they would.'

'Poor Miss Stapleton,' said Mildred. 'She was right after all. She was convinced they were plotting something and we didn't really believe her. But all that snooping did her no good in the end, did it? They must have caught her listening that night and killed her for it. Have they admitted to it yet?'

'No,' said Freddy.

'I don't know why they're bothering to deny it,' she said. 'They're murderers, all right. You know they found Dyer, don't you? Poor thing. I only hope he didn't suffer.'

'Was he really passing information to Intelligence?' said St. John.

'So they tell me,' said Freddy.

'I'm not certain I like that sort of thing,' said St. John. 'Seems a sneak's business.'

'Perhaps so, but if he hadn't, then the plot might have succeeded and Rowbotham would have been shot,' said Freddy. 'I think on balance I shall cheer rather than jeer him.'

'Where's Mrs. Belcher?' said Mildred suddenly. 'She's late. She was supposed to be bringing some printed pamphlets, and I wanted to put them out on the chairs before the meeting begins. And I must just take a look at the subscription book, to see whether it's up-to-date. I do think Mr. Bottle might have given us a little more notice before he left.'

'Left?' said Freddy, pricking up his ears.

'Oh, he's gone abroad for his health, apparently. We only found out about it on Sunday. But it means we have no treasurer now. I expect Mrs. Belcher will bully Mummy into doing it. Come and help me in the hall, St. John. At least one good thing has come of all this: now that you Communists have gone we can have the big hall to ourselves instead of being squashed into the little one.'

She and St. John departed, and Freddy was left in the kitchen with Miss Hodges.

'Can I assist?' he said. He waved away her stammered protests and started collecting spoons and sugar bowls together.

'Good thing they caught the desperate men who killed Miss Stapleton, don't you think?' he said.

'Oh—yes,' she replied.

'Queer, isn't it?' he went on. 'If you'd asked me I should have said they'd had nothing to do with it.'

'Oh, but they must have,' said Miss Hodges. 'They killed Mr. Dyer, after all.'

'True,' he conceded. 'But I still think someone else did it.'

He paused, watching her as she wiped the same small area of table top over and over again. At last she looked up.

'Who do you think did it?' she said, almost unwillingly.

'Well, for a while I *did* think it might have been Mr. Bottle,' he said. She did not reply, and he went on, 'When I first met him I was certain I'd seen him somewhere before, but it wasn't until a day or two before the rally that I remembered where—and remembered, too, something that Miss Flowers once said about your association's never seeming to have any money, despite the subs you charge. I went to dig through our archives at the *Clarion*, just to make sure, but it was the same fellow, right enough. Your Mr. Bottle is an habitual embezzler of money. I last saw him in court about three years ago, when he was charged with stealing funds from an anglers' club in Brentford. He pleaded guilty and repaid everything in full, and the court treated him leniently. It appears he has a fatal weakness for the horses, and is unable to resist helping himself to any sums of cash that happen to pass through his hands in order to finance his hobby. One might have thought that he would have learned his lesson after last time, but it seems not. I ought to have warned Mrs. Belcher when I first realized who Bottle was, but other events interceded, and it slipped out of my mind. At any rate, I telephoned her earlier today and suggested she look carefully through the Association's bank books, but she told me the bank manager had already called her that very morning, as he was uneasy about certain irregularities he'd noticed. If I were to make a prediction, I should say that now Bottle has gone abroad—might I say skipped, even?—Mrs. Belcher will discover that she has not been keeping a close enough eye on the funds, and that her trust in her treasurer has been misplaced.'

'Goodness me!' said Miss Hodges, who had listened to all this open-mouthed.

'Quite,' said Freddy. 'As you can see, this puts Miss Stapleton's death in a very different light. We've all been assuming she was killed because of what she knew about the Communists, but from what we know now it seems equally likely that she was murdered because she had found out what Bottle had been doing, and was threatening to expose him. He didn't come to the meeting that night, you remember, because he was ill in bed—or at least, that's what he said. But it just so happens that I was wandering around outside after the meeting finished, and I saw someone who looked awfully like him creeping out of the hall at just around the time Miss Stapleton died.'

'Oh!' said Miss Hodges.

'Yes. Of course, one might draw all sorts of conclusions from that. The most obvious one, naturally, is that Bottle remembered he had accidentally left evidence that would tell against him at the hall—perhaps a bank statement or suchlike—and came to retrieve it, but that Miss Stapleton found it first, and he was forced to resort to violence to hide his crime. You may remember that a torn-off scrap of paper was found in her hand. One might guess that he took the paper and the takings box from her after he had killed her, then made his escape.'

He glanced at her, but she said nothing, and he went on:

'However, the difficulty with that theory is that the man I saw was certainly not carrying a takings box. Still, it was such a beautiful solution to the mystery that I didn't like to let it go, so I started to wonder whether perhaps Bottle had had an accomplice.'

She shook her head quickly, but he ignored it.

'You'll think it absurd, no doubt,' he said, 'but it was a game that put me on to the other half of the solution. "Hobbes and Descartes Took the 'Bus" is the name. Frightfully silly game, but someone happened to mention it and for some reason it made me think of that night, when I left you at the 'bus stop. I passed that way again a few minutes later and because you weren't there I assumed you'd got on the 'bus. But later on it occurred to me that I might have been mistaken in my assumption. And I was, wasn't I? I don't know about Hobbes and Descartes, but Miss Hodges didn't take the 'bus, did she? I know she didn't, because I tracked down the two women who were at the stop with you and spoke to them, and they were certain that you hadn't got on with them. In fact, they said that not long after I left you, you gave an exclamation and hurried off back the way you had come. At first I couldn't think why, but then I remembered that Mildred told me you were supposed to take the box home and count the subs. You didn't have it with you when we left, but I expect you remembered it after we got to the 'bus stop. That's what you went back for, isn't it? The takings box.'

She stared at him, but still she was speechless.

'So now I have two halves of a solution, but I don't know how to put them together to make a whole,' said Freddy. 'If Bottle *was* working with someone, then why did he drag himself out of bed that night when he was unwell and might just as easily have asked his accomplice to do it? He *must* have come back for whatever it was he took out of Miss Stapleton's hand. So where do you come in, Miss Hodges?'

There was a silence, then at last Miss Hodges spoke.

'Was Mr. Bottle really stealing money all the time?' she asked in a sort of wonder. 'All this time? I can hardly believe it. Why, that explains—'

'Explains what?'

'Nothing.'

Although Freddy was still not entirely clear about what had happened that night, he decided to hazard a guess.

'It wasn't Mr. Bottle who killed Miss Stapleton, was it?' he said gently.

She looked at the floor, and he went on, 'I think you're an honest woman, Miss Hodges, and you don't want someone else to get the blame for what you did. Why don't you tell me what happened?'

'It was an accident!' she exclaimed, and sat down suddenly on a chair. 'At least, I think it was. I'm almost sure it was. I certainly never meant—'

'Meant what? To kill her?'

She shook her head, terrified.

'It sounds so awful, said out loud like that,' she whispered. 'But it was just a *little* push, and she'd been *so* provoking that evening that I'm afraid I couldn't stop myself, and I did it before I'd even thought about what might happen. I don't know how you guessed, but you're right—I'd gone back to fetch the takings box. She told me to count the subs and in all the confusion I forgot to take the box with me, and had to come back for it. I came back in through the side door to the minor hall and got it from the office—I knew she was still about somewhere, because she'd left her keys in the lock of the drawer, so I took them and the box and hurried off, hoping she wouldn't realize I'd forgotten and start telling me off again. I'd had rather a trying day—my sister had been very ill, you see, and I'd been nursing her, and I only came to the meeting because she insisted I go out and enjoy myself a little. But I didn't enjoy myself at all, because Miss Stapleton kept telling me off for getting everything wrong, although it was only because I was tired and my mind was elsewhere. I thought I'd managed to get the box without being seen, but then she came out of the committee-room just as I was passing. She had a letter and the paper-knife, but when she saw me she clicked her tongue and said that was just like me, to forget, and couldn't I do anything right, and perhaps I wasn't to be trusted with the takings after all. Then she tried to grab the box off me, and then I—I don't know—I think something snapped in my head, and I was suddenly determined that I shouldn't let her treat me like this any longer, and that she shouldn't take the box from me. So I resisted, and she kept on trying to pull it away from me. She was still holding the paper-knife in her hand, and I think it must have been facing away from me and towards her—I've thought about it and thought about it, and I can't see how it could have happened otherwise. Anyway, at last I'm afraid I lost my temper, and I shoved the box at her, and said something like, "Oh, there's your silly box!" I thought then that she'd overbalanced, because she sort of stumbled and fell backwards, and I was so sure she was going to get up and shout at me. But she didn't move, and I looked and there she was, on the floor, with the paper-knife sticking out of her and the box by her side. At first I didn't understand what had happened, and I was waiting for her to get up. Then I thought she must have knocked her head against something. Time seems to pass so slowly, you know,' she said, looking up suddenly. 'It felt as though I'd been bending over her for hours, but it can't have been more than a few seconds. At any rate, my mind went blank, and all I could think was that it was terribly important that I take the box home. I don't really remember what happened then, but I suppose I must have picked up the box and run back out the way I came. I walked home after that, I think. I was sure nobody had seen me, and I thought that since Miss Stapleton had asked me to count the subs, then it wouldn't arouse any suspicion if people knew I had the box. It seemed very important to behave as normally as possible. You do understand, don't you?'

'I think so,' said Freddy.

'I didn't sleep a wink that night, but it wasn't until the next day, when I heard that the police had been called, that I realized exactly what I must have done. I should have gone and confessed there and then, and told them that it had all been an accident, but then I happened to open the takings box and saw that the money we'd collected at the jumble sale wasn't there, and I began to think, and to wonder, and to hesitate. I wanted to know where it was, because it seemed to me that if I did confess then they'd say I'd killed Miss Stapleton for the money.'

'The jumble sale?'

'Yes. We raised thirty-five pounds, and Mr. Bottle brought the money here to the hall and put it in the box, as the bank was closed. At least, he said he did, when I asked him about it a day or two later. That's when I became really frightened, because if Mr. Bottle had put the cash in the takings box then why wasn't it there now?'

'You weren't in league with Mr. Bottle, then?'

'No! I had no idea he'd been stealing,' she said. 'Not until you told me just now.'

'Then what did you know?'

'Nothing. But he knew—knew—'

'He knew what you'd done?'

She nodded.

'Did he see you do it?'

'I don't think so. It was when we were at Mrs. Starkweather's house on the Thursday. I dropped my bag and the keys to the box fell out, and he picked them up for me. He must have realized then that if I had Miss Stapleton's keys then I must have the box too. He insisted we take a taxi together, and that's when it all started.'

'Was he blackmailing you?'

'Blackmail?' she said, uncomprehending. 'No—at least, I don't think so. He took the box from me and said he would keep it safe for me. He was very kind. He said he was sure it must have been an accident, but that I was in the gravest danger, and that I mustn't think of telling the police. I'd happened to tell him that the thirty-five pounds was missing, you see, and he looked very sober at that and promised never to tell a soul, only I mustn't say anything either, unless I wanted to be hanged. He followed me around after that. I thought he was concerned about me, and didn't want to see me get into trouble. Oh, Mr. Pilkington-Soames, I can't tell you how many times I was on the point of confessing everything—why, I believe it would have been nothing but a relief—but each time he reminded me that I should be hanged as a common murderess, and everybody should know I had killed a woman for thirty-five pounds. My sister was beginning to recover by this time, and I couldn't bear the thought of the shame and disgrace I'd be bringing upon her if I were to be arrested and hanged. I didn't want to see her fall ill again. And so I kept quiet, and said nothing. But I've been a fool, haven't I? Because he was the one who took the money. I suppose he persuaded me to hold my tongue because he didn't want his own misdeeds to be discovered.'

'I'm afraid it rather looks like it,' said Freddy. 'If you'd confessed, then it would all have come out into the open, and he would have been arrested.'

'Then he wasn't concerned for me at all,' she said sadly. 'And I thought he was so kind.'

'No, he was driven entirely by selfish motives,' said Freddy. 'Quite a coincidence that he decided to come along to the central hall that evening, though. I expect he left the incriminating bank statement, or letter, or whatever it was, there when he brought the takings box back to the hall on the day of the jumble sale, then came back to retrieve it on Tuesday night. I don't know what happened then, but I can make a guess. He found Miss Stapleton's body and took the letter from her hand. I wonder why he dragged her into the committee-room, though. Perhaps he wanted to search her pockets thoroughly in case she was carrying some other evidence that would tell against him.'

Miss Hodges was no longer listening, but was absorbed in her own thoughts.

'But if Mr. Bottle has gone, then that means I may confess now, doesn't it?' she said suddenly.

'Yes, I suppose it does,' said Freddy.

'Then I shall,' she said. 'I shall go and speak to the police tomorrow. I shall tell my sister first. I only wish she were well enough to come with me. I'm a little frightened of the police.'

'I'll come with you if you like,' said Freddy. 'I'll see to it that they treat you well.'

'Oh, would you?' she said. 'That would be terribly kind.'

'Not at all,' said Freddy. It was impossible not to feel sympathy for her.

'Do you think they really will hang me?' she said in a small voice.

'Not unless you're very unlucky. But you won't be, as long as you have a good lawyer. As a matter of fact, I think I know just the chap. He's terribly good in cases of this sort and he'll see you right. They may not even prosecute if you can convince them it really was an accident.'

'Oh!' she said faintly.

The sound of a woman's loud voice could now be heard from the lobby. Miss Hodges jumped up.

'It's Mrs. Belcher!' she said. 'And nothing's ready yet. Oh, goodness!'

She picked up an armful of tea-things and hurried out of the room, scattering teaspoons behind her, and leaving Freddy to wonder whether he had dreamt the past ten minutes, for the whole conversation had had an air of unreality about it, somehow, and Miss Hodges was now bustling about in her usual apologetic manner as though nothing had happened. At length he wandered out of the kitchen and into the lobby, where the first thing he saw was Ivor Trevett, looking as pleased with himself as ever, and holding forth on the subject of the Temperance movement to several young women, who were hanging on his every word. A little way away, Mr. Hussey was watching the little group with some displeasure. Just then Trevett looked up and saw him. The two men nodded stiffly to one another.

'Too funny, isn't it?' came a voice at Freddy's ear. It was Mildred, who was watching the scene with malicious enjoyment. 'The Chudderley has decided she wants no more of him, you see, and now that the Communists have disbanded Trevett's found himself without an audience, so he's decided to fasten on to us. Mr. Hussey is appalled. Watch out for fireworks now!'

'If I thought your mother wasn't listening I should call you a minx,' said Freddy.

'Get along with you,' she said, by no means displeased. She went into the hall, slightly pink in the face. St. John was just coming out, and he smiled at her as they passed one another. He was wearing a slightly sheepish expression that Freddy recognized only too well.

'She's a fine girl, isn't she?' said St. John.

'Mildred, you mean?'

'Of course? Who else?'

'I thought you were in love with Ruth.'

'Pfft!' said St. John in disdain. 'A mere passing interest. I mean to say, she's not quite the thing, is she? But Mildred, now. There's a girl a man could really depend on—sensible, intelligent, and without any of these silly modern ideas. A jolly good sort, in fact.'

'I quite agree with you,' said Freddy.

'She's already come up with some marvellous ideas for the *Radical* that won't cost too much, and she's also thought of some people who might be interested in advertising with us. Ruth hadn't the first idea about money—had to keep reminding her that it wasn't a bottomless well—but Mildred has already been looking at the accounts. My, didn't she shake her head when she saw some of the things we'd been spending the funds on! If anyone can get the *Radical* into profit, she can.'

'It sounds like the perfect match,' said Freddy.

'Do you know, I think perhaps it is,' said St. John. 'Mother knows her, and is fond of her, so I don't think there'll be any opposition there. Everyone's all caught up with Iris's wedding, but who knows—if I work fast, perhaps I can get in before her. And then you'll have *two* weddings to go to. What do you say to that, eh?'

'Splendid,' said Freddy dryly.

———

New Releases

If you'd like to receive news of further releases by Clara Benson, you can sign up to my mailing list here.

CLARABENSON.COM/NEWSLETTER

Or follow me on Facebook.

FACEBOOK.COM/CLARABENSONBOOKS

New to Freddy? Read more about him in the Angela Marchmont mysteries.

CLARABENSON.COM/BOOKS

BOOKS IN THIS SERIES

- A Case of Blackmail in Belgravia
- A Case of Murder in Mayfair
- A Case of Conspiracy in Clerkenwell
- A Case of Duplicity in Dorset
- A Case of Suicide in St. James's

ALSO BY CLARA BENSON:

The Angela Marchmont Mysteries